BOOK 3 OF THE WAIVING PLAINS TRILOGY

OCCUPANT #3

KEVIN MOCCIA

OCCUPANT #3

KEVIN MOCCIA

iUniverse®

OCCUPANT #3

This is a work of fiction. All of the characters, names, incidents, organizations, and dialogue in this novel are either the products of the author's imagination or are used fictitiously.

iUniverse books may be ordered through booksellers or by contacting:

iUniverse
1663 Liberty Drive
Bloomington, IN 47403
www.iuniverse.com
844-349-9409

Because of the dynamic nature of the Internet, any web addresses or links contained in this book may have changed since publication and may no longer be valid. The views expressed in this work are solely those of the author and do not necessarily reflect the views of the publisher, and the publisher hereby disclaims any responsibility for them.

Any people depicted in stock imagery provided by Getty Images are models, and such images are being used for illustrative purposes only. Certain stock imagery © Getty Images.

Cover Art: Keno McCloskey

ISBN: 978-1-6632-4129-0 (sc)
ISBN: 978-1-6632-4130-6 (hc)
ISBN: 978-1-6632-4128-3 (e)

Library of Congress Control Number: 2022911474

Print information available on the last page.

iUniverse rev. date: 11/04/2022

This book is dedicated to my father,
Vito Moccia
Korean War Veteran and Founder of V.M. Modern
Fort Street, Barber
Wyandotte, Michigan
&
Edith Lee,
Longmeadow's maternal sun

Edited by
Regina Marie Gallagher
The pirate queen of words

CONTENTS

CHAPTER 1

The Map Handler

C larence entered the pawn shop which was equipped with a single lift garage bay attached to a bodega that hung off the side of the main structure like the molted shell of a harvest fly. Competing scents of machine oil and bacon assailed Clarence's nostrils as he parted the faded curtain strips that separated the bodega from the garage. The strips were interlaced with long strands of twisted deer intestines, attached to cow bells, their clappers replaced by M-16 ammo casings, which chimed forth their warning welcome.

"Zero eight hundred hours," Clarence called aloud into the store. "Sun's up, big cheese! Time to walk some iron!" Clarence's eyes locked onto the immense frame of the man who appeared to be circling him, frigate-like, amid aisles of convenience goods stacked into estate sale furniture buys, repurposed as grocery racks.

The diversity of the furniture collection in the bodega straddled a fine line between clutter and chaos. Auto and truck parts hung from the ceiling amid sports helmets, cleats, skates, skis and snowshoes. Clarence walked down a library aisle of barrister bookshelves organized case by case with trinkets and timepieces, bracelets, brooches, rings sold at the end of their shine slipped from banded fingers, chains darkened from sweat or dulled from the trace of a civet cat. The pawned jewelry section opened onto a long marble countertop, salvaged from a sideboard, mounted on pickle barrels and bookended by two Vernor's beverage coolers; its perishable contents consumed by a small community of pharmaceutical abuse survivors relying on government assistance, drop box shoes and warehouse running gigs.

Clarence studied the contents of a doorless armoire and a heavily provisioned china cabinet that served as the canned meat and vegetable sections of Buck's Piggly Wiggly Auto Plex. "Did you buy this place because of the bulk rate on Slim Jims?"

A mountain of flesh appeared in front of Clarence Clay. The last person one would wish to see on a stormy night, tapping at your car window holding a tire iron. Large clumps of hair scattered the man's head, reed like, with wide hair plug holes visible as a scalped doll. The sunken right half of the shopkeeper's face, extending down to his chin, had been surgically replaced with skin grafted from his thighs and stretched over a titanium plate. Except for a welcoming ember, burning outwards from the shopkeeper's good eye, the rest of the man's face resembled an embossed battle shield, mounted on a swampwater stump of a neck; squared between the athletic remnants of two mammoth shoulders. The shopkeeper's decorative eye was surgically positioned off the natural plumb line of his face, distorting the Golden Ratio.

"You had both legs when you shipped out? What did you do? Lose one, betting the pot on two pair?" Clarence shared his sense of humor openly with the one man whom he knew he could not offend.

"Diabetes. Still no getting used to it." The shopkeeper offered sparingly, his thoughts damming up against his three remaining teeth, swiping at the air with his prosthetic leg.

The shopkeeper was offline, verbally, since most of his clientele were awaiting their end of the month checks and those that had money were living off stockpiles, avoiding the others that didn't. The result levied a three day, silent pall over Buck's Piggly Wiggly Auto Plex and Pawn Shop, where all supplemental nutrition paper was accepted, but hard luck monologues concerning any extension of non-existent credit were strictly forbidden. Loitering by way of preparing to ask for credit, making inane weather proclamations based on aching body parts, was also frowned upon.

"Pray tell? What brings my savior north?" The shopkeeper propped himself up in front of Clarence, blocking his path, so much so that whatever light was coming in from behind him, was eclipsed by the immense wall of the man's girth.

"I've got an ear stud, bathed in diamonds, with a ruby in it. Anybody out there…you might know…looking for a thing like that?"

"It would have been worth more…had you brought it in…with the bleeding piece of ear the owner left attached to it." Buck's good eye sparkled, knowing the value of the ear stud, speaking in his customary rifle shot delivery, supported by huge krill gathering intakes of breath.

Clarence followed the shopkeeper to a large barnyard door, opening onto a trucking access area where weathered prep tables were visible as well as heaps of cabbage scraps and mustard greens swept into enormous piles.

"Holy Moses, fish meat! You still don't bother to pick up piles? *There's two kinds of men in this world, private…those who sweep piles…and those that expect someone else to sweep up after them… every marine in this company, keeps a dustpan clipped to the end of his rifle...*" Clarence fell into his imitation of their platoon sargent, his spirit lifting out of himself as he transformed into the caricature.

"Didn't Banjo Dave put that speech to song?"

"Last night of Cody's life...dust rifle blues!"

The shopkeeper rolled the barnyard door closed and locked it, effortlessly.

"*Silent National Manufacturing...*" Clarence thought, addressing the rolling door hardware on the ancient barn door; knowing Buck was obsessed with products that remained operational for generations.

"That man out there, with three-fourths of an ear, looking for that stud, he's a hybrid pot grower—mar-i-g-ju-ana. I'm sure a guy, gourmet money like that, he ain't *Holyfielding* it around, with three-fourths of an ear, no more. Man like that...with a reward out...most likely put his ear back together. The lobule...at the flap of an ear...is easier to reconstruct than the sacred placement of a man's glance. Is that stud...shape of a C?" Buck asked, his smile stretching across his face as a ladder spanning a moat, knowing that the right answer was a jackpot jewelry hit, however it waltzed through the door.

"It is."

"The reward's fifteen K. I can give you...thirty-eight hundred now...split the balance from the fifteen K...when the money hits my account."

"Fair enough." Clarence offered.

It had been almost a decade since the two men had stood face to whatever face Buck had left. In the passing seasons, Clarence had gone through his savings planting crops that draped his land with a fragrant bouquet, temporarily staving off the emptiness he felt from the loss of his beloved wife, Clara. During the same collection of days, Buck found his way to the end of an iron rail, six stories off the ground, unwilling to step his mangled body off the I-beam underfoot and add another statistic to the ranks of self-annihilating war veterans. Buck greeted the sun and the arriving iron working crew that morning, with a ritual salutation of the day's welcome, swearing to meet the world as more than a discarded heap of military flesh. The stars and stripes unseen beneath Buck's skin, ran true, much truer than his military scars, which were the outermost strip of his human veneer. Whatever the connection these two men forged it had not altered in each other's absence, uniting their bond as battlefield pawns, re-engaged in the continual tug of war to wield the barbeque tongs and flip another man's meat.

"You didn't come all this way just to exchange jewelry, did you Clay?"

"Would you send whatever my end comes to, to my son, Terrance?"

"Since you never invite me...and you're not going to be there...sure...I'll deliver the balance, in person. You're goin' north, aren't ya'?"

There was much that Clarence wanted to say, but being brought up in a household where words were an unwanted interruption to a loud, deafening silence, by habit, he clamped down on everything he was feeling, silencing questions that would have been an attempt to span gaps of time, and squelching the impulse to wrap his arms around what was left of his old platoon mate. Yet all Clarence could muster, forgetting that he had yet to exchange the ear stud was, "Thanks, Buck…I knew I could count on you…"

As Clarence rushed through the string of chiming, ammo casings, his companion hound raced in from his outside post, coming to attention, staring upwards at Buck.

The dog was predominantly black, with a tan mask that circled both his eyes, adding to his interrogating expression. Each of his paws were tan as well, which made the dog look like he was wearing socks that matched his mask.

"No dogs!" Buck shouted at the uninvited intruder with an intense, immediate rage.

The masked hound didn't flinch, but remained locked in his study of the shopkeeper, cocking his head as a criminal judge might, reflecting upon an all too familiar felon.

"You heard the man." Clarence addressed the dog, who stared Buck down, imploring a poised, silent appeal.

"Stay…but stick to that spot!" Buck commanded, whereupon the dog folded himself flat but remained at attention, following Buck's story as if Buck were conveying it to the dog directly. "I used to take in strays. Took in one…off a couple month bender…Dutch Shepherd, Russian Sheepdog mix…caked with dried blood—mighta' had some Saint Bernard in it. Hosed it down. Remember them…blood streams in drains on bad days? The day Cody got hit, his blood dried to my skin…lifting off in sheets 'cause I'd cradled him. Cody bled out on my lap, like I was his mother's apron. I tossed this mutt in a kennel with twelve other strays I had. The apostles. Used t' walk 'em, unleashed, in a cloud around me. Next morning, through the remnants of a blackout drunk, I see that…Dutch shepherd, mutt…clotted in blood, waiting for breakfast. Haven't taken in another stray...or had a drink since. I do though...I do...I gotta'...tin box full of AA tokens from vets I sponsored—bent prisms—the way I see 'em. I was thinking about stringing them into a necklace. Counseling failure trophies, like them architect rings...made from that bridge that collapsed in Quebec." Buck took a gigantic breath then continued, "North is a three month stint, Clay. Even for guys like us, who live this system...testing drugs...that's a long stretch."

"North is different...thirty K, up front."

"Yeah, yeah, yeah..."

"Thirty K on the walk in, day of—after vitals."

"Second silo...strictly second silo!"

"Sixty grand, at the end of three months—plus bonus money, that's the difference."

"If you make it three months."

"I'll make it..." Clarence confirmed.

"North isn't about *testing* drugs, it's about growing disease. You're walking into a pharmaceutical Petri dish. All of us drug test misfits...we all get the same packets to pick from that you get. Nobody I know is going north, Clarence, just you. You go north, and they'll use some of whatever life you got left...to find out what'll kill someone...maybe...two hundred years from now."

"And what if two hundred years from now, is closer to around the corner then we think?" asked Clarence genuinely.

"Always the hero."

"It's what I do best. Not a big fan of empty parades or red capes."

"So might have said the trophy fish, but it couldn't speak around the bait hook, and all that taste of bloody steel. You know the hair on my cheek, used to be on the back of my thigh…now when my face itches…I sometimes forget…and scratch my leg." Buck stared at Clarence, relaxing all the ugliness that was trapped in his complexion, a dripping wax portrait of war, depicting a face used as a backstop for shrapnel, including a pitcher's mound for a nose with two snake holes for nostrils.

"My heart…used to live in the soil…" Clarence disclosed, almost as a prayer, admitting openly all of what he knew of himself, annihilated by the ugly beauty of his friend's company.

"You think you can find that piece of yourself…going north? Traveling the globe or turning in a circle, what's the difference?"

"I've been onboard, north, since the beginning. I know all about what north is."

"You drew money on your walk-in bonus…and borrowed against the start of the project…what did I hear you were growing after Clara died? Sweet peas and heliotropes? Go home Clay…I'll send you thirty grand tomorrow!"

"It's a Canadian funded experiment, Buck. The food will be airline quality, that's a given, but a hockey game is bound to break out eventually…right? This biosphere is built on Canadian soil. Hockey's on my bucket list—maybe you can throw in some sticks, you got a few here…or this…I would take this with me…if I knew what it was. What is this?" Clarence grabbed an article that resembled a giant wishbone.

"That's an Inuit vise…used to spread open a whale head…so they could work in the head cavity…extracting spermaceti…brain blubber used for candles or oil, it had a cleaner flame. Less smoke. Let's see that stud…you, damn Alzheimer Flash Gordon…forget the thing you came for!"

"Inuit whale vise, this is no...Inuit, whale vise...you Antique Roadsow...crap hustler." Clarence muttered as he replaced the item in question and passed over the stud, retrieving it from the watch pocket of his jeans; haphazardly concealed in an empty candy wrapper.

Buck clamped his good eye into a jeweler's' loupe he wore on a necklace, his bad eye staring aimlessly sideways. "Wow...a piece of ear is still slivered on here." Buck uttered, reaching for his jewelry tools.

"How's a guy...get his ear shot off...on a back road...cut between cornfields on both sides?" Clarence questioned, aloud, while examining the abundant array of different artifacts stored within the bodega-antique-mechanics hut.

"Green thumb, Van Gogh-pot-gangster...who knows? Maybe he was shooting at a rival pot farmer...came at him...on a John Deere drive-by?"

"Inuit head vise..."

"That's what it is."

"Signed by Nanook of the North!"

"I got more Eskimo stuff in my collection, if you're interested? Museum quality pieces. Take some time to drag them out." muttered Buck, cleaning the fragments of cartilage off the earpiece with a pair of tweezers and a tiny putty knife.

Without retrieving any impressions, Buck followed Clarence with the roving replica of his good eye as he searched through the store like an impulsively lost dog, exploring its temporary surroundings. Buck shook his head as he spoke, marveling how Clarence ever made it back to the states in one piece. Wondering too, if Clarence ever turned off his Sargent York switch. "When

I get a sit down to exchange this "C", with this Kush guy…I'll check out…what his ear looks like. A civilian dodges a bullet at point blank range…there's usually a story attached. Maybe…this tomato Kush guy, his heart was broke…he was high…he blew his ear off…because that's where his phone was." Buck said, speaking over the compressor that kicked on and off as he sprayed the ear stud clean with an air gun.

"Clara couldn't wait for me to walk through the door, an hour was like a week to her, a day a month…but she never went near a phone…did you know that?"

"No, I didn't…"

"Woman lived and died…never ordered a pizza."

"My ex-wife Cindy's phone…grew out of her ear like an extra hair curl, hand and all. Me…comin' through the door was the same as leaving…coming back…same thing. Nothing changed… nothing to say…very John Prine. The woman had to take a handful of pills and battle demons just to wash a dish…she's in between her third or fourth kid now, so…I guess…the only demon she needed to get out of the way of….was me."

Clarence rove through the pawn shop bodega speaking into the air, untethered, re-immersing himself in the colloquial pattern grooved out over time with his trusted compadre. "I think it was with Clara…her folks were out there somewhere, they moved on…but never called. We eloped, she gave birth. If the phone rang…she never answered it."

"Here's your end, up front from the reward." Buck counted out thirty eight, one hundred dollar bills onto the eight foot slab of marble; crowded with Slim Jims, homemade fishing flies, and at least a single dose packet of anything one might find at a corner drugstore.

"That'll get me as far north as I need to go, and then some. The final three month payment, after the experiment, that'll set me and my kid, debt free—unbeholden. The second thirty thousand I drew on...for the kid—just in case. In three months, after the experiment, I'll own all my earth again. My family and wife's grave. After the experiment, anything I walk on, under my feet... will be mine."

"It's all mud when it rains."

"Not if it's fertile—and if it's "not" mine...it just mixes with everything else."

"You need a lift north?"

"No, I have to register the dog, he's new. Then we both get on a train and eventually cross water."

"That ain't your dog?

"It is now."

"You got any papers for him? You can't get him into the *germ sphere* without papers? Find yourself a place to put your feet up... I'll microwave us some breakfast...I got peach cobbler and fresh trout patties...I'll draw you up some dog papers."

Clarence wanted to question Buck about the words he used, especially the two loaded ones, *germ sphere,* but Clarence knew if he stayed, Buck would find a way to talk him out of going north.

"I won't need no dog papers. Me and this hound just finished the last of some rabbits I jerkied."

"You can leave the dog with me...even last minute. I can pick him up at the launch point...if it comes to that."

"I'm not going into that biosphere without this dog, that's why…I won't need no papers."

Buck came to himself in Clarence's presence, recognizing the man standing in front of him as his friend, an addicted assassin who lost his mind tallying abandoned supplies in military burn pits.

"He's a keeper that's for sure. How'd you come by him?" Buck said, hoping the story was a long one, pouring Clarence a Dixie cup shot of chilled Jagermeister from an unseen cooler. Buck grabbed an imported six ounce juice box of sparkling cider for himself, using his jewelry tools to peel back the foil lid.

Clarence pounded the shot then motioned for Buck to pour him another. Buck knew Clarence only drank to contain his emotional awkwardness in social situations, but never for answers, to chase away shadows, or before breakfast. Buck was betting the Jager shots would slow Clarence down and uncork his tongue.

"What was it Banjo Dave used to say about you, Buck? That you could talk the horns off a ram!" Clarence pounded the second shot then burst out laughing, like he had not laughed in years, savage and wild, then in a single gulp his eyes spit tears that dried, as a sun shower does on late summer asphalt.

Both men laughed and sobbed embracing their estrangement from Banjo Dave, who ex-communicated himself from his military service family.

"How'd you come by that dog?" Buck asked, clearing his throat before pounding his apple cider juice box and pouring Clarence another shot, which Clarence accepted, waving his hand over his Dixie cup, to convey that he had reached his limit.

"Two a.m. Back of a convenience store, a little different from this place, no hockey sticks or Inuit brain spreaders. Dog was wedged behind a dumpster and a wall. At least two waves of coyotes, seven in the hunt, four scouts, maybe six…moving in for the kill…comin' across this ball field. Dog didn't have a scratch on him."

"Did you name him yet?"

"The dairy farmer's daughter did…me…not yet."

"Stay away from bandit…where you're going. Pick something nobler. He's already got the mask but Bandit's too easy and Socks or Boots is worse than Bandit. Sock Bandit, that's out too."

"Buck…

"If you can stay, or you *need* to stay, stay. I know you're up against the north launch…come see me, on your return trip—if your compass bends you back this way."

"I don't own a compass…if I knew where I was going…it would defeat the purpose."

"Take this then…*put away childish things*. You remember it? My granddaddy's from WWI." Buck handed Clarence a military compass, a standard issue from the First World War. "In the back of this compass, Clarence…there's a list of coordinates. It's where you'll find food stashed. North ain't gonna' be no…company picnic. Take this, too. It's a map…commit it to memory…then stick it in the mail…and send it back. The postage is on the cylinder. You don't have to destroy it, but don't try to sneak it past whatever checkpoint they send you through. If the people who built that *germ sphere* find this map…they'll know the cartographer, and how he came by it. This map will give you an overview of what you're walking into, but there's no scale. After ninety days, if you find your exit to that germ sphere locked...get yourself to the last set of coordinates in the back of that compass...and you'll find an alternative exit—left...pried open for you there."

Clarence pointed over his Dixie cup, waving his hand, vigorously, encouraging Buck to pour another shot as he opened the back of the compass and studied the coordinates.

"How did you know I was coming?" Clarence asked.

"The only person that didn't know you were coming here, was you! The ruby stud with the Chippewa C, was a bonus surprise, I'll give you that, but not you. Hold your britches a second here..." Buck peeled back the lid of his juice box with his jeweler's scalpel, his massive thumbs dwarfing the entire box. "These eyelash seals...are so annoying...a toast, to Banjo Dave—wherever the sun finds him, God's gift to modern warfare! How many bullets missed that man's head sticking out of a Humvee, with fifty state flags waving on his helmet?"

"To Banjo Dave and this...and this...I greet you father sun with all my human strength, embrace and welcome you, as the one true source of light." Clarence solemnly recited Buck's morning prayer back to him, then dashed the shot, bringing his hands together at his chest and saluting upwards—crushing the Dixie cup between his palms and discarding it into a circular bin, hoping, mid-bank shot, that the bin was for trash and not an Inuit artifact.

"You remember my morning mantra!" Buck said, slurping the entire contents of his sparkling apple cider through the straw in one mighty sip-toke, then crushing the empty carton against the metal framework of his skull.

"Just one more then. One more!" Clarence shouted.

Buck poured Clarence another shot into a new paper cup; the booze beginning to swim through Clarence's bloodstream as he watched Buck peel the foil lid off another juice box.

"Your thumbs, man, your whole body has evaporated...but your thumbs are still the size of freaking baby shoes! Bro, you could Little Jack Horner...bro...you could Little Jack Horner a freaking truck tire with those big ape lugs, you got for thumbs, bro!"

The two men traded barbs and laughed, coming to a halt as wild horses do, feeling the terrain shifting below them.

"I know I asked you...not to save me, Clay, but I'm glad you did. I was in church when I first got back, and there was this girl singing. No more than seven years old...and I thought...*If any piece of me made it back to hear that angel sing...it was worth it.* You never listened to me anyway, probably why you ain't got no metal...in your head...welded beneath your leg skin."

"How about Zorro?" Clarence erupted, off topic, changing his attention to the dog, and feeling the rush of the alcohol crashing against his funny bone.

"Project Zorro? You don't want to drink anymore Jager, but you want to talk about Project Zorro? If we get into that, I'll have to start drinking, too! We prepared for everything in all the heat that day...but snow..."

"Zorro for the dog's name...not Project Zorro."

Buck thought about it for a second, looking at the black dog with the tan, dime store mask, staring up at him, then replied, "Zorro, yeah, I guess then...we'll both hang a tag on him."

"This dog ain't about Project Zorro." Clarence said, summoning drunk Nostradamus through the early stages of a solemn, alcohol induced haze.

"Zorro's like hero, with a Z."

"Yeah, so…just Zorro, then."

"When you bring me back my granddaddy's compass, come stay at the house. There is no history in my home. We'll take the boat out and meet the sun. I got a place for Zorro on my craft, aft. All my apostle fishing crew hounds sat aft. I got so much fish in the freezer, Clay—fresh. You want? All the last two days, I can fry you up some road sammies'? Bass? Porgies? My cellar's stocked, cukes, pickled beets, three kinds of slaw. I work, yankin' on trucks—towed off the interstate; but anytime I want…I can melt down…all my gold…all my silver…pop all my jewels from their settings…walk into the mist and disappear. When you get back, come stay…then I'll ferry you home to your boy, or have the barber bring him here. You might need the R and R after your span ends. Indulge me some time, would ya', Clay, if your compass points you back this way."

"Your compass…"

"Mine—on loan. WWI standard issue. It's been through the mud. That's how I know it'll clear passed check. When you come back make plans to linger…it would mean a lot to me not to have to wrap my ahead around everything I might want to say."

"For the record, Buck…saving you was the only thing I don't regret…I do regret taking you to the hoop on your two weak sides, when you had both legs, and winning large parts of your service pay…well…you…pretty much gave your money away at cards… but I don't regret listening…whenever you mapped the stars."

"I don't know if I became a better astronomer studying the northern hemisphere…or just an alcoholic?"

"You ever hear from Banjo Dave?"

"Just that postcard…on the wall there…outa the blue…about three years ago."

"Man knew a thousand songs…"

"He could pick, couldn't sing though."

"Just to wake the dead and discourage the locust revival. That's this year, you know?"

"Locusts revival is this year?"

"Every seventeen years…this is the year. Clarence, make sure they pull you out of that germ sphere before they kill you…you get yourself back here in one piece…and I'll ferry you home."

"We'll have that meal I promised…my grain…my cattle."

"Me and you and your boy, Terrance. Zorro…he'll fetch all the bones. I'll reach out to Banjo Dave…see if he can make the trip. It's been a few years since I tracked him down. He wasn't so happy about it the second to last time I found him."

"Tell Banjo Dave he's welcome in my home…his dirt road of a voice and any member of his first band…Locust Revival! They're welcome, too!"

"Yeah…Locust Revival!" Buck chuckled.

"You remember when Banjo Dave told us that was the name of his first rock band? Locust Revival?"

"Yeah."

"You remember how many times out of nowhere one of us would say it…Locust Revival…and we'd all laugh."

"Yeah…"

"You remember how Cody laughed…how he sounded, when he laughed?"

"Yeah…"

"My son's learning guitar…at least I know I left him one. I put that in his way, I didn't know what else I could lay hands on to slow him down. Anything that kid touches comes to good use. Maybe it's better I do call this dog, Project Z, make his mark with that?"

"No…Project Z's a bad name for a dog. Where you're going… Zorro, will be easier for everybody to remember. Make sure you don't forget this." Buck handed him the map, enclosed in a cardboard poster tube that Clarence had left standing on the counter. "Commit that map to memory."

"I will…"

"You're welcome to study it here…I got breakfast, lunch… plenty of fish and Jager?"

Clarence waved his hand a final time across the marble counter.

"No thanks. How did you come by the map?"

"It's a long story…take about a week?"

"For another time, then…my grain…my cattle."

"There's more things in the universe, than what's grown… outa' all God's green acres, buddy boy. Stuff like that map, and those coordinates on that compass. They're grown in the dark corners of the world…off the grid…near good fishing holes…and Inuit head splitters!"

"Look in on my son when you drop off my end of the ear money, will ya, Buck?"

"I gotta' barber friend in your town, he looks in. Your boy… musta' been all Clara's side…his brains. That last set of coordinates, Clay…tattoo them into your head…just in case you lose that compass, but don't come back without it, if you do. If you have any problems, get to those coordinates. There's a signal flash kit stashed at every one. No matter what you run into…get to that last coordinate, and you're home free. Too bad you ain't goin' in with Banjo Dave to that germ sphere. Banjo Dave was the only sniper target, ever made it back to the states in one piece. Hiked the steps of John Muir…that was the last I heard from him. Postcard it's on the wall there. I am the mongrel of the earth! Hiked the steps of John Muir…that's all it says on the back."

Clarence walked over to the wall and studied the postcard, a clean cut portrait of Banjo Dave was smiling behind a Lone Ranger mask.

"Locust Revival…"

"It's their cycle…"

"Locust?"

"Every seventeen years, this is the cycle. Locust Revival…what a great name for a rock band!"

"Yeah…"

"How come, Buck, you bein' in the steel workers union, how come you joined the military then? You had a steady gig for life? You said yourself you loved a perched view from an I beam—four, five stories high? How come you enlisted when everything you ever wanted was walking rail?"

Buck took a deep breath, uncorked the Jager, poured himself a shot; ceremoniously poured the shot back into the bottle, then wiped his mug as if he drank before he spoke, "Every military cemetery is scattered, up and down. Ain't no different, spaced out, head to toe…separated by wars, four score years later, less or more. Like all my kinfolk…and yours…a call goes out…we don't question back…we follow. We're the Guardian Class. That's how they can do all the stupid things they do, siphon war chests into ex-president's pockets, because all of us rank and file…from the Guardian Class…we can't help but be Americans…it's in our blood to die for what we're lead to believe!"

"I'll see you in three months' time, Buck…my grain, my cattle."

"If you know what's good for you, you'll come back with my grandaddy's compass."

Clarence eventually worked his way out of the bodega through the side exit, screaming back at Buck through a tear in the screen door, flapping like a sea anemone, in a tide of mindful neglect.

"You make sure you fix this screen before I get back…it adds a damn ghetto trash look to the damn ghetto trash look of the place!"

"Why don't you fix it yourself?" Buck shouted back. "I got the screen tools…right next to my Inuit head spreader…besides… ghetto trash is cheap camouflage! You think that map comes with a signature! Dumbass, you never could spot a real sniper! It was me and Banjo Dave that was your eyeballs…you were always just a lucky farm boy…three tours and you never stepped in a fire fight…deeper than geese crap! You went through your time with the dust pan side of your rifle…carrying a clip board and sweeping up!"

CHAPTER 2

Flying Imposters

The train jolted Houdini awake, causing his head to roll off the makeshift cushion fashioned from straw, goat, and feather donations by the message carrying sparrows that slipped their square nest under Houdini's head, hoping to soften the golden rabbit's fits of terror.

"You were having an audio nightmare!" bayed Sampson, the larger of the two goats, often misconstrued as a bully because of his satanic green eyes and Indian corn speckled horns. Sampson was known for keeping his opinions as short as the beard on his chin, never needing to validate himself as other species might by baaahhhing and baying on, beaver-splaining. Beavers being the *mammal proclaimed* know-it-all's of the animal kingdom.

Sampson was the custodial protector of Dandelion D. Delilah, Three D, Triple D, Single D, or any combination of Ds for short. Dandelion D. was a star-gazing nannie, lean from consistent night wanderings, her coat was bluish-flame blonde in sheen, and her ice watering eyes that sipped the night sky, were seldom fixed on mud. Sampson and Dandelion D. were inseparable, ransacking root cellars and stealing pies, known for wandering shank to shank beyond the boundaries of their pasture, seeming, to the farmer who raised them, that the two came and went as they pleased, which they did. D. had a penchant for traversing the stars while following the center line of the interstate. Sampson, steering her onto the shoulder until the crawling headlights flashed over them.

"It wasn't a d-d-d-ream or a n-n-n-nightmare..." Houdini burbled, trembling, waiting for the leeching tentacles of the journey to release his frozen body. The golden rabbit's "after vision thaw" went paw and tail with a list of other side effects Houdini incurred, crossing back from the psychedelic death plains of the Kush fields.

"You were howling as if you were roasting in a human fire!" quipped Liondra, the red-tailed hawk, fluffing her wings in a circular rotation—calming her itch to fly.

"I don't remember a single lick of howling?" said Houdini, whose mind took the form of a bur and detached from the golden hare's body when he slept, waking, exhausted from a full night's chase.

"Last night's howling session was nothing!" chuckled the lead guiding fox, Ghostress, through her sparkly, toothed grin. Ghostress recounted the howling she had heard emitted by Houdini on other occasions as she slunk herself like a wisp of white smoke, through Houdini's triplet protectors, born identically marked from separate litters, seated upon the hay bale steps along the albino, red fox's descent.

Most of the animals were nestled on the hay bale stairway, which was stacked like a pyramid against the boxcar wall. In front of the hay bales was a cable reel spool, three feet high and eight feet in diameter. De Gama, chipmunk, master of seeds, divided the travelers' meal portions on the platform top of the cable spool. The giant wooden spool served as a gathering table for the travelers and was secured to the ceiling by a steel cable, to keep it from rolling about the car. The rest of the container was empty, except for a thorough scattering of straw mingled with the rusty train travel detritus that coated the floor.

"A dusting of snow mild howling, if that!" seconded Ghostress' trailing partner, Slickbend, as he instinctively echoed the movement of his guide mate, completing the same S curve through Houdini's three identical guardian hares before settling, side by side, with Ghostress, on the bottom step of the hay bale risers.

The hay bales were stacked from the floor of the boxcar to the ceiling, reaching just beneath the head of the great horned owl, Bob, who swooped down and released his highest perch rites, followed in flight by his lifelong mate, Dylan. The pair of great horned owls settled upon the cable spool wire, slung just above Houdini's shivering body, continuing their two headed inquisition.

"Are you sure your mother wasn't part coyote?" hooted Bob, his eyebrows connected to his ears, meeting at the point of his hooked beak in the mark of a cursive V.

"You have a jackal's bugle in your lungs!" colorfully embellished his partner, Dylan.

"It was frightening…"

"Even for us…

"Seers and knowers of the night!"

The owls communicated through a wedded mind, which was their tandem custom, rotating their heads in the opposite direction of the other as they hooted their shared thoughts.

"Hearing the noises that came out of you…"

"As if you were possessed by something evil…"

"We were afraid to wake you…"

"Lest we bring the horror here among us…"

"Like a human virus!" The owls completed their final phrase in unison, rocking up and down along the wire on their nest smashing talons.

"I've plucked peeking squirrels from tree holes. Their shocking cries were morning songs compared to your pitiful beg-fest! *Cluck, cluck, cluck!*" quipped the hawk as she opened her wings, glided the perimeter of the boxcar then claimed the apex, hay bale spot, made vacant by the wedded owls.

Liondra, the red-tailed hawk, was the most feared huntress to ever dot the sky, extinguishing several native species from her surrounding territory until the animal council offered her Central Park as her sole hunting ground, guaranteeing the hawk open season on a limitless supply of rats and setting up her residency, as a perk, on a Madison Avenue window ledge, knowing the hawk's fondness for catching her reflection off penthouse glass.

"Why squawk of killing squirrels? When we asked you to join this mission, we told you there would be no bloodshed between species, we made it clear. I've fainted from the shadow of an oak leaf…floating in the wind! You don't know the fear your talons hold!" hissed the chipmunk, hopping up and down hysterically on the top of the cable spool.

"I'll do my part rest assured! *Cluck, cluck, cluck!* I will eat my corn, dried beans and seeds, but I will wish for squirrel blood! Squirrel blood's my jam!" squealed the hawk.

"You don't have any idea what it's like to be preyed upon!" rapidly chattered De Gama, shadow boxing and throwing combinations toward the mighty huntress, queen of the sky.

"Every beast is a meal for a different master! My feathered bib's as blood smeared as any lion, egret or lamb!" declared the hawk, sizing up the chipmunk through her predacious glare, converting the taste of her jam from squirrel to chipmunk.

"Don't you dare look at me like that! I'm the master of seeds, for chrysalis sake! Keep it up, keep telling us all how squirrel blood's your jam, and I'll deduct a pumpkin seed from your meal pile, for every utterance, and divvy up your loss among the rest of us, that don't want to snack on their neighbors!" vehemently chirped the chipmunk, puffing her cheeks and flipping her tail in an agitated manner.

"Not a single rabbit more…no more! All this gnawing metal!" howled Striker, having wandered away from the group, pawing at his snout as he stared mournfully through the crack in the boxcar doors, reading the smells off a passing breeze.

"I don't ever remember howling. Cabbage veins—that's how distinct these visions come, sometimes, like a mess of sprouts—wadded to no end. In my journey from the Kush fields I returned to the crystal precipice of golden ice. That's where my mind was, while my body was being chased, screaming…my mind was submersed around speckled opals and reflective gems, dripping and melding into unrecognizable colors…gem sparks flying off in multiple hues!"

"I recall that part of your journey…" offered Barrister Holmes, heartily fluffing every wrinkle of his fur while reclining in a receptive posture.

"The precipice of golden ice!" hooted both owls, Dylan and Bob, "twit-too-woo—the jewels on that ridge were fired anew!"

"The crags of the cliffs and stockyard crowds…" included Delilah D, staring into the crags of the mountain herself, which is where Houdini left her off in his story.

The sparrows, the hawk and the crow had never heard Houdini's tale of his return trip back from the Kush fields, but the other animals all knew the golden precipice Houdini spoke of—all listening intently with their senses, knowing very well that they themselves might be called upon to recollect a missing element when the story was retold, or recount the tale themselves, if the guardian hares failed and Houdini were eaten for his brightness.

Striker, lay down with his paws folded over his snout, following Houdini's tale with his eyes while forcefully pressing his nose to the ground, subduing a roiling metallic scent trapped inside it as a foe.

"At the brink of the precipice was the most spectacular vision… unimaginable…without comparison to anything known—in the fur. I was afraid to hold witness to all of what was beautiful unfolding before me, so close, yet I was cowering, crowded with other animals, all burying our heads into the crags of a cliff, until somehow I found myself at the very edge of the thing I was afraid of. Looking out…that's when I woke up. I had forgotten my own fear, not wanting to see what was beautiful—closing my senses from its calling. There was a monstrous purple hornet too, that flew above us, on watch, over all, and above the hornet, there was a single bird—we could feel the thrust of its wings. When the bird flew against the sun, an older, bluer burning sun than ours, we froze in the place where we stood. Our very beings cracking inside out from the searing cold penetrating into us as a crowding sleep. In the same instant, whatever sun it was that stood above us, returned, and we were all thawed. Every traveler that ventured forth with me was frozen to its marrow and warmed anew, by the passing of the great bird flying against the sun."

"Caw, caw, caw!" the enormous crow exploded, perched on a bolt head that protruded into the boxcar at the furthest distance from the arrangement of the other animals, popping her hooded head in and out, concealing her pecked out eye in the corrugated wall shadow. "I have heard many stories of this great bird, many stories. I have heard too, that at death, we fly in its sight, and feel the power of the great bird's wings—soaring through us, from an unreachable height in the sky!"

"Groundhogs speak of the Grand Weasel escorting the dead through a golden maze. Animals that are eaten...go in pieces." recalled the feisty chipmunk, expertly sorting various seeds into calculated piles, as if she were dealing a paw of poker. "Some turns of the Grand Weasel's maze, are stockaded silos of thoughts," De Gama spit three concealed pumpkin seeds into Liondra's pile, exchanging a wink with the feathered huntress. "These... cupboarded thoughts, sprung open at death...lead to blood curdling predators, built from unquestioned things. Other ways lead to banquet tables filled with bushels of silver grains and mother of pearl coated almonds."

"I can't confirm knowing the Grand Weasel's path, but the great bird is alive...from the world I visited...living in my hackles!" said Houdini, as the memory of frost thawed from his marrow and he began to contemplate moving.

The three message carrying sparrows crisscrossed the boxcar, as the rumbling sound of the train, bending around a river curve, sang its rattling hum, accented by the siren sound of the steel wheels, stressing the rails.

"Has anything changed since we gathered our last news?" Houdini asked, taking a few short hops from the place where he first awoke, while nonchalantly dodging a diving sparrow and then another—having moved somehow directly into their flight path.

"These annoying sparrows, flying about, they brought the last word in, then stayed. They've been circling the car ever since." answered Barrister Holmes, stealing a glance at his own meal pile, counting the pumpkin seeds that like Liondra, were also his favorite.

"Nothing's changed?" inquired Houdini.

"Everything's the same." confirmed Veshnuk, the bravest and emotional strength of the triplet troika.

"Same ol', same ol'." added Durgan, shiftiest of Houdini's identical protectors.

"Same grass...different fields." concluded Rishna, marked, blemish for blemish as his fellow guardians, impossible to tell one from the other, though Rishna had an aversion to cilantro, Veshnuk and Durgan's chew-to-the-root favorite herb, which tasted to Rishna, like soap.

The triplet hares, born with identical markings from different litters, were absolutely indistinguishable, which helped in their protective duties overseeing Houdini's safety. Whenever Houdini was cornered by a curious predator, which was often, the hares implemented their momentary diversion by simply appearing. The foe would then be forced to reconcile its drooling vision of the golden rabbit, surrounded by hares, replicated in triplicate, followed by Barrister Holmes' orchestrated escape plan, leaving Durgan to lure off and shake the predator.

De Gama, having nearly completed her seed rationing duty, vanished through the shaft of the spool and re-appeared, hauling a dog mauled, white Frisbee, into the center of the boxcar. The chipmunk then log rolled herself atop a full liter of bottled water, bringing the bottle to rest, without spilling a drop, at the edge of the Frisbee. De Gama tipped the contents of the water bottle into the disc until the watering trough was filled to its grip.

"Who wants to drink first?" the chipmunk inquired, as the three sparrows swooped in and begin filling their beaks. "Just drink it! Don't bathe in it! Who sent these messenger sparrows? It's as if they were schooled by a herd of lemmings!" scolded the chipmunk, having magically appeared back at the edge of the cable spool, returning her attention to completing her seed tally.

"Striker, we've mounted this enterprise to rescue your offspring. If there is anything you've found flawed in our plan— bark the alarm. It's in our best interest to avoid dire combustion and confused events, lest we all end up encased in sausage!" sounded Barrister Holmes, noticing that Striker had removed himself from the arrangement of the group, who except for the birds, were all den curled in different spots among the hay bales. Holmes was lounging against the base of the cable reel spool, underneath the rim. De Gama counted out seeds above, using the velvet softness of Holmes' ears as a work tarp.

Lying flat at the door of the boxcar, Striker crawled toward his companions. Half of the warrior beagle's face was separated by the teething wound the yellow eyed wolf had scraped across his scalp, dragging his countless other scars with him, tail to snout, Striker emptied his mind, "I keep smelling the rabbits I killed escaping your entrapment! They all seemed…peacefully engaged…the blood metal scent coming off their bodies—keeps pulling me back!" Striker howled.

"Metallic! Copper! Iron-bronze!" answered each of the three guardian hares in unison.

"I keep smelling gnawing metal…running through them! Each kill a different metal smell, locked in my snout!" Striker answered, dredging the side of his snout against the hay scattered floor, pawing at it, as if he were trying to remove his muzzle from his head.

"Did you find anything strange in their prevention of your escape? Anything peculiar?" asked Barrister Holmes, his ears unfolding over the top of the cable spool, between the many seed piles.

"Why didn't they get out of the way?" barked Striker. "They risked their lives forming a paper barrier? And they come dragging their metallic scent back into my snout today—on the brink of my pup's rescue? Why today?"

The giant Flemish hare unstacked his body from underneath the cable spool, hopping reassuringly toward Striker, in his lumbering, wrinkle-furred way. "The hares stationed outside the area where you escaped were all terminally ill. Those hares that blocked your path, volunteered for those positions."

"The hares I killed at the end of my escape…were all sick? You never told me that?" queried Striker, perplexed to the point that it was evident to the other animals that he was suffering, as they uncoiled their bodies, anticipating the need for an emotional animal huddle.

"Those ten blocking hares were all bonded in various stages of withering, unlike other species, we hares gather our sick together..." responded Rishna.

"So they can drive us all crazy! Standing in the hurried way! Old, slow chewing hares are obnoxious!" interrupted Durgan.

"Our toothless hares remain the strongest links in our commmunity. Their tunneling days displayed in the passages they built, exemplifies how the cherished sun sets within each rise!" continued Rishna.

"Old rabbits clutter the way and slow everything down!" erupted Durgan, running his ears through his front paws, kicking his hind legs over the edge of the hay bale.

"The root of all evil for a hare...is haste!" measured Barrister Holmes.

"They make us all crazy..." added Veshnuk, seated beside Durgan and above Rishna, though none of the other animals, by sight or scent could tell any of the three hares, the one from the other, or which was seated where.

"But we accept them..." said Rishna, "Knowing they mirror what's to come...we are all living under the same canopy, the ancient Philosopher Hopprates was right, *a rabbit can't expect to find radishes digging in a turnip bed...but it can happen...the wind carries and plants more seeds than human kind!*"

"Those hares that chose to meet you, where you met, were useful up until the very last twitch of their whiskers." concluded Barrister Holmes, trying to steer the conversation back on point and away from the guardian hares, who held radically different opinions and would argue to great end over the length of straw.

"That doesn't make killing them easier—for me!" Striker growled, almost inaudibly, as he began trotting along the rectangular outline of the boxcar. The tracking foxes took their positions, Ghostress maneuvering her way in front of Striker, and Slickbend taking his post on Striker's tail. The hay bale stacks were converted into the obstacle course portion of the animal chase as Slickbend, Ghostress and Striker, leapt around their nestled passenger mates, while opening up speed on the walls that offered little resistance in the way of barriers. Sampson chose to chase the three participants *ram-dumbly*.

"My good hound, though their efforts to you seemed futile, it was anything but that to them! Our blocking hares volunteered!" shouted Barrister Holmes to a place where he felt his friend's snake bitten ears were headed.

Striker and the tracking foxes reached top speed, lapping the perimeter of the boxcar, turning their pursuit of each other into a syncopated dance.

"That's different somehow from being murdered?" Striker barked, stretching out his strides as he once did busting headlong for a kill from a hidden trail.

"Many of your victims were in pain, their death at the force of your skull, was an option they weighed, equally; universally consenting to the possibility of that very outcome. That's mercy, my friend, twice blessed. *Blessing him that barks, or she that screeches.* You brought swift death to them, crushing the shell of that slow, timeless snail! A hound's mercy is weighed as light as a lion!" answered Barrister Holmes, passionately, remembering each of the ten blocking hares as he spoke, whispering their names under his breath.

Striker ran full speed circling the boxcar until a thought pressed its way passed the surging flood of anger that consumed and drove his limbs. Exiting the draft established by the two tracking foxes, Striker leapt atop the cable spool and struck a defiant stance, the multiplicity of his scars glistening in a widening crease of light that yawned through the crack in the boxcar door, bathing Striker amid a momentary break from the unseen clouds above. "The blocking hares volunteered to die but I killed them all intentionally! Nothing changes my intention!" Striker was overwhelmed by a penetrating, metallic scent, forcing him to buckle forwards, pulling at his snout, flipping off the cable spool, landing on his back! Dragging himself the length of the railroad car, rabidly struggling to separate his own head from his body.

"There's not a single wasp that can repel their sting, yet bees lose their own life in the same display of anger. Yet the wasp... flies back to its nest with a story on its mandibles and often dances a wing-jig for its queen, declaring its antics, sting by sting! The story the bee tells, maybe Houdini will recollect what the ruptured bees sing...on their way to the hives of Valhalla!" offered Barrister Holmes, his long antenna-like ears raising and lowering as if they had minds of their own.

Perhaps..." answered Striker, shaking his entire body thoroughly then padding off, snorting and pawing at his snout on his way to the Frisbee trough. Striker was met there by the rest of the travelers that all drank together, lapping at the water Frisbee, pack thinking.

"So is the thing you think you see, from the death of our blocking hares—that didn't block. They chose to impede your escape because their time for digging radishes in a turnip patch had past. When the mystery of life has shed its casing, then one is overwrought by the calamity of all that looms mundane. There was nothing new for the blocking hares to experience…except more pain."

"How is their sacrifice, throwing their bodies in my path, different from a human terrorist?" Striker asked.

"Those hares chose to defend our community with their own lives, from you. How can you call that an act of terrorism?" asked Barrister Holmes, shrugging both of his ears separately, then forming question marks with each.

"But I was running in the other direction!" Striker validated his argument, trumping Holmes' ears by using his body to point itself.

"Where is the terrorist element in that? You ran in a direction that our blocking hares met you in…that's the question you need to consider." answered Holmes, the gentle wrinkles of his fur fluttering like lake ripples.

"But it's suicide. Isn't that the same human thing?" howled Striker, the question he harbored rattling through him, his scars scattered about his face and limbs, attesting to his collision with life. His coat, speckled with so many missing patches, that the raw, pinkness of his flesh, added another color to his fur.

"Where in the actions of our blocking hares, can you find any measure of destruction or malice towards another animated soul?" cross-examined Holmes mildly.

"What about me?" Striker barked, releasing a low beagle howl, which mournfully grew louder.

"How can that be violent? You said yourself that our blocking hares, served as a paper barrier. Aspiring towards the greater good, isn't any living thing made more whole by being connected to something greater than the sum of all its parts—as well as... the sum of all its parts? Tending smoldering embers to blaze a stranger's fire?"

Striker mooed, blocking everything rushing through his snout from the outside world in order to follow Barrister Holmes reasoning, moaning from his belly as a cow.

"Even if it's unexplainable...doesn't the good in this life, echo and inform the next, beyond evil?" asked Barrister Holmes, lying flat in a cascading puddle of his own fur.

"Humans call them recipes! Unlocking a flavor from a written list!" bayed Sampson, remembering how Delilah convinced him to snatch a window sill of pies, made from *recipes*. Sampson received a corn broom thrashing for his actions, cleaning his beard of rhubarb while he manipulated the blows to rout his fleas and unsettle flies.

"Surely any evolving species responds to its own wish..." hooted first, Bob, the great horned owl and then his mate.

"Recycling itself to the best of its own abilities."

"My migrating ancestors, caw, caw, caw! Instilling flight paths...from one generation to the next!" pecked in the giant crow. Enlisted into the task at paw, rescuing Striker's offspring, because of her excellent stealing skills, returning half of her branded face back into the corrugated ruffle of the railcar wall.

"I was wondering how we were going to pass the non-foraging bouts of time...riding this iron horse! How deliciously exciting!" bayed Triple D, who set out in search of a second portion of cotton candy made from maple syrup, before acquiring a taste for the patterns of the sky.

"Let's define the argument down to its roots…" stated Bob, turning its head from its mate.

"So we can measure where we start…" Dylan replied.

"To where we finish." the owls completed in unison then added.

"For anything left undone…

"Is purely a fuse…"

"Lit by the mind and left astray!"

"There's no argument. It's a clear cut thing." Rishna stated.

"Either you're in for the sake of another, or you're out. No matter who you serve, you serve or you resent serving." expressed Vishnuk, passionately.

"I choose to serve the golden rabbit!" rallied Durgan.

"As do I." matched Rishna.

"All of us, born as one to serve as one…" swelled Vishnuk.

"For the sake of the golden rabbit!" the identical, first born kits from separate litters began chattering against each other's teeth in a tribal male-rabbit ritual, their mirth spilling onto their feet, thumping rhythmically with the irrepressible joy of a shared cause.

"Hold off on the tribal chattering or you'll fill the whole car with the smell of burning teeth! Serving isn't the argument here." stated Barrister Holmes.

"Cluck, cluck, cluck, an argument has to have at least two sides and possibly threeeeeee! Unless, you've no mind to mind, sitting all day on a clothesline, crow squawking over each other in atonal opinions!" screeched the hawk, clutching her throat.

"I knew this trip wasn't going to end, without some animal making a crow crack! I might have guessed it would spill out from the blood striped bill of a hawk!" cawed the crow, thrusting her head out from the crease of the boxcar wall, exposing her blind eye.

"Then let me ask you this crow, to make our own argument smooooother. Why are you here, and not on a clothesline, or a telephone wire? Cluck, cluck, cluck!" questioned the hawk.

All the animals were silent, until the crow let loose an unflustered, feather curdling guffaw, "Caw-caw-caw-caw!" the crow exploded laughing, drawing the animals to join in.

"What is the argument, Striker?" Dandelion D, bayed to the great warrior.

"How is the cause of a terrorist, different from the cause of a blocking rabbit? Is that simple enough?" asked Striker.

"Are you asking...that...if the value of all life is equal, are the actions of all animals measured equally in the eyes of the animal kingdom? Is that your question?" asked Barrister Holmes, broadening the idea in order to make better use of the argument, lumbering a few wrinkly hops back to the base of the cable spool.

"I was thinking of human terrorism as a blight." answered Striker.

"Are there terrorist blights in the animal kingdom?" asked Dandelion D.

"Termites and long horned beetles maybe they are some..." reflected Holmes, making a spark from a flint with his back paws, catching his fur on fire in order to light his long horned pipe and taking in a deep draw of the many dried herbs he smoked. The second paw clouds that Holmes emitted, produced a calming effect on the surrounding animals, the scents varied magically from cinnamon to vanilla to licorice, all sparked from the same bowl. Barrister Holmes told anyone who asked that he smoked corn powder, after catching himself feeling fatigued one day, explaining the many intricacies of his personal blend.

"A terrorist commits his life to a cause at the promise of something greater, beyond any plains known or wandered." offered Striker.

"No use of raven witchcraft could transform the good will of our blocking hares to something other than the core root of their own choosing—which my hound friend, is worth dying for...not once...but as many times, in as many lives, as is required!"

"I'm not following you..." Striker whined, the scented smoke from Holmes' pipe clouds taking Striker back to the most primitive recesses of his mind.

"Choice! The ten blocking hares you killed, died living "in" their right to choose. They wagered their own lives defending the living!"

"Rec-i-pes, rec-i-pes, rec-i-pes!" Sampson bayed, in a peanut huckster's cadence.

"Good will is eternal. It has no end." continued Barrister Holmes, letting out a juniper, sage cloud.

"But isn't that a terrorist principle as well? Rewarding a full belly on a desired plain? So there is never any unrest food searching, fed and catered for?" Striker asked, "Where nothing can be verified in the fur, except the rubble pile, left as the result?"

"To the effect of what change? Isn't that part of the question, too?" asked Dandelion D.

"You call it sacrifice. A terrorists calls it the same thing. Death to the declarer can't be equal to both parties? Are you saying that Great Nature chooses sides?" Striker asked. "Is that what you're saying? That if Great Nature flipped a stone, it would land neither on the side of good, nor evil, but in between the two—standing on edge?" Striker stopped for a moment, standing deathly still, and then, as only a hound can, he howled! "Without a greater influence, there is no difference!"

"You've said it before…" hooted Bob, interspersed by his partner Dylan.

"The path of an ant can't be observed…"

"Inside the head of the traveling insect…"

"Looking to pick up something ten times its own weight…"

"But from the color of the sunflower petals above!" concluded both owls, accompanied by the she goat, Delilah, seconded in turn by each of the guardian hares upon their own concurrent reflection.

"Precisely! Recipes! A thing written down in human scrawl, left on a window sill, passed on…in taste," cooed Dandelion D.

"Sticking to ones' beard!" bayed Sampson, remembering the rhubarb taste and the beating he received, bundled as one.

"The difference is like the waves in a pond that branch out in a circle from something as simple as a stone, thrown by a child from the shore. Those waves go forth gently, orchestrated by Great Nature herself—they can go, no other way—no matter the size of the stone. But the ripples of terror spread out indifferently. There is no touch of nature's handiwork in their progression, only misery and anguish—the seed from which they're sprung. What kind of manmade element, infiltrating the soil, can grow from there? Nothing that should be fed or found on milk teats, tickling the tongues of babes. Mankind lives in its own path, whether he chooses or not to get out of his own way, that's the human condition."

"And the metallic smell?" asked Striker.

Durgan, perched on the hay bale, above his other two mirror reflections said, "The animals you encountered…"

"Killed…" corrected Vishnuk.

"Thought he killed…" countered both Barrister Holmes and Rishna.

"They were let be in mineral halls…" continued Durgan.

"That section of our lair has healing powers, its walls are impacted with quartz, zinc, copper, iron ore…" interrupted Vishnuk.

"They didn't smell of blood, they smelled of the minerals their halls were layered in." concluded Rishna.

"But why is their scent impacting on me, now? I haven't thought of those blocking rabbits for months? Ever since we got into this railway car, I have thought of nothing but those ten blocking rabbits…and their haunting, metallic stench!"

"What's beneath the idea of their death, their scent, the action of killing them…look beneath their scent to perhaps…hear what they meant?" inquired Barrister Holmes in a soft penetrating way, his ears escalating up and down.

"You mean…my question?" asked Striker, turning his head as all dogs do when they are apt to encounter a crayfish scuttling across the floor in front of them.

"Without an inquisitive mind, thoughts circle for the taste of their own tail! A fish isn't born with a hook in its mouth—what is your question, Striker? Yours and yours alone?"

"How is it...that in one moment I can escape your capture, thinking about separating myself from my role as a murderer and then...within a few full strides, kill ten more hares as easily known to me as treeing squirrels?"

The question the great warrior regaled upon his companion didn't fluster the Flemish hare, a rabbit native to all surrounding habitats. The rest of the animals stood at the ends of their fur waiting for Barrister Holmes' response.

"Those ten blocking hares you "think" you killed...how is it they remained inside your snout? Visiting you with their metalic scent, on the very brink of our rescue?"

"I don't know..."

"I see the pattern!" said the youngest traveler, Dandelion D. Delilah, exploding with uncontainable enthusiasm. "Striker is keeping them alive...breathing them still!"

"Is that possible?" asked Striker.

"Do you think it's possible? We never expected you to escape. The path the blocking hares met you on was theirs and yours, combined. We didn't send them. They waited to meet you where you met." Barrister Holmes concluded, filling the car with a vanilla, cinnamon waft.

"Live a thousand years...I never thought I'd be schooled by a goat!" howled Striker.

All the animals let out a large laugh, chasing each other until their mirth subsided; agreeing that Striker's argument was concluded, they set upon reviewing their rescue plans, for each had a very specific role to play in order to complete the task at paw. Most of the animals ate their seed piles as Striker outlined the plan, the goats ate plain straw flavored with garbage. The crow flew away from the safety of its bolt head and settled upon the cable spool, joining the rest of the company, picking around the pumpkin seeds in her pile, hiding her face in her wing. When thirst came upon them as a pack, they lapped at their communal Frisbee, the sparrows drinking off the bowed heads of the others.

CHAPTER 3

Occupant #3

octor Schworlitzburg was the tallest of the one hundred bio-medical professionals who were each assigned to individually monitor one hundred of the total ten thousand case specimens. The case specimens, recipients, were enlisted, like Clarence, to survive as many days of their upcoming experimental internment as possible. Schworlitzburg stood toweringly erect at six foot seven, an overstretched unpainted canvas of a man, with an NBA wing span, unruly Sephardic-fro, and a horseshoe crab sized nose, that crowded most of the man's face, visible to Clarence behind a transparent goalie shield, fogged at the nostrils.

"I'm Doctor Herman Schworlitzburg, (snort, snort) thank you for your service to this country and for volunteering for our three month internment program. The information we intend to gather from the large group that you're a part of is vital for what we'll be facing in the impinging years to come, but…(snooooort, snooooort)…."

After what Clarence surmised was the unanticipated summoning of a king through the doctor's nasal passages, Schworlitzburg's fingers skipped across his keyboard, his eyes shutter speeding through images of patients flashing against his face shield. The visor reflected a computer screen, dropped from a low ceiling and partially separating the two men in the sanitized room, where every corner folded onto itself, like the inside of a milk carton. Schworlitzburg labored under the white flag of millennial etiquette, whilst simultaneously navigating the galactic pathways of the sphere mind. Schworlitzburg's hands twitched from his keyboard to a Kevlar enforced pen pocket, which housed five Ibex tipped, twenty year, "game" scalpels, used to post and remove decals. After hyper-fondling each scalpel, pondering moves, Schworlitzburg appeared cornered, smiling as if someone had tossed a false expression across his face from the bottom of a paint can.

Clarence followed an impulse to crowd the doctor, rising from his chair and thrusting his hand over the white rectangular desk that marked the boundary between the two men in the scrubbed white work quadrant. Clarence's aggressive gesture sent Dr. Schworlitzburg spinning into a lion tamer of a tizzy, rolling his chair in front of his body from behind his desk and flapping the arms of his laboratory coat, his movements constricted amid an area built for laborers to code while remaining seated.

"We don't shake hands here, Mr. Clay, that's one thing you'll soon understand about the environment you're entering. We don't unmask—you won't want to, and we don't do human contact. How about we start you off with an elbow pump? How is that my man?" Doctor Schworlitzburg bent his back oddly along the distorted angle of the ceiling as he stood up to his crunched height, presenting his elbow to Clarence, who obliged him, butted the doctor's pterodactyl wing and then observed Doctor Schworlitzburg burrowing himself back into his imaginary bunker on the other side of the table.

Doctor Schworlitzburg kicked on. The features behind his mask narrowing as he spoke, reminding Clarence of the final blind turn in a slaughtering pen. "Our terrain is constructed to grow disease, Mr. Clay. You'll come in contact with things…we'll cure them, and if we need to, we'll take you out and reinsert you back into captivity as many times as you consent. As long as we feel your safety is not at risk…we'll keep you healthily employed, in our captivity structure, accruing bonus dollars, for the next ninety days…you and your…" Doctor Schworlitzburg's convivial momentum derailed, as if he were a carnival ride bereft of power. Amid a background of patients' faces, Dr. Schworlitzburg clicked open a file revealing a puppy channel feed.

"Dog…dog!" barked Dr. Schworlitzburg, retrieving his keyboard from Clarence's perusal, Clarence noted that the keyboard was covered with tiny micro stickers. There were moats, bridges, army outposts and villages, meticulously decoupaged under, on top of and along the sides of the typewriter-high, fingerboard panel, culminating in many fortified cities, stationed along the ASDF, JKL; home row, surrounding detailed castles positioned on the GH keys. "Of course…yes, dog! Dog!" repeated Doctor Schworlitzburg, abandoning the file he had opened while reciting scripted material, tarantula dancing his hand across his game scalpels, pondering moves then reluctantly excising a brigade outpost decal from the Z and question mark keys of his finger panel. "We have a full emergency medical unit on hand in our biosphere, supplied and staffed to treat any internally created pandemic that we induce. We're testing things here, Mr. Clay, that we feel will have serious repercussions in the near, or not too distant future. We have adequate vaccines pre-supplied to minimize recipient casualties…all we need to know…to study…is how fast a virus tags to its source and spreads. Thanks to you…and the other nine

thousand, nine hundred and ninety nine prescribers like you…
we can follow enough people…living in a definable proximity
to each other, to monitor and test our laboratory contagions, in
motion. We've simulated a normal living environment within
our terrain that patterns a general life cycle—ninety days, being
the maximum time before the center relinquishes its hold and…
the falcon cannot recognize the falconer. Translation being, Mr.
Clay…we can't keep our information pure. The knowledge *we* seek
to obtain is under constant attack by technophile pirates. Ninety
days from now we scrape our experimental plates clean."

"*Whatever* I need to know, *whenever* I need to know
something…I'll ask… you'll answer, agreed?" Clarence interrupted
forcefully.

"By all means." The doctor's nostrils bristled behind his goalie
shield, his singular expression returning for a curtain call as he
reached for a game scalpel, removing two fortified bridge decals,
from opposite sides of his keyboard.

"I don't care who pays you to shoot information up the chain,
but I want my contact point to be you. Can you confirm that?"
Clarence ran his callused hands across the fresh shaved baldness
of his head, stroking the grain stubs that formed a landing strip
down the center of his scalp while rolling an acorn through his
knuckles.

"Every medical scientist on this project is assigned to follow the
data provided to each of us by one hundred resident prescribers.
We're responsible to track our prescribers, individually; but
as the conditions in the biosphere are scientifically harshened
incrementally, the number of our prescribers…will decrease. The
greater amount of data could fall upon the burden of a random

few—but that's unlikely. What's more conceivable, Mr. Clay, is that our study will marginalize around a rare number of survivors. If there is any way I can assist you…in getting through as many days as possible…consecutively…I'll be available to you, as well as the professional depth of our medical and psychiatric staff…"

"Do you know how I got here, Doc?"

"Please…enlighten me, Mr. Clay. We've been several decades preparing this study…I confess my head is significantly…piked… atop mounds of endless, preparatory details—maintaining only half a step ahead of prying phaantoms!" Doctor Schworlitzburg raised his shield, feeding his nostrils air before lowering his visor back into place. "Lazarus was called back to life…to code… instructing us all to keep one foot out of the grave…serving both God and PMeister and Schoemann in balanced strides!" Overcome by his own joke, Doctor Schworlizburg battled against the struggle to strangle his own mirth, accompanied by a circus collection of apologetic gestures, speaking through hiccup burps of breath, his fingers pondering choices over his game scalpels. "If you have a superpower, Mr. Clay, I hope it's not leaping tall buildings in a single bound!"

"When I was a kid, I wanted to be a part of those hometown parades…waving back to the crowds…in uniform. Full military cabbage on display."

Doctor Schworlitzburg rolled himself as close as possible to Clarence, not listening, but studying him as a specimen, his fingers floating from his keyboard to his Ibex tipped scalpels, repeating the process while checking his fingers for tack. "Now…I'm happy to sweep the streets after the celebration passes—it's more honest work. Seeing all the garbage left behind, that's where the truth is. If...*if* I could save thousands of your so called specimens with a single teaspoon of my own spit, I wouldn't bother. I'm on a selfish mission. I don't care if you kill all nine thousand, nine hundred and ninety nine recipients in this tower...but me. I'm done collecting medals for squeezing people's heads together, only to have them curse me out, all the way back to Jesus, when their morphine's cut. Ninety days and a wake up, Doc. You get your data, I get paid...and me and my dog...we go back to the farm. I survive...that's my superpower."

"The longer you can endure the internment, the more data we can obtain. We insert our medical chip into you and your... *animal*...on the train, leading into the biosphere. Painless. From that chip, we can monitor your every pulse. We collect our chips after your internment expires, then write you a final check, based on the amount of days you participate. The information obtained during the next three months will save..."

"What's the whole financial enchilada come to, Doc? My end, bonus cut and all?"

Dr. Schworlizburg's fingers set upon his keyboard, gushing code into a collapsing fire wall. "As well as your ninety day internment here, Mr. Clay, you will have the ability to serve as a possible resource for many years to come. Most of the information that's to be obtained from this experiment can be transmitted orally...over time. We're not savages, Mr. Clay. We're scientists working against a clock wound by the idle hands of modern man consumed by distraction. Modern man that has squandered his instinctive sense of reality for a peek into a black hole...shrinking the vastness of his mind around the idea that only his phone can convince him of who he is and where he's going." Doctor

Schworlizburg's attention switched to the overhead screen, then flooded onto his keyboard, his face contorting behind his shield, "With the help of you and your fellow prescribers, we hope to gather enough information to help us outrun whatever it is we can't see. I can guarantee you one thing, Mr. Clay..."

"What's that, Doc?"

"Anything you might come in contact with during your ninety day internment, or anything you take with you that you might end up harboring as a direct result from your internment here...God forbid, for the rest of your life...you will be attended to, Mr. Clay, and compensated for. You have my word."

"Sounds...all too familiar, doc. What does the bonus money amount to? You neglected to say."

"It's set at a manicured suburb wage." Doctor Schworlitzburg replied, his nostrils smothered against the shield.

The two men in the sanitized room stared across the rectangular desk at each other. A flightless bird of a man, with a paperweight for a nose, seemingly set in place to keep the rest of his features from sliding off the blankness of his untraveled face; seated across from a third generation farmer whose brown scalp, leathered from the sun, sported the beginnings of what would become his signature red, white and blue mohawk.

"It's six hundred dollars a day. The more days you remain in the quarantine structure of our biosphere, the larger your bonus money...lumps. Bonus interest is compounded daily. I can schedule an appointment for you, if you wish, with one of our payroll accountants, pre or post span?"

Clarence studied the packaged office space, following the seamless corners that overlapped and folded around the ceiling and floors. "This structure of yours, your biosphere...it's in Canada, aye? I was going to bring my skates." Clarence pressed.

"Our bio-structure Mr. Clay, isn't built on Canadian or American soil. We've constructed our *environmental complex* on a ten mile, private bird sanctuary. Huckleberry Island is uninhabitable, except for the migrating flocks following the southern trail of the Atlantic Flyway...which we have accommodated, based on MBI considerations. If you make it with us, Mr. Clay, to the end of your full ninety day span...you'll witness...under the recycled plastic of our dome...the birds flying over. They land in flocks of thousands, several species, three months to the very first day of your internment...which will start officially tomorrow. Today is a day outside of time and off the proverbial clock."

"I'll be on hand to verify the last species that flies in for a landing, Doc. Seems there can never be enough landing spots, for what's considered *foul*."

Doctor Schworlitzburg hovered over his keyboard continuing at where he left off in his admission speech, all the while fumbling over his pocket scalpels, selecting and twirling them individually, contemplating moves and checking his outer extremities for tack. "You'll be living in a ten thousand prescriber confined community. We've been training teams of suppliers to work in this environment, so it's already sustainable. Some of the people you'll be coming into contact with are directly employed by us, in order to maintain an immediate flow of perishable goods into the terrain, as well as directly monitoring the health, safety, and wellbeing of you and your fellow prescribers. Your role for the next three months is to bring us information, through your own biological experience, within our applied environment."

"The fifty-four K bonus, Doc, that's outside the guaranteed ninety K bonus for the initial sign up and…what did you call it?"

"Internment, Mr. Clay. The bonus amounts to six hundred dollars a day—tax free. Do you have any other questions, besides money?

"When do I get to see my dog?"

"Your animal ships out with you, on the same train. You'll be in coach, in a single dwelling compartment designed for us to gather all the medical vitals we need, up to the very moment of your initial entrance into our biosphere. Your animal companion will be lodged with other domestic transports. We suggest a mild sedative for the…" Doctor Schworlitzburg became completely derailed, until he found his synthetic footing and continued, without recognizing that he'd disappeared into a spiritual glitch. "…dog prior to travel, that way, your living cargo will arrive a little groggy…but safe. Groggie doggie…but safe. You can give… the dog…the dog…the pill…along with an immunity packet in a snack bite, or we can administer the sedative in a meal tin… chicken or fish. We also carry a plant based sedative…in case your dog is gluten free."

"I'll give the dog the same pill I take, only half. You can arrange that?"

"I'll see to it. I just need to enter the dog's name?"

"Zorro."

Doctor Schworlitzburg's nostrils flared with interest, as if detecting the rarest of scents, his body booming over his desk toward Clarence in a crane-like fashion.

"Your dog's named after Project Zorro?"

"Just Zorro. Project Zorro…is a long time gone, Doc."

"You had a friend die in that battle, didn't you a…Sargent Sheldrake? Died in command of the company you were later awarded command over? Then you worked as a supply manager?" Doctor Schworlitzburg persisted, his nose, from behind its plastic sheath, wriggling like a gerbil.

"Citizen Sheldrake is alive and well, living off the grid… following the steps of John Muir, last I heard, with our platoon mate, Banjo Dave."

"Very well then." Doctor Schworlitzburg blazed his fingers over his keyboard, clicking and snorting, madly. "I'm glad to hear Citizen Sheldrake is surviving…did you say, Shelldrake was traveling with Mr. David Banjolaro?"

"How much extra money do I get for the dog?" Clarence asked, shifting the control of the inquiry, playing his dog card.

"Excuse me?"

"The dog? What's his salary?"

"The dog's *salary*, Mr. Clay?"

Doctor Schworlitzburg appeared to be under attack, fending off a security invasion with Rachmaninoff inspired defensive flare.

"Aren't you gonna' take the dog's vitals, well as mine…" Clarence continued, "Track his progress? Man's best friend and all?"

Doctor Schworlitzburg fondled his pocket scalpels, removing another decal from the bottom row of his keyboard with a skilful swipe.

"We're able to offer you an extra bonus scale for the dog. Doubling yours, unless the dog has its own social security number? Or is a member of any union?"

"Double my bonus for the dog, but not a separate salary?"

"That's correct, Mr. Clay. The dog doesn't receive a salary for being a dog, just a bonus."

"Can we sign something...so it's documented? Then we can bounce elbows again...alright my man?" Clarence said, charmingly, as he slid his elbow over the table, stealing another glance at Doctor Schworlitzburg's keyboard.

"Is there anything else we need to go over before we split your pill and sedate your animal, Mr. Clay?" Doctor Schworlitzburg asked, swiping off three more decals from his right and left flanks.

"No...just the chance that you might grant me an extra hour or two before we shove off...so I could rustle up a few bonus cats!"

"The biosphere is plenty supplied with cats, Mr. Clay. Few... canines...yours being a fifty-four thousand dollar exception."

"Why so many cats and no dogs, doc? Have you cloned a bunch of old ladies in this sphere you're not telling me about? I saw a Twilight Zone episode like that—a whole planet full of old ladies and cats...no dogs."

"I hope you don't mind cockroach beetles, Mr. Clay? By the end of your internment they'll have the full run of the place. They always do. We breed the cats to help keep the cockroach beetle population under control. In the end...they serve as the bug's last meal...as well as everything else in the sphere. There will be a more extensive, video indoctrination on the train. Unfortunately, we've run over our opening...wedge of time together, Mr. Clay."

Clarence felt an emotional surge flowing through him, a confused morass of mangled feelings that amounted to his need to secure his return to his son, manifesting in an unwillingness to lift himself from where he was seated until that bond was met. "I won't need to contact anybody…"

"You can't. Once you progress this far, it's strictly forbidden."

"I understand…but I want to be able to do any personal banking, from your *germ sphere*…day or night. In case of emergency."

"Of course." Doctor Schworlitzburg agreed, trying not to extend his nostrils too wide he added, "The term *germ sphere*? That's a term I'm unfamiliar with….where did you come by it, Mr. Clay?"

"After you inject your chip, you'll know my pulse, morning noon and night, but I'll always know how to find my way back to this room, that's my other super power…I only hunt to kill." A cryptic change rolled through Clarence's demeanor, dissolving right before Doctor's Schworlitzburg's, Ritalin popped eyes.

"The term germ sphere is a term we're not supporting at this time." Doctor Schworlitzburg said, his cheeks twitching nervously as he struggled to uphold the ends of his used car salesman's grin.

"Why is that?"

"It circulated back to us through a rather…unsavory group of…meddling, bio-tech-pirates…if that makes any sense to you, Mr. Clay."

"It resonates."

"Anything else?"

"If the term *germ sphere* came specifically from meddling mercenaries, what's that make you and your cadre of lab partners,

Doc? Some...new breed of scientific capitalists? Replacing newsstands on every street corner with opioid huts and vaccine kiosks? I could be wrong, Doc, maybe that's not who you are, but what you've become?"

"You've ingested a twisted bit of disinformation, Mr. Clay. I'm the man standing between pillars. Cut my optic hair...and everything crumbles. Any more questions?"

"I am holding you responsible for the welfare of my dog. That's clear, isn't it?"

"Crystal clear, Mr. Clay. It's why we picked you and prepared ourselves to tolerate your insolence. I'm honored to experience your abrasive nature first hand. It's a splendid taste of what we're paying you and your dog an extra fifty-four thousand dollars for. You have a very rare immune system, Mr. Clay. What we call... Platinum Immunity. You're of maximum value to us, Mr. Clay. Within a week, half of our prescribers, once infected, will be transported out. Most of the recipients will be too sick to transport back. We don't expect more than a handful of prescribers to be fit enough to see the bird's land and collect full bonuses. Everyone's on a sliding pay scale, you see. We're not in the smiley face business here, Mr. Clay. We're in the stark, worse-case scenario business. What we learn in the next ninety days...will keep people breathing healthily among each other...far beyond the 26th century. We're testing things in this environment that will be on the horizon...hundreds of years from now...unless...all of mankind backs into each other...going full throttle...in a mass back up camera outing...like the ice age...everyone dying at once, going backwards, taking selfies..."

"I've known my immune system was rare…since the day I enlisted. Any time I had a scratch, I was treated different from other soldiers. Tell me…in your medical records, Doc, do I carry my Christian name, Clarence Woodrow Clay, or a number? What is it, Doc? I'm curious? Christian name or number?"

Clarence could see the flashes of information notices reflecting off Doctor Schworlitzburg's shield as he galloped his fingers across his keyboard.

"You're Occupant Three with an asterisk, Mr. Clay. To the staff here, waiting for this day, and we have been waiting for this day for a long time…you were always Occupant Three with an asterisk, but starting tomorrow…you'll be Occupant Three without an asterisk. One of nine thousand, nine hundred and ninety nine other occupants…without asterisks."

CHAPTER 4

Cage Keepers

"Be mindful nothing happens to that black dog with the brown mask—some kind of Border collie, beagle mix!" Full House, one of the two transport workers manning the final inspection end of the loading dock bellowed, pseudo officiously, as he watched Jucco deftly clear a dolly filled with animal cages stacked four wide and three high.

"I can spot breeds, the happier the heat the merrier the puzzle! The only breed I like is any dead breeding kind! How do you think I met these scars?" Jucco said, scowling like a badly carved pumpkin as he cleared another dolly with an effortless ballet mix of strength and agility, lining up the cages by way of a colored SKU. "Gamebred...damn...slobber-drowning, demon!" Jucco sighed aloud, as if clouding a mirror in the sky, arching his crisscrossing map of a face into the sun, the intersecting divots connecting the stitched lines where Gamebred's teeth had punctured his flesh. The dog having changed grips many times.

"Gamebred...oh boy, here we go!" Full House whispered under his breath, then enunciated more clearly, bullfrog croaking, through his tobacco coated throat, "Your dad, he trained mixed Rots and Pits—Rots and Pits, was it? Gamebred was a Russian mongrel?" Full House Carlson sparked a bowl of pipe tobacco with a fresh match, adjusted his admiral's hat then shifted his belt around his back to support his belly, digging a considerate trench in his mind, for what he hoped was the shorter version of Jucco's Gamebred jag.

"One hundred and twenty-five stitches…my tongue was in so many pieces I couldn't pronounce words full until I was seven. Formed words slow…never finished a full thought." Jucco grumbled from the more pliable side of his face, his lips curling in a jagged weave as he glared at the black dog with the brown mask; crouched, sphinx like, studying the stitched lines of Jucco's face from the center of his cage. "That's the brown mask in here for ya, Cap." said the spine-masted, merchant marine, who carried miles of traveled water within his stride.

Jucco separated Zorro's cage from the featherless chickens with serrated teeth, bred partly from lizards with thick hides; fierce, spur wielding birds, able to fly their gaunt leathery bodies, high enough off the ground to avoid the only other cockroach beetle eating species, native to the dish; the acid crapping, skinless cats.

"I'm going under to my earbuds. I downloaded a fresh bootleg! Billerica Forum, May, seventy-nine. I was there, but I don't remember the set or most of anything else…until about… eighty-three."

"Roger Cap, take your Casey Jones…Dead river groove."

"When you pull out them cat trays, make sure you flip the fans on before you roast any of that acid scat! God help us if those fans aren't on full blast! Second shift contaminated the place to toxic hell, last night! We're lucky the whole station wasn't yellow taped, and all of us marched into white zip suits, head to toe! Damn Toxoplasmosis nightmare!" Full House reckoned, puffing his pipe as he searched his olive green, corduroy suit coat, fifty-two long, for his earbuds. The earbuds, if they had a life, might very well have been hiding. Full House's ears were as big as hanging bats and his canal passages were overrun with a jungle of Venus flytrap-like man hairs.

"Aye, aye, Cap, aye, aye, I'll put the fans on before I toast the cat scat!" Jucco said, as he set to work dragging the cages to the spot where they were to be loaded onto a compact supply train, which docked directly from the tracks onto a cargo ship.

Full House and Jucco inspected all living cargo before any shipment entered the sphere's import hub, located at the base of the pharmaceutical structure, beneath the dish itself. All supplies and all living cargo passed into the base of the sphere by way of radio captained ferries. No one traveled back and forth from the island, once the span was set. Crews were divided on land and attached to the sphere itself. Zorro's passage was linked to the final stream of reptilian chickens and skinless cats. Both species were restocked throughout the duration of the span.

"Gamebred was my stepdad's big money earner. Tried to take my face off before I ever had a chance at having any good looks! I have to pay a high price for someone to find my beauty now! Who wants to fill wedding frames with this golf course face?" Jucco said, separating Zorro's cage from the others.

"Your stitches set you apart from other men—you could never be condemned for a crime you didn't commit, or do another man's time, just because your prints matched—they'd have to match you, stitch for stitch! You're a free man because of those scars, Jucco, making above average, free man's wages! Life's a full kettle of scars, ice skates to first loves! You got all your scars, up front. I stumbled into mine. Rubbing the frost from a car window. Three red haired gingers, Jucco! Sisters! Irish triplets, eleven months apart from the county Cavan! Asphyxiated, blue as berries—wrapped in ruby locks. A mother's nightmare to behold—all mine...catering for a buck. A truck backed against the girls' trunk, idling through the cold fog. We were all parked in a Delaware mushroom field, paid in weight for what we picked in bulk. Temperature dropped forty degrees, too cold to camp. Anything we didn't pluck from that cycle was dead!" Full House rambled on, while imagining himself standing, bare-chested, in the middle of a putting green, coaxing an orange breeze through the center of his chest, his hand waving over an imaginary grill, testing the heat as Jucco spun the first spool of his Gamebred yarn.

"I was a tall freak with stitches and with Frank for a last name...I didn't stand a chance. Coo-coo Jucco Frank-en-*stine*... *took the candy, drank the wine.* Coo-coo Jucco Frank-en-*steen*... *ate the baby, scared the beans!* I heard all the poetic nickname songs. Sung myself to sleep on my own taunter's rhymes, they were so catchy—until I joined the Merchant Marines at seventeen. Went OS to Third Officer by thirty-two. My first trip on the Mississippi was on a corn syrup barge, summer heat, so stale...I had to cut my own breath with a knife! I spent decades zigzagging the great lakes, cracking frozen chunks off my beard! My stepdad wouldn't put Gamebred down. Let him earn and burn, earn and burn! That dog kept me and my stepbrothers and sisters...stepping in church shoes and sneakers. Step-d put him to stud when the steroid dogs took over. The zombie dogs, wrapped in muscles, with extra teeth. My stepdad didn't want to see Gamebred shredded by them pill-muscle hounds, but I did! Every Friday night I waited for the truck to pull in...hoping to see Gamebred, coffin carried off the tailgate.

Shotgun riding, face chomping, head-teether! Anything we ate fancy...came from that dog's purse—every bit of steak, every amusement park ride, all of us, kids...on our knees...making change at Gamebred's dog bowls! Damn fur devil attacked me on the fourth day out of my stroller. I was late to use my legs. Gamebred was waiting for me to get out of my stroller, waiting... for my first run! Tracked me down without any get away speed... with only four land days under my onesie!"

"Oh man...my batteries are dead!" Full House Carlson exclaimed aloud, knowing that Jucco went through days where he talked non-stop about being attacked by his stepfather's dog, it was a verbal, childhood jag Jucco got hung up on—his mind skipping endlessly over itself. Full House Carlson realized that it didn't matter if he listened or not, Jucco would talk himself through to the end regardless of his participation. "*Something must have triggered it...*" Carlson thought as he watched Jucco crouching at the waist and circling through the animal cages, looking for a target, his taut frame offset by a rusted blond ponytail.

Jucco was very sensitive about his skin, not going in for tattoos, he wore other peoples ink on his clothes, preferring hot wax to razors and donning silk screened, hand painted outfits he ordered from a woman he met on Facebook. Today's theme featured a blaze of satanic symbols, horned gargoyles, devils wielding pitch forks, the design conceived in the poorest taste imaginable, but it worked as a complete, off the rack ensemble. The outfit included, Day of the Dead bandana, pocketed retro bowling polo with famous Hollywood dark side actors, Beast of Revelations vest, black work bibs with hot rod flames along the seams, hem to pocket, complemented by hand painted work boots.

Full House Calrson figured Jucco's Gamebred jags were separated by the days that fell before Jucco had his head chewed on by a pit bull, Rottweiler mix, and the days after. Jucco recalled being inside the dog's mouth, feeling it changing its grip, and at times Carlson felt that his own perception of Jucco, was that Jucco was still peering through Gamebred's teeth and slobber. In an odd way, Jucco and Carlson were the perfect tilt of the planet match; Jucco staring at the world through a dog's mouth and Full House Carlson, waving his hand over the imaginary flame of a propane griddle, a gesture he repeated several times a day, checking the temperature, prior to cracking eggs he purchased forty years ago.

"I wonder what a camp side egg goes for today? Camp side egg, without cheese on toast?" Carlson thought, as he followed the primitive dance Jucco made out of inspecting the cargo, slinking around the animal cages, shaking his keys as he retracted them back and forth along a chain, while spinning counterclockwise on his heels, provoking the animals as he progressed forward on his black work boots, painted with crammed souls suffering in hell on each shaft and across the steel toe caps. "You're a darn boardroom carnie, that's what you are, Jucco! I've been around thousands of warehouse men, nobody moves freight and totes the company line with as much pride and Coney Island bravado as you do! You're a damn, freight moving legend! If you were my chief second I'd work until I was eighty! Drop dead routing something bound for a place I'd never stepped near of…scan me…once I flatline…and ship me off!"

Jucco flashed his hatchet lipped grin as he pulled the rest of the cages down the dock furthest from Zorro's cage, which he let rest a short pull from the platform edge.

Full House Carlson and Jucco had only worked together for a few months, but they adhered to the three unwritten laws from PMeister and Schoemann's short stint manifesto. *Law number one*, bond tight, *two*, know your partner's load, but pull your own, *three*, talk about getting together over the holidays, but never do. Both Carlson and Jucco were overqualified for the jobs they performed, but PMeister and Schoemann, the pharmaceutical company that employed them, had a lot of loose ends that they didn't want unraveling into the tapestry of other things they were involved in, like supplying the military with toiletries, condoms, and anti-depressant drugs. PM&S always hired up. If either Jucco or Carlson knew anything about the inner workings of PMeister and Schoemann it was because they'd worked enough spans to become familiar with other tradesmen. Jucco played Halo with a contractor hired to trouble shoot the sphere and keep it operable, Full House had a *taster's pass* to the "shroom room". His bridge partner was one of the chefs in charge of cramming tanker loads of empty crab legs with fish paste for the gong feast. Anything Full House and Jucco could ever surmise regarding their employer, was a reflected glimmer of the thousand-sided, behemoth that was PMeister and Schoemann. Grand architects of the Obelisk Project, aka, the germ sphere.

Full House thought Jucco called him Captain because Carlson wore a pristine admiral's hat. But Captain Carlson was either in fastidious preparation, prior to a mushroom trip, or in mid sail, surfing psilocybin winds. The two hadn't been paired before this present PM&S work stint, but they were amicably engaged, seeing each day through to an impeccable end—as a standard. Carlson hadn't lost a package in thirty years, Jucco never recorded a single accident on any vessel he ever worked transport on—not a scratch. In the Merchant Marine pool, Jucco coo coo Frankenstein, was always considered the uber-sober, but most likely to go postal on the high seas—hire. Having abandoned land for water, Jucco's was the unheard voice running his Gamebred jag in the uninhabited corners of the engine room.

"He waited for me to get out of my pram…to get comfortable with a little head start…then he tracked me down. I thought we were playing…I was laughing. Left me no escape. All I had was that fresh out of the pram head start. One hundred and twenty five stitches. Cut me down on my first day on two legs. Can't stand dogs ever since. Only at the end of a syringe, or near a handful of pills I can feed them, or when I can cap their skulls with a bolt gun! Right in the spot where their owners' kiss their heads for smells!" Jucco took out his cattle prod from his police belt and zapped the side of a cage sending dozens of cockroach-beetle-eating-cats, hissing, spitting, and caterwauling as they leapt in midair from the shock. Sterile male and females mixed, turning their frustrations upon a cat with one eye, swiping the blind side the cat used as a shield, but regretting their aggression after receiving the one eyed cats rebuke, dealt out evenly, separately and savagely. The skinless cat cage vibrated with violence and the expectation of horror that hung between one unsettled score and another, until the final culprit was dealt the one eyed cat's last dose of wrath. "The crap from these cockroach eating cats is toxic! I hate these hairless mutants! I can't stand frogs, turtles, birds, beetles or bats, but I hate dogs worst of all!" Jucco said, spreading his scarred smile as wide as he could, glaring at the masked hound while sliding a tray out from the bottom of one of the cat cages. Jucco fed the tray into a machine that swept, disinfected, and cleared the tray before spitting it back out. The machine was a portable cat furnace that cleaned the trays and incinerated the toxic cat excrement.

"Mark that black dog with the brown mask. He gets the royal treatment until we're up rail. Anything happens to that dog, on our watch, and we'll be sent into the germ sphere to bang the feast gongs, or ladle out solvent green muckidy mush muck—whatever it is they serve. Melting down those big blocks of sludge for watery soup. I prefer to work transport, ship in, ship out—stay off the inside grounds. I'll take my dodgy, Motel Six kitchenette digs for six months, hot plate and a bunk on this side of that eighty story, plastic kettle, and all its workers' suites. I don't want any part of what goes on inside that dish—my luck I'd catch some future disease, living out of there…between gin rummy rounds and bridge hands. They'd bury me in the rainforest…where they harvest all their voodoo—name a mushroom after me, when the stools grow up from my bones in tie-dye patterns…humming… bootleg jams!" Full House croaked on, puffing at his pipe, his fingers counting egg carton stacks. *"Twelve dozen flats…"* he marked off in his mind.

"When you die, there'll be a congealed spore where your bones lay, from all the psilocybin you've ingested in your damaged case of whiskey drinking life!"

"Part of the perks, working this side of the devil! Barrel whiskey, tapped from the crate! Plenty of state of the art mushrooms, lab fresh! You got your chain hooked up?" Full House commanded, merrily.

"I do."

"Chain that masked dog, if you would sir, when you take it out to lose its bowels, to the hook teeth on your gargoyle belt for safe keeping. Soon as that dog is back in its cage and loaded, safe and sound, I will help myself to three experimental mushroom buttons I plucked, a la carte, to melt in my tea!"

"I thought you drank that tea an hour ago?"

"You're right…I did!" Carlson let out a loud, cavernous laugh that rolled around his guts and echoed throughout the empty loading dock. "Part of the perks, working this side of the devil!"

"Let your mushrooms sail Cap, I got this."

Full House puffed his pipe beneath his admiral's hat, waddling about the loading platform issuing orders to Jucco like a wine lunched duck, his broad shoulders tucked behind his unconditioned frame. "We got orders to walk that masked hound until he poops himself out from the pill they gave him. Then we give him the second pill after we shove off. Give him some time to get hungry. Feed it to him with nothing in his guts, so it works straight away and has plenty of time to do its business. It's rattlesnake heart attack syrup…that's what we're feeding that canine raccoon! Works like a charm—reads like a fatal claustrophobic reaction to confined spaces. Cramped death they call it."

"No more dogs, that's the order!" interjected Jucco.

"One of the ferry engineers sent a load of dogs supposed to be green gassed, back into the dish. Now there's a pack of dogs, let loose in the sphere by mistake. The crew on the kettle side had just broke a twelve hour shift when the ferry went out. The ship never docked, circled back, first boat in on the next shift! The fresh crew read the ticket and sent the dogs on to desert release. Any domestic strain…won't survive the cockroach beetles in the end, but I'm glad none of that dock end hubbub leads back here to us!"

The chicken lizards protested Jucco's presence, making a hideous roil, combining long exasperated sounds that warped into yipping clucks. Jucco talked above their discordant squabbling, while he removed the fecal trays from beneath the animal cages. "Blame it on the toxic cat crap or the cockroach beetles, however they do it. We don't package the freight, Cap, we just move it. I've seen them though, in captivity, big cockroach beetles, in structures at the end of a span…abandoned, as far as I knew, but I've seen cockroach beetles, Cap, come outa this one sphere, smaller than this. This tower is massive, eighty stories high, eight miles square—it's built on a giant pedestal, and it spins, Cap! The elevators go up and down the sphere, in some areas, and revolve around the sphere, three hundred and sixty degrees, in others. That sphere that I saw these cockroach beetles come out of, they were as big as dachshunds, Cap, I swear! We cooked 'em with flame throwers! Some of them we cooked in the air when they flew off! Their eggs exploding from the worst smelling, death metal carcasses. That sphere was a Sputnik motel, compared to this. This is all state of the art—land of the FEE, home of deductible equity. Once the span is over…poof. This whole plastic Petri kettle comes down. They're going to clear this out, did you hear, Cap? Implode it, that's the plan. Bring it all down, in one fell swoop, like it never was—poof."

"That's always the plan…but it's really none of my business to know what they do, that's what they hired me for, to cash my checks and forget. I'm a long term, part time employee, with a short memory." Full House boasted, puffing on his pipe and taking a pull of whiskey from a Grateful Dead Tombstone flask. "I'll do three more years, short stinting gigs for PM&S then re-retire…find myself a time machine…take all my mushroom stash, from my in-house contact buddies here, and follow a Dead tribute band…in a Winnebago. Do upscale breakfast sandwiches off the grill." There was a sadness in what Full House expressed, in the surreal honesty of wishing to go back in time and start over in an era that had already existed, waving his hand over an imaginary grill.

Jucco's continual flow of words flooded their way into Full House's reverie, peeling his mind away from the last morning he spent, selling breakfast sandwiches, following "The Dead". Always the last breakfast. Rubbing the frost from a car window to wake his customers, peering into a full seat of blue skinned, ginger haired girls. All devouring egg sandwiches…only a handful of tour stops before…melting acid together, trippingly off the tongue. "At the end of the span…they're going to vacate the entire sphere—seal the top…soon as the birds go…'cause the birds are coming, Cap! This is *their* path…then poof! This whole place is built out of some kind of gas infused, plastic. A military grade, contact lens material, stretched over an eighty story eye! They're going to vaporize everything inside, then shatter this entire kettle into a pile of plastic sand. I've got thirteen months in, prior to the span, three months running, and serious overtime…during the span to come. Then another thirty days doing maybe nothing…"

"The first samples won't be coming out of the kettle for a few days…we'll be running crews back and forth, light freight—short runs…after the span. We can snag all the OT we want, since second team can't remember to turn the damn fans on before they toast the cat scat! They leave those fans off one more time and I'll slice that crew down to straight eights, from here till the end of the span! They won't see a damn dime of overtime between their brainless skulls!" Carlson foamed angrily, saddling a recollection of how the frozen dew crunched on the ground the last morning of the Dead tour, and how each of the individual twelve dozen eggs he cracked, sold, fried, flipped or scrambled, seemed to have a separate identity.

"I'm booked three months after the span…"

"It'll turn into six…"

"Always does." Jucco said, retightening his hair, pulling his reddish, blonde ponytail, through his skull and bones Scrunchie.

"Easy pay—samples coming and going—crew transport. Nothing heavier for you to lift, Jucco, than a sample kit."

"The rodents and pests will all be gone that first week. The first wave of gas…brings 'em all crawling out for water. The second fumigation stage, the green gas, they seal the top—to keep the bats in. I don't know what that second green gas is, or why they send the bats into the kettle, but they do. They always do."

"It's a milky green gas…I don't know either…about the bats." Full House added, delighted that Jucco was off his Gamebred jag.

"Toxic crap—lays waste to everything. It can take up to three days for the green gas to permeate the seal on the lid."

"That's a week you could take off, if you need to—remember that, Jucco. It's not officially on the calendar, but corporate knows there's three days set aside, for that second stage gas to fill. We're just on call, during then. A kettle this big…"

"Eighty stories…"

"Who knows how long it will take for that second gas to rise. Could take a full week. Either way, you could make a vacation out of it, with a couple of sick days strung together, take a jump to Toronto, visit the woman you got your threads from, if you need to. I'll be on hand after the green gas settles…my mark will be on the last box of explosives shipped in to implode this jug!"

Jucco stared into Zorro's cage, sliding his right hand into a protective mitt, "I'll have a good laugh putting this dog or any other dog, cat, or pet goldfish they want put down! Any time I spend killing an animal, is time I spend smiling. Smiling as far as the scars on my face allow me to smile!"

"Nothing happens to that dog until it's booked for storage. The order is to put it down on the way up rail—then it gets the pill. No more dogs. No exceptions. Not after the ferry mix up. No more dogs that's final."

"We follow company orders here, Cap. That's how we earn soft clearance…with no need for blank faces, judging down, to answer up to! Always counting the lines in my face between questions… walking the course with their eyes."

"If the next six months of my paycheck is determined as to when and where that dog gets its pill…"

"Trust me, Cap, I swear, by every bad weather mile I ever crossed in prayer—that mutt will get its pill. I'll wrap it up in salmon, if I have to. No hungry mutt can resist fresh salmon stink! If I want to, Cap, I can get that hound to lick that death pill, right out of the tooth divots in my face!"

"You can mash it in a tin—half chicken, half fish, pulp it all up—mashed good, and remember to put the drops in the water we give him, too. Either hungry or thirsty…that masked hound has to show up in the sphere…dead on arrival! Final orders. No more dogs!"

CHAPTER 5

Animal Rescue

The crow tightened the half circle she flew in, holding her good eye over the ponytailed man loading cages at the end of the platform. The crow fixed her gaze on Jucco's left hand between his finger and his thumb.

Liondra perched herself atop a flag pole, anxiously folding her wings, itching to signal screech and soar. The trailing foxes, Dandelion D. and her watch-goat Sampson, De Gama, Striker, Houdini (Durgan, Vishnuk, and Rishna, attentively positioned at the golden rabbit's side), all awaited the hawk's screeching descent to set Striker's plan to paw! The owls served as alternate fowl, in case the hawk failed, and a militia of local blue jays were on wing, willing to accept full payment in seed, risking their tail feathers for the beagle's cause.

Liondra took serious umbrage at having the great horned owls as her backup. Their species known to target the huntress' offspring, smothering nestfuls of hatchlings with their gorilla talons. Barrister Holmes unruffled the red-tailed hawk's feathers, convincing her that Dylan and Bob were vegetarian converts, who were crewed on to back up the crow's part exclusively, and not hers. The white feathered lie that Barrister Holmes stretched to calm the tempestuous hawk was partially true, since the owls both observed the animal Lenten season, which fell just after cherries and in between corn. "Figures, cluck, cluck, cluck!" spit the arrogant hawk, "All that twisting of their brains can't be good for thinking! This plan *caws* for a swift theft, their claws are too bulky for such fine work! Better they back up that disabled nest robber than waste their doubled wing snaps, sparing me!"

Jucco's keyring held his master set for the cages and a taser button for collars similar to Zorro's. The keys were attached to twenty-five feet of retractable, number thirty grade, dog chain. Jucco kept the chain on his police belt—long; so that any animal he clipped for transport that happened to get away, received a short feeling of freedom before Jucco timed his sadistic, end of the chain, yank. Jucco relished each job perk yank, having spray painted the last five feet of his chain link red, to accurately determine his escapee's run length, doubling the effects of his cruelty. Jucco's police belt also holstered his taser, a flashlight, his cattle prod and a six inch hunting knife. One of three other knives, four box cutters and two carpentry blades that Jucco carried on his silk screened personage at all times.

Jucco's attention was drawn to the red-tailed hawk casting a startling shadow against the sun as she took to the sky, accompanied by the smack of her wings. The hawk flapped through the echo of her own progress, each pound of her wings folding into the returning crack of the other. "Top of the food chain for Colonel Sanders!" remarked Jucco, shielding his eyes, watching the enormous red-tailed hawk flying upward, her white wings and paunchy, well fed belly; reflecting silver in the sun.

"What a specimen! Red-tails are rare lakeside. More inland birds, hunting among trees. That one's a prehistoric female, with a Lead Belly gut to boot! What a giant!" exclaimed Full House as the hawk's flowing white chest feathers intermingled with his pores, morphing feather for feather with Full House Carlson's casino carpet skin. *"Take me, hawk! Take my spirit request! I will gladly visit the shadowland, riding your neck as my guide! I can change my spirit animal for lighter freight—I could go as a stingless bee! Easy carry...no ego just the weight of my striped fur!"* Full House Carlson spoke through an opening he had constructed intangibly in the center of his chest, where he imagined, if provoked, he could double any one of his five senses, or summon a sixth sense into play.

Jucco extended and retracted his keys along the twenty-five feet of chain as was his habit. Wiping his hands clean on his Charlie Harper retro bowling shirt, careful not to smear any of the Hollywood celluloid ghouls silk screened on the shirt's extended tails. Jucco amused himself, calculating the many ways he could kill the masked hound as he reached down for the key and the button to Zorro's cage and collar, positioning himself to grab Zorro and chain him with his right hand, which was covered by his protective mitt. Jucco kept his left hand gloveless, in case he had to draw his cattle prod or any of his many accessible blades.

The moment Jucco opened Zorro's cage the crow executed a perfect assault dragging her beak across the valley of flesh between Jucco's index finger and his thumb. Liondra, dodging the three sparrows who appeared in the hawk's flight path, screeched in behind the crow, snatching Jucco's keys before any shift in gravity dropped them from the air.

Jucco's quick reflexes enabled him to catch the crow with a vicious backhand, slapping the bird into the pavement on her blind side, shortening her bill as it snapped against the loading platform.

The crow rolled onto her inner and middle toes, straightening her tarsus as she toppled over, almost unconscious, onto the tracks, then scrambled back to her feet, rocked onto her hind toes, dug in her claws, and tumbled, bullied under the railroad car! The crow was groggy from the blow, but still could not raise her wings to fly, as one of the messenger sparrows, who had knocked the crow onto the tracks and flew the crow, under the train car, had progressed his grip to the back of the crow's neck, pinning her head with his short beak, flapping his wings against the crows, flap for flap, clinging to the crow's back with his claws, fighting with all of his strength to keep the crow grounded.

The other message carrying sparrows arrived from opposite sides of the railroad car and immediately set upon the crow, clearing her free of her good eye, taking turns pecking it out until the socket was as round and clean as a spoon. Finished with their mission, the assassin sparrows flew out from beneath the railroad car together; the third sparrow, held his grip on the crow's back, stinging the stunned crow, repeatedly, with a hammering succession of beak pecks. The third sparrow didn't escape until the crow broke free, and flew herself, sightless, against the undercarriage of the train car.

The crow, finding herself back between the rocks of the tracks, almost unconscious, stood and gripped her claws, rocking on her tarsus, awaiting the assault from the other sparrows, she flew up out of rage, grounding herself once more.

Clutching Jucco's keys, Liondra climbed toward the clouds, assured she could break the attached chain through the force of her flight. The chain whined as it ran through Jucco's retractor, affixed to his police belt. At twenty-five feet the red-tailed hawk looped backwards against the force of her own momentum, meeting the end of the chain's length, yanking Jucco upward; teetering him like a long haired baby.

Fearing that the hawk would pull him off the platform, Jucco made his way down the steps, fighting against the red-tailed hawk to keep his feet on the ground, stumbling across the tracks until he made his stand in a dense patch of rail side weeds and scattered brush.

Releasing a blood curdling screech, Liondra swooped back down towards Jucco, who face planted amid the thistles, flinching as the hawk's talons whisked along his spine. Angrily Liondra roared upward with an even fiercer burst for height. Jucco was yanked off the ground as he scrambled to his feet, receiving an atomic hawk-wedgie, as Liondra flew with all of her weight against the chain, looping in small circles, frantically pulling Jucco upward as she climbed, refusing to believe that the chain would not submit to her will and snap. Jucco dug in his heels, while twisting backwards, reaching for the chain to pull the hawk down.

Carlson's mouth fell agape as the mushroom buttons overwhelmed his bloodstream, the red-tailed hawk converting into his spirit animal, a peacock, flying upwards in plumes of color trails with Jucco's keys grasped in her talons.

"The clasp! Release the clasp!" chirped De Gama, who raced from her concealed position, climbing straight up the hot rod flames of Jucco's pant leg, traversing an image of Barnabas Collins, than crossing over three Revelation beasts before leaping off the platform of Jucco's shoulders onto the chain, tightroping her way to the clasp which was tucked below the hawk's talons.

"These mushrooms are morphing things into Colorforms!" gasped Full House, questioning the reality of the fluorescent chipmunk scaling along the dog chain in the sky.

"You're ground crew chipmunk, stick to the weeds and the low grass—leave this work in the clouds to me!" screeched Liondra.

"It's only a tiny clasp! You can't expect me to go back!" replied the master of seeds, making steady progress streaking toward the clasp on the keychain, hind legs over forepaws.

"Go back to the grass where you belong! You measly rodent, you're not part of the sky plan!" clucked the hawk.

"I am now!" chirped back De Gama, holding the chain clasp in view.

Striker reached the front of the cage and Zorro escaped, following the scent of his father. Leading Zorro to safety, Striker caught a glimpse of De Gama, racing along the chain in mid-air, when Striker turned to address his offspring his snout was overwhelmed by the smell of his pup, having fallen behind, half squatting and running, his bowels discharging a bright orange exhaust.

"Man-dammit!" Striker barked, "Head straight for the clearing...look for a flower crown or follow the smell of wrinkled rabbit!" Striker commanded to his offspring, his eyes bouncing wildly behind the pink scar mound that divided his muzzle.

The clearing was beyond the end of the train platform. Zorro, running as he pooped, could see a crown of daffodils, tied off on the head of a stick, being raised out of a small copse as he followed his father's request, messily doing his business along the way.

Striker let loose a long howl summoning the squadron of blue jays as he chased after the chain line, tripling his speed, nearing the spot where Jucco was stutter stepping in small circles.

Liondra, flying against the end of the chain, in short thrusts, twisted Jucco's hips, throwing the seaman off balance as she repeatedly swooped down, then pounded her mighty wings upward, each time meeting the end of the chain's length in vain.

Twisting, like a contortionist, Jucco got hold of the chain and began yanking against the hawk, pulling her toward him, reeling the great huntress in.

Striker, without breaking stride, leapt at a taut spot in the chain line, grasped the chain into his mouth, as a bit, and severed the links in midair with a snap of his neck, combined with the force of his bite and deer bone honed teeth. The shredding metal smell joined in his snout, activating his muzzle memory, dragging the blocking hares back through his senses as Striker hit the ground, flattening himself out and shielding his eyes with his paws, dodging most of the severed chain Jucco managed to whip his direction, except for a nick from the severed end that slit a fresh gash on the beagle's snout; opposite the side where the dairy farmer's daughter shot out three of his whiskers. Striker leapt to his feet, dodging under Jucco's lunging kick as the beagle raced to meet his offspring in the clearing where Barrister Holmes was stationed, holding his welcoming yellow crown.

The squadron of blue jays took turns dive bombing Jucco at consecutive intervals as the tension released from yanking the severed chain sent Jucco tumbling backwards, whiffing on his steel toed chance to soccer kick Striker's head. Coming to a kneeling base, Jucco extended his leg and reached for his hunting blade, kept in a sheath, above the "crowded souls" painted on his work boots. Unsheathing the blade, Jucco received a tremendous blow upon his kidney, a direct Nosferatu "bull's eye" upon the image of Max Schreck, administered by Dandelion D. Immobilized, writhing in pain, Jucco managed to bring himself to his knees, leaning on all fours, where he was met at full speed by Sampson, who butted Jucco flush on the nose, jerking Jucco's neck back, crumpling his body, almost unconscious, blood gushing from both nostrils, his exposed leg tucked beneath him, precariously.

"Surely...this is the son of agony!" Full House exclaimed, confounded by the antics of the kamikaze blue jays accompanied by the goats pummeling Jucco to the ground in a two butt tag team event. Full House made a move toward a toolbox where Jucco kept a firearm, coming face to triple face with Houdini's three identical guardian hares appearing from their stations, blocking Full House's path. Full House removed his hat reverently and backed away, merging into the spiritual lane of his mushroom trip, not sure if he voiced his questions aloud or in a language spoken only on psilocybin plains. "Three identical rabbits... warning me...not to take that pistolero? Te envio, aque? Hetuba Chorray befobbu? Speak perturbed rabbits, speak! Come into my chest and speak! Bila-cha-la-hutchie-chilli-atchie-bay! Why are you beating the stitched face one? Have pity—he was a chew toy as a baby! Hetuba Chorray befobbu? Bila-cha-la-hutchie-cha-cha-cha-chilli-atchie-bay, Befobbu, parque?" As Full House intoned his mushroom gibberish, the rabbits vanished. Full House advanced again toward the firearm and Houdini appeared, his coat glistening in all of its auriferous splendor. "The lost Inca Hare...and three reflections barricading the weapon! The cook warned me these mushrooms had Imax appeal! Have mercy, my mind is impaired! Bilamu-cha-chu-chilli-atchie-bay! Bilamu-cha-chu-chilli-atchie-bay!" Full House intoned his psilocybin chant as he crept down the platform, pulling up his drawers scuttling toward Jucco, tripping over himself as he pushed back against his own fear, stealing a final glance at the toolbox where the golden hare had vanished.

The chipmunk hanging from the chain upside down, scaled it much like a telephone wire, claw over claw until she reached the clasp, unclasped the chain from the keys then plummeted, head over tail, with the keys firmly in her grasp.

The hawk let the chipmunk fall, waiting for the chattering rodent's tail to make a complete, counterclockwise circle before she snatched her up, securing Jucco's keys in one talon, and the volatile chipmunk in the other. "Didn't think that one quite through, did you, chipmunk? Brilliant move, brilliant! Cluck, cluck, cluck! Only you forgot your species doesn't have wings— only the greatest of great nature's creatures have wings! Remember that, chipmunk whenever you find yourself looking up at the sky, from the mud—in awe of my domain!" gloated the hawk.

The chipmunk struggled to straighten out her facial features as the hawk narrowed her sight on Full House's cap, singling out a campaign button for Jimmy Carter in the shape of a peanut. Tapping out at a downward speed of one hundred miles an hour, the approaching hawk caused Carlson to shield his partner's body with the entire tarp of his sloth, laying the accomplishment of his life's work, avoiding manual labor, over Jucco's body, as Liondra buzzed by them, smacking De Gama in the face with her target, sending the captain's hat flying from his head.

Feeling vindicated the mighty huntress soared upwards, chipmunk and keys in talons tow.

"Just remember hawk, the greatest of great nature's creatures didn't know how to open a human clasp!"

"It was out of my reach, I don't have a prehensile tail, only my lovely wings!"

"It was above your brain grade! Fur over feather!" De Gama continued, causing Liondra to treat the rodent to several loop de loops, which only encouraged the master of seeds. "No human fire for you, blood breath! Luckily you let survive a rodent species from the low grass, to bail your slaughtering feathers out!" the chipmunk chirped off, attempting to make a chaise lounge out of the hawk's talons, while dolling out her two nuts worth of sense.

"Are you comfortable chipmunk?"

"Getting there…except for the company…little drafty."

"What was that you said chipmunk, I'm sorry I couldn't hear you? Did you say you wanted to get off here?" the hawk released the chipmunk, letting De Gama slip into the air head first, then recaptured her with ease. The two females flew in silence the rest of the trip.

Zorro reached the clearing the same time the hawk flew in with the chipmunk.

"What were those sparrows doing in my flight path?" screeched the hawk, ejecting her passenger and hacky-sacking the chipmunk with her talons as she landed. The two goats jogged in behind Zorro, dodging De Gama as she tuck and rolled herself to safety.

Zorro wagged his tail, effusively, kneading the ground, standing chest to chest against the mass of scars that carried his father's scent, then he welcomed the two goats, the foxes, and the three guardian hares, having all arrived from different paths to the clearing, following Barrister Holmes' daffodil crown.

"You're the golden rabbit?" Zorro said to Houdini, putting his paw on Houdini's shoulder. "I wish I had time to hear your tale. I've heard others tell pieces of it. Another time, I'm sure…but not now…oh, no…not again!"

"What do you mean, *another time*?" inquired Barrister Holmes, keeping his distance from Zorro who trotted out of the clearing, pointing the pooping end of his body away from the other animals.

"We rescued you from the experiment you were being sent into?" chirped the flabbergasted chipmunk, spitting stored seeds, dislodged from being spun upside down in the air.

"It's a long way to Sullivan County, offspring…there's plenty of time for Houdini's story." howled Striker, joyously, dancing in a circle as hounds do, loving every part of the reunion, trailing in and out of the other animals in a four legged, dosey doe.

"Especially if we take the train!" Dandelion D bleated in, shoveling her hooves in the dirt.

"I came with you…I followed your scent…you're my father… but as soon as my human whistles me back, I've got to return. Regardless of where he leads…he's my human. Where he goes…I follow."

"We rescued you because we don't think your human knows what he's getting you into! Let alone himself. Just because he's a human, doesn't mean he has a brain! I don't mean to pull rank here, but everyone knows rabbits are the most evolved species in the animal kingdom!" exhorted Barrister Holmes.

"How do you know your human isn't a canine meat peddler?" anteed in Durgan, followed by Vishnuk and Rishna.

"You could end up on a menu making your human a healthy profit on your flesh!"

"Your bones sold for dog soup and your belly fur for bedtime slippers!"

"It's not a home or a shelter you're being lead into…it's a disease hatchery. It's no place for a farmer, let alone a farm animal. I hope you don't take offense in me calling you a farm animal, you mammals nowadays, you're all so sensitive about your origins, forgetting every strain of history but the last five minutes." backtracked Barrister Holmes, carefully.

"I go where my human goes. And when he whistles…I'll follow."

The small pack of animals surrounding Zorro and Striker felt a stillness engulf the air around them, unanimously agreeing, without making a sound that Zorro had the right to his own choosing, and there was nothing they could do but to welcome his choice, huddling together to wish him well.

"It's as the leaves fall." said Barrister Holmes, wistfully.

The understanding shared between the animals resonated, as they could only imagine what it would be like to be in service of their own humans, except for Liondra who promised herself a pigeon liver feast when she returned to Manhattan.

"Is there anything we can tell him?" offered Striker, sniffing his offspring neck to neck, taking in Zorro's sweet, first born scent. Zorro reciprocated, feeding upon his father's woodsy stench, licking the bleeding wound on his nose.

Barrister Holmes immediately thought of Polonius' *"To thine own self be true"* speech, yet due to the severity of the situation the Giant Flemish Hare ruled against it, speaking extempore instead to the dangerous nature at paw. "Don't eat anything that smells of anything manmade, or has anything to do with man. Don't drink from anywhere you see water come from, unless you see humans drink from it first. If there are no humans around to give you water, and you're thirsty, and you find water, stir it with your paw to see what lives in it first, even if it's a puddle. Stick with your human and live by your nose…you can't go wrong…if your heart is true…following the mind that dominates your senses."

Zorro acknowledged Barrister Holmes with a short appreciative bark, then turning to Striker the wayfaring mutt relinquished his feelings. "Tell mom…I didn't know what I was looking for…until I found my human. Mom's herd protector, for her cows, I can't spend my whole life sitting with those cud chewing, butt belchers, too stupid to lay out of the rain! The rest of my litter has your fields to patrol. I have my human and where he goes…I go. I promise… when my human takes me home, I'll visit mom and all my litter, neck to neck, you have my bark on it!"

"Your human lives by our fields?" asked Striker, wildly wagging his stump of a battered tail.

"My human…is the planter of smells!" Zorro trumpeted, proudly.

"Your human is the planter of smells? All this way? The fragrance grower?" questioned Barrister Holmes, in an astonished manner, his ears forming two question marks, pointing in opposite directions, standing back to back as he spoke.

"I saw him when I investigated the sweet smells. Rolling in them...to take their scent to my mother...I came upon the same man, under a moon snarl...he took me off the coyotes' menu—when I had my tail backed into the best defensive position I could find."

The sound of Clarence's whistle swept through the clearing, as swiftly and directly as Ulysses' arrow pierced the ax handles at his great hall in Ithaca.

"That's my human!" rumbled Zorro, trying to sound brave, yet apprehensively whining quietly.

"Perhaps there was some good in us being here after all..." Striker howled, then joined his offspring whining, reassuring the pup of his own feelings.

"It was worth the trip...to reunite our scents..." returned Zorro, nuzzling his father.

"For me as well!" agreed Striker, standing chest to chest with his offspring, feeling each other's hearts, filling their snouts and wagging their tails high in the air.

At the sound of the second whistle Zorro turned and headed toward the platform, the two tracking foxes, Ghostress and Slickbend, escorted Zorro, their bodies smothered together in a tilt, parting company beyond the edge of the platform.

Heading back toward the spot of the original placement of his cage, Zorro crawled under the train car and came upon the bloodied crow, flying blindly against the underside of the train. Zorro picked the crow up in his mouth, and continued onward, answering his human's call.

CHAPTER 6

The Acorn Whistler

Full House Carlson, though he fancied himself a psilocybin sommelier, was tripping his brains out as he walked Jucco back to the loading dock. Carlson's chemist friend who supplied him with the same mushrooms which were integrated into the sphere reservoirs, advised Full House to only sample one, Carlson took three. Carlson wasn't expecting the new batch of mushrooms to be so powerful, he also didn't expect a sphere prescriber in a blue transport tunic to be waiting for him and Jucco when they retreated back to their command hub at the end of the platform.

"Come to see my dog. He's a black dog with a brown mask." Clarence called aloud to the two men approaching him.

Carlson and Jucco halted their progression and exchanged a Pyrrhic glance, then looked back at Clarence, a beanpole of a man, lean as dirt, standing on the edge of the platform, nervously rubbing the edge of an acorn down the skid patch of his two-day old mohawk.

"Mister..." Jucco began, tilting his head back, slightly, so it didn't gush blood, "If I told you I was attacked by a half blind crow—tore part of the flesh off my hand...then had my keys snatched by a red-tailed hawk, big as a brown eagle, working with a circus chipmunk, and a dog full of scars, you wouldn't believe me now, would you mister? I mean, I wouldn't expect you to...but

I got bucked in the kidney by a goat…then rammed…flat on my snauz-o-la by another goat!"

"He didn't know what run him over, but I saw it happen. I'm the one told him…it was goats." Carlson thought about including the three identical rabbits and the golden hare gathered around the toolbox but held his tongue. Full House had learned while tripping through hours of tedious staff meetings that he could be perceived solemnly wise, as long as he kept what he said to the absolute minimum, exuding the least amount of human participation possible; if less were more, Carlson's life, never happened. "*Did I already tell him it was goats?*" Full House wrestled in his mind, holding firm to his minimal speaking theory, encouraged by the phosphorescent liquid leaking out of Jucco's body, experiencing his partner as a cracked thermos.

Clarence sized up the two men and concluded that Full House, sporting a protruding belly and a non-violent tell, was incapable of doing the damage that appeared evident to Jucco's face, the bruise tint widening amid a pirate's map of stitching trails. "Does the fact that you got attacked by a half blind crow have anything to do with my black dog with a brown mask?" Clarence watched Jucco's face fill out to the full span of its sidling stitched grin.

"Mister, soon as my nose stops bleeding, I'll have a look for your dog and I'll find him. You have my word. Just give me a minute until my face stops leaking…and I'll commence the search." Jucco lay flat on his back, putting pressure on his nose with a bandana featuring various skeletons playing instruments.

"My dog…he'll be along. Mind if I wait? Acorns…follow me… never had to learn to whistle without one." Clarence revealed the large acorn from the center of his fist, gently working the seed of the acorn and tossing it aside, then he placed his thumbs around the acorn cap and blew into it, emitting a hollow whistle. "People call me, Clay—no relation to the soil. He'll be on his way my dog... he'll be along."

"I'm Jucco, that's my boss, Robert Carlson." Jucco said, talking around the blood backing into his throat while applying more pressure to his nose, attempting to sit up, his face swelling as it throbbed.

"People call me Full House…" Carlson added, squelching an itch to chatter.

"Is that a poker given nickname? I played a lot of poker in the service. If I had a nickname it might have been…Chip Daddy, or Trip Jacks, somethin' like that!" Clarence shared, knowing the familiarity would draw the workmen in.

"I lost a trailer home on a full house. Queens over nines—name stuck."

"Damn nickname's an albatross if it's a bull's eye!" Clarence offered.

"Tombstone for life!" Full House gushed in agreement.

"You lost a trailer home with queens over nines?" choked Jucco, coughing up blood and gagging.

Clarence put his thumbs around the giant acorn cap and blew into it a second time. The sound musically rolling off the walls of the transport hub.

Full House felt Clarence had signaled him out and was staring him down, but he was determined to hold his tongue, until he realized he was listening to himself speak, already detailing what he thought he had suppressed himself to say. "Pot winner had a Dodge Ram, drove from the poker table to the trailer park. My rig was hooked and gone before the sun rose. My layaway fiancé was sleeping in the trailer, but since I was sworn off gambling and hadn't been home for three days, I figured by the time it took to pick her up from wherever they discovered each other...I was hoping that would be enough time for her to calm down...but she was long gone before I wrote that marker. Full House stuck to me like rib sauce after that."

Jucco noticed Clarence's posture shift, as Clarence caught sight of Zorro crawling under the railroad car and coming down the tracks; Jucco's master button and keys affixed to the dog's collar, the crow's head and tail, sticking out from both ends of the dog's mouth.

Zorro trotted past Jucco and Full House, joining Clarence back at the platform dropping the crow at his master's feet and taking his rightful place, seated beside his human.

"You said the crow that ripped your hand had one eye?" Clarence stated, rolling the blind crow over with his shoe.

Jucco and Carlson made their way onto the platform where all the cages were lined up for final boarding. Seated by his human, Zorro fixed his attention entirely on Jucco.

"This crow here, if it was half blind before, it looks freshly blind now. You think this is the crow, with this grapefruit scooped eye, ripped that chunk of meat from your hand?" Clarence asked.

"Let me see if that's the culprit...see if it's got any life left." Jucco mumbled.

Under Zorro's watch, Jucco labored to where the crow was splayed, choking back blood, looking all the part of a beaten man, then he slid on his knees and snatched the crow up deftly, stuffing the crow's head directly into his mouth, feeling the bird twitching with life against his tongue. Jucco pulled the crow through his jagged lips, wetting the bird's head like a painter's brush, then he placed his thumb around the crow's cracked beak, pressing down against the nape of the bird's neck to keep it from moving. "Fresh dead! Just new…maybe thirty seconds since the weight flew! I couldn't taste any life left…not a wiggle! Too good to waste!" Jucco flung open the feeding hatch of the cockroach beetle eating cats and chucked the crow among them. The crow's feathers flew as the cats tore at its flesh, the half-blind cat feeding first and often, the others, fighting among themselves, in turn, for claw-fuls and cat bites of crow.

"Mr. Jucco, Mr. Full House—queens over nines, respectfully… change of plans." Clarence declared, as a puff of the crow's feathers spilled out from the cat cage, still shaking from the feeding frenzy. "This dog, his name is Zorro, he rides with me, first class, or I ride with him—coach! Tell your superiors I came and claimed my dog, and we will forget about the hawk and the chipmunk and the circus dog full of scars—capiche? Capiche, that's Italian for, *what are you planning on a' doing for the nexta' ninety days, while you're nota' getting paid? Capiche?*"

CHAPTER 7

Covenant of the Eye

The blue jay squadron flew in for their seed payment, scattered by De Gama over a raised manhole cover. The other animals regrouped around the Frisbee, lapping water and making plans for the trip back to Sullivan County.

"Master of seeds, what's our trip count?" inquired Barrister Holmes of his chipmunk companion.

"After paying off the jays, we have less than half the seeds we consumed along the way. If we share by merit, based on the success of our rescue, I'd say the hawk would have to make her banquet on whatever scraps dropped from our shells, especially mine!" chortled the chipmunk, causing Sampson to spin in a circle, kicking his back hooves dizzily in the air, while Dandelion D. bulldozed the earth with her forehead, her goat mind, spinning between the nubs of her horns, trying to hold the idea in her head that a chipmunk was plucking down a hawk. These food chain squabbles were common within the company of Barrister Holmes' small cadre of animals, herded together, without range, by Houdini's return tale from the Kush fields.

"You weren't making jokes when you were climbing through the clouds, flying on your tail, were ya' chipmunk? You would have bought a parachute then, for all the seeds you'd see in your rodent life, and spent the rest of your days collecting them back to me, sky pharaoh, to pay your debt! Cluck, cluck, cluck!" squawked the hawk, sending a piercing screech through the sky.

"Re-seed, re-seed, the sunflowers are blooming—full on, in the Ukrainian fields, where the train rests, adding cars!" interrupted Barrister Holmes, interjecting between the two species to ensure that chipmunk didn't end up arguing herself down the canal of the hawk's throat. "We'll eat everything we have now and feast on the sunflowers when the train rests, restocking our provisions there. Are all of you okay with sunflower seeds the rest of the way—I know that's not what we originally promised?" Barrister Holmes asked of his rescue pack, as any mission guide might inquire about pizza toppings.

"It's not a victory dinner but twill serve—*cluck-cluck-cluck*! Eventually I'm going to need some blood to oil all these seeds!" protested the Hawk.

"The sunflower heads are shedding at the touch of a breeze! Flap your wings, peck your fill, and make it rain!" chirped the chipmunk, undulating her entire body as she flipped in circles, contemplating the provisions she would be able to gather with the help of the birds.

"We need to find out what happened to the crow." whimpered Striker, pointed in Zorro's direction, gripping his quivering leg muscles. The once great hunter restraining himself from sprinting after his first born. *"Of all the things I've chased...to leave off following the thing I love?"* thought Striker, his hind legs, targets of the quarry snakes, trembling.

"Crows don't tip their wings into the wind for pleasure!" quipped Liondra, creating a stir amongst the jays as she snatched one of their pumpkin seeds, tipping it into the air, high enough for all of the jays to have a swipe at, then splitting it in half with the point of her beak, letting the shells fall, sending the jays fluttering after the scraps, soliciting an angry protest.

"Keep out of the jay pile, hawk!" ordered Barrister Holmes.

Sampson maneuvered his body over the blue jay pile, watching guard as they devoured their earnings, sending him snacking after a while on a milkweed patch, circling back to the manhole cover on a bitter trail of poison ivy.

"Crows have little or no sense of loyalty—she probably just flew off. That's what crows do! They fly off one thing to the next, looking for other crows to fly off things and argue with! A crow amongst crows, is still a crow, down to its last feather! What's to miss? Divvy up her seeds!" added the indignant hawk.

"But she wasn't among crows!" snapped Striker. Relieving himself of the emptiness he felt for his offspring. Echoed back by a short, affirming bark from the platform.

"She never partnered, that crow—the disruption she spread was personal—nest after nest…raging out a lonely vengeance against the unborn. Devouring the hatchling hopes and feeding on the suffering of others. She wasn't our choice for this mission, but when she caught wind of our enterprise, she insisted she be counted in." Barrister Holmes spoke reverently of the crow, almost eulogizing her with the solemnity of his tone.

Striker barked in agreement, sulking toward the Frisbee bowl, the warrior's body shaking from its reunion with adrenaline and feeling the emptiness the assassin had first felt, waking in a root cellar, without the warmth of his siblings surrounding him.

"Maybe I misdiagnosed her willingness to change feathers quicker than I should have." Barrister Holmes concluded, hanging his large head in despair, his ears bending against the ground and folding upwards, a poorly measured curtain, bunched above the hem.

"She was enthusiastic about helping, I don't think she just flew off or flew home!" Striker added, licking Barrister Holmes' giant ears to console him, nuzzling the rabbit, head to head and scratching the giant hare under his neck with the length of his scar.

Houdini looked on, feeling the crow confused, flying upside down—inside his own head, but Houdini did not wish to reveal to the others that he could see the crow flying, because the crow's journey was the first flight he ever experienced—outside of himself, through another animal's body. Houdini was unsure at first *how* he was traveling with the crow *and* standing in the copse, but it was clear to the golden rabbit, upside down or not, the crow was no longer flying among them. Houdini was uncertain how far he would be paired in the crow's mind, but he flew along, listening to his friends, taking in the kaleidoscopic path the sun winged bird migrated through from the crow's perspective.

"Why wouldn't she return with us to share our gratitude?" pondered Striker.

"Her pumpkin seeds!" De Gama piped in, "She made me put her pumpkin seeds aside, for all of us to share on the return trip!"

"That's a crow thing! Spreading dumb mysteries and filling the air with putrid sound! She's a crow! It's what crows do! Caw, caw, caw! No music! Do you really have to chase your tail about it, more than that? Crows will be crows! Maybe…she flew past a telephone wire and landed into an argument!" squawked the hawk.

"Did any of you see, hear, or smell anything in the scuffle with the ponytailed human? Any of you?" barked Striker.

"His nose was no match for my horn crest!" mused Sampson.

"The sparrows flew right into my flight path. Who authorized that?" Liondra squawked, unwilling to give any animal a single breath of air time.

"Sparrows? What sparrows?" questioned Barrister Holmes, every furrow of his wrinkled pelt, percolating with interest, his ears twitching like divining rods, sensing the missing element to the mystery.

"The sparrows flew out of the train door and off as soon as we left the boxcar?" barked Striker.

"The very same sparrows flew right through my flight path! That's why my original thrust upward to break the chain was cut in half! I flew around them going in and I had to fly around them going out!" squawked the hawk, conveniently linking the sparrows to her failure to separate Jucco's chain.

"When I was crossing the chain, I looked back and didn't see the crow. I thought she flew on to the clearing. We could all see the daffodil crown marking this spot." chirped the chipmunk.

"I may not be a warrior, like Striker, or be able to out run the yellow eyed wolf as many times as Durgan, but I held down the clearing with a stick and a halo of gold…she never arrived." ceremoniously concluded Barrister Holmes, out carrot-ing carrots.

The impulsive owls hooted together, enlisting their dual headed services, volunteering for an immediate reconnaissance mission.

"Never needing to implement…"

"The backup plan…"

"Which was our part to perform…"

"Our services were never…"

"Caaawwwed upon…

"Or rendered…"

"We will scout the grounds…"

"And contribute…"

"A full two beak effort…"

"Unlike the half beak services…"

"Performed by the unchained hawk among us!"

"Chain, chain, chain…chain of fools!" The owls, rocking on their talons, concluded in unison.

"Prove it four-clops! Let's see how empty your talons are, when you come back, and then we'll mark your score! Either way…I've got first dibs on the crow's pumpkin seeds!" claimed the hawk, spitting as she screeched.

"We'll fly back and see…"

"If some mishap has befallen her…"

"We'll scout the area and rendezvous back…

"Where the wide river bends…

"We'll meet you …"

"Where the train drains its whistle…

"Where the chicken stench blends!"

"We'll rendezvous back…

"Before the last whistle ends!"

The owls flew out of the clearing and headed toward the area where the crow had performed her part of the mission.

"Thanks for reminding me, checkmark heads! I think I'll stretch my wings where the train rests and snatch me a farmer's bird, there! Get me one of them grass fed…chickadees! The seeds

in my stomach are binding up for blood! Blood's the organ's oil!"
screeched the hawk as she fluffed her feathers then flew upwards,
circling the blue jays, still battling over the remains of their reward.

"You've got chicken blood on the brain!" chuckled Ghostress,
accompanied by her trailing partner, Slickbend, giggling fox yips.

"Don't think you're riding all the way back to Sullivan County,
smelling of poultry blood!" chirped De Gama, "You snack and
murder, sister, you fly home alone! We've survived different
winters, hawk. Mine spent digging nuts for share—you thinning
the woods of anything that struggles. The thinner the beast only
leaves you wanting more!"

"That's me, the reliever of living grief! I do my part to mitigate
the suffering of lesser species, and thank you for acknowledging
my contribution to the overpopulation of your own! By order of
the animal kingdom I now spread my table, over Central Park,
not the smorgasbord of species I had in the woods, but lucky for
me...I never spawned a taste for dog...no offense, beagle." Liondra
squawked, addressing Striker directly.

"You would eat dog?" growled Striker, rising up on his hind
legs aggressively.

"I would...but it wouldn't be tasty. Dog is...dingy meat. I
prefer squirrels and blood-plump, pigeons. Rats I kill to stay sharp,
dropping them live from high heights for...flaps and splats! Cluck,
cluck, cluck! They're shifty targets, rats, but their addicted to
repetitive trails, so they're easy to train on. The animal kingdom
will never protest the death of an extra rat! I stay sharp targeting
their tails, other times I target their ears, some days the left, other
days the right...their death depending on how the wind tips my
wings!" clucked the hawk.

"And dogs?" inquired Striker.

"Gotham is a feathery town, grime on the outside, plush posh in the middle! I'd be stuffed at Gracie Mansion for hunting dog! Simple fare, too, in their fenced-in parks, and soft leash hours, but pigeons and squirrels are part of the daily blood, killing what one kills to survive—that's koooooosher—it's what's happening behind every window, stacked to the sky! The shadow of billionaires' row darkens my sunny grounds. Cluck, cluck, cluck! But ahhhh, the building baron's view from that Central Park South perch, I can count a raccoon's tail rings from there, all the way from the Conservatory Gardens! They'd make a fat feast, city 'coons, but I don't like their dining habits—knowing they've gone loopy sharing dumpster trash with rats!"

"So dogs are off the city menu?" sighed Striker, exploring the scent of a poop trail left by his offspring.

"Gotham patrons have precious ties to their animals. I admit, I do fly up the Hudson for rabbit, but I wouldn't fly around a city block for dog."

"Really? That's such an unpleasant surprise!" quipped Barrister Holmes, wringing his ears and noticing that the hawk's company was wearing on his patience.

"I fly up the Hudson, but I don't cross the Hudson, as sworn and promised to the animal kingdom—honest raven!"

"Anything else on the menu that we should know about?" asked Striker.

"I like a good snake. You've tasted snake haven't you, Striker? I know they've tasted you! Cottonmouths in the quarry say… they just haven't bitten you enough times yet, to kill you! How many snakes or rabbits do you think you've licked your chops on? Once a killer…always a killer, beagle! Cluck! Cluck! Cluck! You corralled my services, and I delivered, that doesn't mean I'm changing diets. Soon as we get train side…I think I'll snack me one of them farmer's birds! A grass fed chicken would be worth the long fly home!"

"You've found your species eating species home; in the tombstone towers of New York City, hawk. The dock and subway rats there, always pressing the east coast cats for war! In the country every animal lives within its boundary; in the city—nothing remains off limits, as long as you get to it first!" chortled De Gama.

"I've never been to the city. I don't think I'd like hearing strange noises I couldn't define." pondered Striker.

"I'm a novice in death compared to you, scar head! Your coat is covered with missing pieces! I'm curious, beagle, in winter, do you feel the cold, biting through the missing patches of your fur?" questioned the hawk.

"Never judge a bird by its feathers or a dog by its scars. That wound that splits Striker's muzzle, he earned for me." declared Barrister Holmes.

"That's the work of the yellow eyed wolf, the alpha forced from their pack." interjected Vishnu.

"That wolf's always slobbering after the golden rabbit, tracking us for a snack!" added Rishna.

"Wolf? Oaf! Woalf! How many times have I run through his legs to distract him from the kill?" boasted Durgan.

"Do you have any scars on your feathers, received in the service of another species?" Rishna asked, judiciously.

"No, and I don't plan on collecting any. Besides the hunt and kiting winds, I like pulling nervy meat from bones. You forbid yourself the kill, beagle, I understand that, wandering around with the *Dali*-rabbit and the chirp-*monk* here, but do you miss the hunt?" asked the hawk, trying somehow to reach her talons under Striker's fur and gouge her mark beneath the warrior's tattered coat, scattered with patches and scars from muzzle to tail.

"I think…" Striker paused for a moment, looking fondly at the small cadre of animals that Barrister Holmes enlisted to rescue his pup, then up at the hawk circling around them. "I think this hawk is hungry and we should eat our seeds before we go any further, as Barrister Holmes suggested, and share them too, with any beast that lands or crawls in range."

The animals broke seeds together, chiding the hawk for being cranky, going off about eating animals that just so happened to be among the species she was traveling with. After they devoured their trip supply, they caught the train heading back toward Sullivan County.

At the point where the train came to a midway stop the owls returned and regurgitated their findings, vomiting the contents of their investigation onto the corrugated floor of the railroad car. In the owl's collection from their scout, Dylan and Bob revealed the entire eye the sparrows removed from the crow, the crow's final feather, retrieved from the platform, a piece of the crow's shattered beak, and the remainder of the crow's neck vertebrate, picked clean by the hairless cats and the few wild chickens that struck the final pecks.

When all the animals were convinced that the crow had met her end, and that the sparrows were possibly responsible, they allowed the hawk to eat the evidence, easing her hankering for grass fed chicken, a craving that would have coveted a bullet through her senses. The crow's pumpkin seeds were divided evenly. Houdini split a portion with the crow, who though blinded, recognized the seeds as her own.

The feather, bones, and part of the crow's beak, the animals brushed out of the railroad car while crossing over a wide stream, aided by the help of the long mated owls, fluttering their wings in unison to push the remains of the crow back into the wild.

CHAPTER 8

Gerba

Zorro standing on Clarence's chest, waited for his human's eyelids to open as Clarence struggled to arrange his own image which was reflected back to him through his dog's glare. The duo awoke in a room the size of a large sauna complete with its own recycling apparatus.

The hovel dwellings were comprised of polyethylene blended resins, extracted primarily from water and sports drink bottles, twist off caps, beach raked soda containers, aluminum cans and booze nips. The dry erase walls replicating worldwide trash peddling restrictions were layered over with expiration stickers from perishable items including country of origin tags and barcodes. Trademarks were lifted from glassware, then pasted onto the recycled walls, presently thick with five layered spans of label pastings.

A hinged countertop serving as a desk and a kitchen table was made from compressed cardboard. It locked into place above a solitary chair pulled out from the floor by use of a handle. The chair was comprised of single use wrappings, plastic bags, prepared food containers, takeout lids, deli straws and cellophane wrappers from condiment packets. The self-composting and energy producing toilet pulled up from the floor for use, then flushed when reinserted.

Clarence's domicile merged step-less, without a porch or platform, into the main passage way through a vulcanized rubber pocket door which led directly into a congested clog of prescribers, making it impossible for Clarence to avoid recipient contact. This exit slid out from the wall accompanied by a security bar that fell into interior brackets when the door sealed. Aligned by a series of deadbolts and a police rod, moored into the composite floor boards. A food sack of perishable items hung from the ceiling as promised to all prescriber's within the orientation video; each item laced with an overdose of junk food pheromones, plugging recipients into an immediate addiction to span meals. Though the bag reeked of rock candy, buttered corn, fried chicken, cheese burgers and buffalo jerky, the duo left the sack hanging and exited through the rubber pocket door, which locked into place behind them.

Clarence and Zorro funneled into a tangled flow of rickety limbed humans. Their pallid skin shades glaring out from sunken skulls as pigment flags. Their eyes bulging above their burlap curtains, drawn as protective coverings across the multitude of panicked faces twisting in anguish to avoid Clarence's unmasked "pie hole".

These living hovels drained directly into what was more of a cobbled gorge pass than a street, paved with thermoplastic block. The hovel quarter walls, also built of plastic, were constructed to help guide the mass of humanity, sliding them along the forged corridors, aiding the forward motion of the human cattle swirl; the men clad in mallard green, the women in dull brown. Traveling amid the nightmarish pull of the crowd, Clarence studied the eyes of the people smothered around him, their eyes seemed to be cantilevered out of their orbital sockets, as if to pour out and empty what they had seen. Etched upon them all, from the patch of their faces visible from the crease of their nose to their eyebrows, was the patina of human suffering.

"Where is everyone going?" shouted Clarence into the throng crowded around him in a coil of bony cobwebs.

"Mask your piehole, dough boy!" an answer returned as the sound of voices in many languages converged, the multitude calling out names, shouting over each other in song, and reciting religious incantations, all assailing Clarence's ears, forming a maddening cacophony of disgruntled babble.

"*We go, but to go…follow to the end and back…don't buck the flow…What is a man, what has he got…I lost you to the summer wind…hallow be thy name…draw your face curtain…pasty giant… devil curse your sun strength! We never know when the first dark ends…living without spoons…I hate the early days… following until the tide thins! Fruit, fruit, fruit! Beware the stampede rush when the crab feast gongs are bled! Cover your pie hole, you pasty clown!*"

The mass of grumbling voices sent Clarence veering into a divergent push, covering his ears he was sucked into a surge of bodies that branched off and descended a deep flight of stairs, leading into an underground subway station. The station was packed as two emerging sunflower colored subway trains arrived; crammed with recipients. Clarence forced his way into one of the cars as crowd control officers, in full armor, resembling metallic flies, pushed people clear on both sides of the closing doors— using hydraulic extendable jousting pads.

Clarence could barely turn his face to the inside of the packed train car as the doors closed, when a thought raced through his mind…"*My dog!*" Clarence felt at his legs, and there, between them, having followed Clarence through the flooded stream of bodies, was his bandit eyed partner, Zorro, his ribs pounding for breath against Clarence's calf muscles. "Up, up, up!" commanded Clarence. Zorro scaled Clarence's body until his front legs were balanced on one of Clarence's shoulders and his back legs on the other. Clarence bent his head slightly so the natural bow of the dog's body fit along the nape of his neck.

Peering through a contorted cluster of torsos and limbs, Clarence spied a coal skinned girl calling out to him without the use of words. The girl focused her gaze primarily on Zorro, her emerald eyes, unlike the other cantilevered recipients, were as hopeful as unfilled stockings, blazing out from a patchwork of industrial facial scars. The girl spoke to Clarence by telepathy, imploring him to save her.

A portion of an hour prior to waking up in his hovel suite, Clarence had experienced his life harshly divided between growing up on the farm, traversing seasons underfoot and through his hands, and his baptismal into the immoral expense of the military complex. In a sunflower colored subway car filled with human beings clustered upon each other as Christmas tree spines gathered for mulching, Clarence understood his immediate purpose as his heart and mind coalesced, forged by the plea of a helpless child. Clarence made a press toward the girl but it was impossible to move through the rickety thickets of bodies clumped between them. "Come to me! Climb up on everyone's shoulders and come to me!" Clarence beckoned to the child, without speaking.

Zorro fixed his own bandit gaze on the little girl, applying canine telepathy, imploring the child to do as his human commanded.

The tiny speck of a girl remained motionless, pleading for help with the entirety of her will, which was mighty for a human being weighing no more nor standing any taller than a mucking boot.

Clarence determined that the petrified child was unable to give name to something lurking in the pack of bodies wedged between them. "Bring her to me, Zorro! Go get her!" Clarence commanded, his senses tingling as he scanned the bodies looking for whatever phantom he felt the child feared.

Zorro raced atop the shoulders of the sphere prescribers packed in the subway car, the same way his father escaped Meteorite Hall on the day the rabbits assembled for his trial, only Zorro caused more damage, scalping an elderly woman, exposing her head to the elements with his back claws, as she continued singing "Let me call you sweetheart" at the top of her lungs. The bodies Zorro traveled on were feeble and undernourished, his paws met faces that tore easily, lacking sunlight and there wasn't enough room for any of the recipients to avoid Zorro's path, nor space to fall forward after he trounced over them. Zorro reached the girl then wove through the thicket of limbs that entangled her. The girl latched onto Zorro's hocks, following Zorro upwards, hugging his neck, riding along the trail of other recipient's shoulders, until she was swiped off by a burnt skin man with bug slit eyes.

"Where in God's name did he come from?" Clarence thought, having thoroughly surveyed the area where the man was currently standing.

"I claim this child mine! What are you willing to trade for her? Pale devils…you always have something you can trade. A giant like you can carry many things? Empty your pockets! I'm hungry for carp! I'll trade this girl to you for a can of carp—fresh or farmed! Water or oil!" screamed the burnt skinned man, dressed in a mustard brown tunic with a ruby red turban and a bright gold sash.

"I can give you all my delicacies still hanging from my ceiling, every special item! I have hamburgers and chicken." bargained off Clarence quickly.

The entire train load of passengers emitted a horrendous screech of laughter, chanting, "Chickens and burgers! Carp, carp, carp! Bang the gong and start the crab feast!"

"Everyone has hamburgers and chicken! I want fresh carp, water pressed or oil! Trade me the girl for a carp pouch or can!" the slit eyed man shouted back.

Above passengers bellowing meal orders and names of loved ones; two muffled barks were heard.

The child's silent pleading was deafening to Clarence and the sight of the bug slit eyed man holding her for ransom for a can of carp made his blood freeze.

The bug slit eyed man's glare rolled off Clarence and followed the sound of Zorro's barks through the cluster of bodies until they focused upon the hound, brandishing his teeth, vibrating with anger between the man's legs; preparing to latch on to the abductor's privates.

The man in the ruby red turban lowered his burlap mask, licked his finger; drawing a cross on the child's forehead with his spit, then released her. She shot from his grasp bounding on her hands and knees across the heads and shoulders of the crammed recipients.

Clarence made a bridge for the child with his arm and she leapt upon him, wrapping her skeletal body around his neck and plunging her sharp ankle spurs deep into his armpits.

The subway doors opened. Zorro, Clarence and the child, amid bodies pressing in and out, spilled off the train car. Clarence rotated his head around his shoulders, seeking the burnt skinned man with the red turban and golden sash.

"Nothing good can come from a man...who ransoms a child for a can of carp." Clarence thought, sensing that the passenger on his shoulders agreed, as the child clicked her bony heels into Clarence's armpits, commanding him forward while answering his second question, by speaking into his mind...*"It's a delicacy, carp. You can eat it...right out of the pouch, with your fingers or from the can..."*

The trio exited the subway tunnel then merged into a passage clogged with human bodies madly foraging onward in a nomadic pack. The child guided Clarence as if he were a camel, steering him through the crowd with a tap of her heels while pacing across his shoulders, maintaining a vigilant watch for any miscreant pedophiles slithering amid the swarm. After weaving in and around meandering streams of bodies and many times having circled the ramp the child eventually steered Clarence onto, he found himself standing in front of a hovel door, similar in every aspect to his own, but six flights up an exterior stairway. Clarence's passenger leaned over his head, using his clavicle bones as stirrups, rapping out an entrance code on the door with a fist no bigger than a plum stone.

"It's me...Gerba!" Clarence could hear the girl say into his mind, setting off an echo of hushed voices from behind the door.

CHAPTER 9

The Pedophile Tribe

The Volcanized rubber pocket door slid open, exposing a room identical to the one Clarence had woken up in. It was occupied by a faun bearded adolescent, shielding three children peering curiously around him. The children raced to restack several sandbags against the door after it was bolted and police locked. There were extra sandbags scattered around the hovel, strung together as couches and solitary flop spots.

A peanut skinned boy stepped forward addressing the stranger. The boy's eyes were similar to the eyes of the crowd that bogged the passageways; swollen, thrown forward and bulging out from the young child's aquarium sized head, the speed of the child's mind flashing across his eyes like tropical fish.

"Thanks for bringing her. We didn't know what quadrant they set her in. Is your dog from the pack that escaped?" Rognar asked, breaking the ice as spokeschild for the pack, putting his trust in the tiny passenger riding on the giant's shoulders.

"He doesn't look like either of his parents...or any of their litter. He has a brother, Ajax, two times his size." Clarence said, jokingly. Clarence couldn't determine the boy's age, but the child's head was so disproportionate to his frame, that Clarence marveled that the boy didn't capsize leaning forward as he spoke.

"I'm Rognar. This is Tweeker, he's from the sun like you..." said the child referring to a slightly older boy, draped in a St. Louis Cardinal's home uniform and camouflage fatigues, whose gaze was affixed to the plastic floor. "That Eritrean flower on your head, that's Gerbra, the other lotus tiger, is Shin Yen, and our own protector of the realm…this is General Kubrib."

"I didn't bring her, she brought me." Clarence said as he knelt down to offer his passenger the opportunity to exit his shoulders. Clarence sensed the young girl's hesitation, digging her trembling ankles deep into Clarence's armpits until she dismounted; commanding him to wait as she disappeared into the children's welcoming scrum.

Each child stroked the many industrial scars that scattered Gerba's face, holding her head in their hands, covering her face with kisses.

Perched on his haunches, waiting for his rider to return, Clarence heard words whispered into his passenger's mind…

"You smell of death, my friend…of fading blooms…"

Gerba's answer came swiftly in reply.

"This too, my friend…is what I also know. Dead blooms have followed our colorful spoils!"

When the greetings were complete, Gerba saddled back onto Clarence's shoulders, her bottle green eyes blazing, the height of her nautical snail patterned cornrows grazing the ceiling above, her palms resting on Clarence's head.

Zorro sat at Clarence's feet, stifling his tail from wagging as he shifted his attention to the different children, staring them down, projecting his stoic, bomb-sniffing demeanor, accented by his dark hooded head and tan mask.

"This is your first sphere-go? Your first forty-eight hours! You can forget about time from here on in…even a sundial would go cuckoo here!" remarked Rognar, examining Clarence thoroughly.

"He's from sun life!" spoke Shin Yen softly.

"You're from the sun life? That's why you're so freaking big! Your bones are massive. Feel their density." said General Kubrib, as the small circle of children closed in around Clarence, poking and prodding his bones and catching his eyes in furtive glances. "Sun bones..." said General Kubrib, a mountain region child with rugged features.

"He smells like muddied earth." giddily shrieked the ashen waif, Shin Yen, using the knowledge she gathered through her senses to create a dance, spinning in the air amid a sequence of round house and axe heel kicks.

"Petrichor...the first *wish* to smell after the rain..." Rognar exclaimed, reaching out with his mind through his nostrils to smell the idea of rain coming off his own sod pieces, which he nurtured in between spans during quarantine.

"How do you know what muddied earth smells like? You'd have to have been in the rain to smell muddied earth. When were you ever in the rain?" lovingly chided Tweeker.

"Sky eyes, you think you're the only one who's ever smelled muddy earth? I've been through mudslides, where there was nothing to grip but sliding earth and last week's cabbage! Muddied earth, that's what's him, I smell! Popping from methane bubbles bursting in the rain!" shrilled Shin Yen with a joy that churned against the hearts of the others like a shell gathered surf.

The children were raw, their feelings unbridled and savagely displayed, yet the kernel of their bond was evident to Clarence as he watched them dilute the uncertainty of their existence, parceling it off equally among them.

"He's from the actual life…outside of here…look how deep the sun soaked his skin." added Tweeker, his crystal blue eyes sparkling beneath his soot, blonde dreadlocks, twisting out from his head like yucca roots.

"Most of us…sphere breeds, we're born in the span of captivity." explained Rognar.

"I had a mother, too! I had one!" blurted General Kubrib, his Baltic features pinched in a hostile, puzzled look. His heart gushing with rage, turning the skin visible above his burlap mask, flush red.

"We all did." concluded Rognar, moving across the room and placing the palms of his hands upon General Kubrib's chest, then resting the crown of his massive head like a wrecking ball in the center of the young man's sternum.

Rognar appeared to Clarence as the leader of the group, practicing survival love upon the experimental battle plain the children were bred into. Clarence took an immediate liking to Rognar, whose body reminded Clarence of a water tower, every sinew pulling against itself to support the child's head, which he hoisted between his shoulders as his own banner.

"But I remember her!" screamed General Kubrib, unable to control himself, his voice filled with strangled anguish, his limbs triggering through a progression of military postures. "I remember her! I remember!"

"In order to survive…we work together." offered Tweeker, breathing in the visitor's earthy scent, his eyes like minnows darting beneath his dreadlocks.

Clarence watched Tweeker push his head against General Kubrib, grapple-hugging him with Greco Roman maneuvers as

Shin Yen crushed herself into the mix; both of them smothering General Kubrib, who twisted and writhed until he sobbed and laughed and cried out for chocolate.

"Have you eaten anything since you woke up?" asked Rognar, quick to shift focus off the General, whose feelings towards his mother were linked to a smell off the stove and a greasy apron.

"No." answered Clarence.

"And the dog?" continued Rognar.

"He hasn't eaten either. I didn't know if we should."

"Can we touch the animal? There's a name for touching?" asked Shin Yen effusively.

"Is *petting* okay?" asked Rognar.

"Go on, boy!" Clarence commanded.

Zorro dropped his canine Fakir Façade, crawling forward, his tail thumping, rhythmically, as the children swarmed him.

"There was a meal..." asked Rognar crouched over the dog and falling backwards as if propelled by an electric fence after petting Zorro's head cautiously with three fingers.

"In a sack, strung from your ceiling this morning?" continued Tweeker rubbing the entire pineal quarter of his head down the dog's spine.

"Did you eat any of it, even a bite or a nibble?" General Kubrib asked while placing the entire lower part of his jaw into Zorro's mouth. Undisturbed, Zorro teethed the young man's beard with affectionate chomps.

"You'll be twisting like an addict in a few hours if you ate anything!" cautioned Tweeker, as Zorro rolled his belly fur across the young juvenile's face.

"The sack had all your favorites foods...chicken and cheeseburgers...corn on the cob? I stole corn ears from pigs, skinnier than me!" Shin Yen said, bouncing her eyes up and down and smiling as she knelt on top of General Kubrib's back, squishing the meat of her face, then her shoulders, into the nape of his bulging neck; washing herself lovingly over him as they buried their faces together into Zorro's flanks. Sharing the dog's smell and kissing his fur.

"How did you know what was in my food bag?" asked Clarence.

"Did you think I was a witch? I'm a fly painter, waiting for wings! But I would bust a pig, flat on the nose, to feed someone I knew was dying! Feint with my left, in the southpaw stance, then switch to orthodox, so I can land my right! My right hand's the one I use for punching pig snouts away from corn! I didn't know you shouldn't eat the cores and you could cook corn! I'd never eat raw corn again—but I could bite a person's finger clear through to the bone, after chewing cobs!" declared Shin Yen, flaring her nostrils at Clarence, attempting to look scary. Clarence guessed the child's age, though frail, to be nine to eleven, but Shin Yen had just reached the age of reason, wet nursed by Gerba and other members of her industrial tribe.

"All wake up sacks are different, depending on who you are... but most of the bags have cheeseburgers, chicken and corn!" offered Tweeker, longingly studying the depth of the sun's stain on Clarence's skin, until it pressed him back, summoning the vision of his father's hands turning the helm.

"Each basket is different—but my basket is still my basket! It's mine! I always look into it because it's mine! It's mine!" concluded

General Kubrib, hollowing himself out as if he were a canoe, discarding his own innards in order to keep himself afloat.

"That's how they get you…in that first bag…they lace all of your favorites with chemicals that keep you addicted to the sphere menu to come—wedges of protein blocks…soup-loads of gruel. We survive and hold out for stashed *greals*." said Tweeker shyly, but informatively.

General Kubrib rushed headlong toward bonding with Clarence. Tweeker's efforts were less hearty, having first learned to swim with his father amid layers of trawling nets sprawled across the family pool.

"I didn't touch any of the food." offered Clarence.

"Fasting the first forty-eight hours is crucial to surviving the initial span week." said General Kubrib, gently holding Zorro by the neck as the dog lapped his, Shin Yen's and Rognar's faces, all smooshed against each other as Neapolitan flavors.

General Kubrib struggled to strip his mother's image from the traces of his memory—knowing all too well, that within these memories, stirred the depth of his inconsolable sorrow, causing the cannonball framed youngster to short circuit emotionally, seeking to locate a body through a waft of stew.

"A lot of the viruses they're testing, they set out in the first cycle—spraying them on food. During first night…people pace the dark…wondering when the light will come…then they wake up hungry…and they eat." offered Tweeker, as Zorro crashed against his chest, causing the twelve year old boy to topple happily backward. Zorro passed Tweeker's guard and lathered him with kisses, the children all tumbling together with Zorro rolling between them.

"Every seven to fourteen days...there's a new virus introduced into the sphere. If we can avoid the first wave...depending on the amount of data that needs to be assessed, especially if the first wave is a bad wave...that could mean a respite for us, between cycles, anywhere from fourteen to twenty-one days. Of course... if that were the case...after twenty-one days...Satan's cupboard would be sprung wide!" Rognar said, having rolled backwards out of the tussle and rushed to rejoin the other children car washing Zorro with pets.

"Every seven days, new viruses, whatever they're introducing into our systems..." continued General Kubrib, howling with laughter as Zorro nuzzled his earlobes.

"The initial load for the first cycle, they lace into greals." added Tweeker.

"Greals?" questioned Clarence.

"It's what we call meals." answered Rognar.

"Gruel...and food..." added Tweeker.

"Greals. It tastes worse than it sounds. Even in your language." Shin Yen concluded, as her stomach let loose a sawblade growl that echoed through the hovel.

"All of us...accept Tweeker and General Kubrib, were conceived in captivity, so our immune systems are off the charts compared to a sun drencher like yourself. But it's what we've learned...together...that's what keeps us alive—not just surviving, but finding a way to share the sunlight off the reflection of a can!" opined Rognar.

"Learning how to care for each other." interjected General Kubrib.

"Not just care—you can say it! Say it! Care is a substitute word!" urged Shin Yen, afraid to speak the word herself.

"That's not dirt…it's manure! That's what it is! It's manure!" exploded Tweeker.

The children rushed to Clarence, drawing in deep snorts of his skin.

"The first forty-eight hours into a span, we fast—we hold out…for stashed greals." informed General Kubrib.

"What about water?" asked Clarence, standing patiently among the pack of children smelling his skin.

"Only drink water once it's been boiled, mixed with quinine and strained of plastic…" cautioned Rognar.

"Other wise it will hurt like heck for a sun drencher like yourself to take a whizz!" informed General Kubrib.

"And never drink water once the hovels are quartered off." added Tweeker.

"The varied levels of cyanobacteria and psilocybin, from quadrant to quadrant are intolerable to anyone outside the cycle." explained Rognar.

"Do you have any?" asked Clarence, his mouth and lips parched.

"Plastic, sure. It's layered in my DNA. It's why I never cry, I can't. My ducts are blocked with plastic." said Rognar, onion eyed, puffy and swollen; with eyes like the swarming mass of recipients that Clarence first encountered stepping out of his hovel.

"Cup your hands, cup them! It's not safe for you to drink from my water supply with your sun lips!" said General Kubrib, pressing to convince Clarence that he was a good soldier, as well as fighting the impulse to give voice to his wounds, release the anguish that burdened him and wail. The boy's struggle to form a relationship with Clarence touched upon the scorched earth that held his mother's memory.

The children gathered around and watched Clarence drink as General Kubrib thrust his metal canteen over Clarence's hands.

"Can you pour some for the dog?" asked Clarence.

General Kubrib looked toward Rognar, who delivered the go ahead nod.

A silent web of normalcy spun around the misfit children as they sat mesmerized, watching Zorro drink water from Clarence's hands, marveling at the dog's lapping prowess. The children took turns thrusting their faces under the makeshift "hand bowl" to experience the tickling dog shower, resulting from whatever water drizzled from or splashed over Clarence's fingers.

"Remember...every day in a germ sphere...is a super spreader event." cautioned Tweeker, meeting Clarence's eyes briefly then shifting his glance.

"Dog drinking is the best sound. Human data. Only human data. He's smiling!" uttered Shin Yen, with gusto, as she studied the moisture droplets on the underside of Zorro's snout.

"Our days aren't numbered like calendar days...under the sun. Our days, for sphere borns like us, they're tallied off, without marks. Survival; that's the only human trait we share, under the sun—human insects as we are." expressed young Rognar in a princely manner.

"Like the Daytona Five Hundred..." interjected Tweeker, "It doesn't matter to the data collectors, whether we finish the race, it only matters how many times we go around the track until our wheels fall off."

"Human data. Only human data." uttered Shin Yen. "Can you make this doggie make doggie yells? What do you call the name for a dog song, Dog-Nar?"

"It's called barking, Shiatsu!" Rognar retorted.

The children's eyes widened with excitement as Zorro complied with his human's request, drawing their glee into a hysterical crescendo and inspiring dance moves from the children as Zorro tapped into his Sullivan County roots, looking to close out his performance with a treed squirrel howl.

Gerba interrupted the reverie, commanding Clarence to halt Zorro's howling.

The children froze in place, staring up at Gerba, who was standing on Clarence's shoulders, bending under the ceiling, listening. Then she settled down around Clarence's neck, staring directly at Rognar, obviously unnerved.

"Is there any food that you can give him?" asked Clarence.

"We fast during the first forty-eight hours of any new span… until we locate stashed greals." answered Tweeker.

"If we fast and he's with us, the dog fasts too. It's safest for the dog to experience its first forty-eight hours in a kettle on an empty stomach." added General Kubrib.

"If the wave from the first virus, doesn't lessen the amount of bodies in the sphere to half…then we do another three day fast on top of the first forty-eight hour fast…" said Tweeker.

"We know from other spans…they don't grind enough greal to feed everyone…only for the first few weeks." explained Rognar.

"We've been in smaller spheres…where there were silo raids." offered General Kubrib.

"A friend gave me a map to this place with coordinates for food. He said the food was stashed. Does that mean anything?" offered Clarence.

The children closed in as a pack around Zorro and Clarence.

"Where is this map?" asked General Kubrib, his stomach growling at the mere mention of stashed greals.

"It's all up here." Clarence said, pointing to his head, Gerba nodded in agreement.

"My friend told me not to try to sneak the map past my check-in point, but he scrawled safe house coordinates into the back of my compass case. It's a World War I standard issue, he said it would pass check and it did." Clarence reached for the compass and began to remove the covering.

"There's a group of rebels that know about this sphere. Somehow…they get in and they store things for us. The greals they store keep us alive. They go out of their way to help us, that we know, and we're grateful, but they don't want any of us near the light of day—ever!" offered Rognar.

"This is where we belong…until…we don't." concluded General Kubrib, doing his best imitation of an adult.

"None of us has ever gotten ill eating stashed greals!" said Tweeker, trying to put a spin of hope on the grim reality. Though Tweeker was born in the light of day, he split time between sphere span shifts and intertwining months of quarantine.

"This daylight, under this…plastic cup here…it's…"

"Filtered…" Rognar finished Clarence's sentence then continued, "The sun shines through the plastic barrier that keeps us from the outside air. It's duller from what you might have experienced but most of us wouldn't know what that's like."

"I can't remember what it felt like anymore…" uttered Tweeker.

"What what's like?" asked Clarence.

"Sunlight." answered all the children, even Gerba, who erupted aloud and into Clarence's mind.

"How is that?" asked Clarence, trying desperately to get caught up to speed.

"All of us…we go from one sphere to another…between experiments…we're sheltered in place, tending to our sod pieces. If our living plots go unwatered and die…once obtained…they're always replaced."

"Quarantined." General Kubrib added as Rognar continued.

"What we've come in contact with…the viruses …"

"The lack of love and Vitamin D…" Tweeker wisecracked.

"Whatever we've become they don't want out there where you come from. With what we've been exposed to we can't "be" anywhere but where they put us "to be"…or in Shin Yen's case… not to be." concluded Rognar.

"Where do the crowds come from?" asked Clarence.

"Where do you go, when there's no place to go, or no one to know that you went somewhere? The downtrodden, profiting upon the more impoverished, holding that one rung from the bottom, against the throats of anyone a rung behind!" Rognar said, encompassing the fractured reality of their own coin slug existence in a cashless society.

"Human trafficking." General Kubrib added.

"Infants born for test use without breasts to suckle…" Shin Yen concluded.

"Away from the sun…it doesn't take too far to fall from grace. Icarus wasn't the first passenger to cook his wings and end up here." Tweeker the prisoner of circumstance offered, serving out his sentence based on his father's debt, paid in human bondage.

"An extra crust of bread and a few heavy coins, go a long way for a family with too many hungers to manage..." Shin Yen declared, voicing other recipient plights unlike her own.

"Poachers, too..." said Tweeker.

"I got poached." added General Kubrib.

"Poachers?" questioned Clarence.

"Poachers sell bodies by the pound, in shipping containers, cheek by jowl." said Tweeker, projecting his voice in Clarence's general direction.

"Sphere-borns..." hushed Shin Yen quietly.

"We're the Rosetta stones of the future...providing data, under a number given to us at birth, then erased with the back of a pencil. Those eraser shavings, that's the ancient language we're used for. Human sacrifice is another name." Rognar proclaimed.

The conversation was interrupted by the stroke of a distant clock, sounding off ten bells.

"We're up against the last two bells..." said General Kubrib.

"On the map, there were seven hills to cross to reach the final coordinates before my ninety days are up..."

"What if this sphere is smaller than you think, and you cross the seven hills, you say are there, in three days? What if the distance from one coordinate to another is shorter?" continued General Kubrib.

"What do you do with the other eighty-seven days?" said Tweeker.

"I don't know. I've been standing in one place going nowhere for a long time." answered Clarence.

"The drive-ins are closed, but in movie town…films are shown any time…day or night. Modern Times with Spanish subtitles was our group favorite. Seven Samurai was mine." said General Kubrib, reciting several lines from the film in Japanese while maneuvering through sword tactics.

"Creepy claw Nosferatu…Jean-Luc Godard." Shin Yen added.

"Certain quadrants are policed and protected…because the information obtained from there is critical…movie town, gym town, workers-ville, are all policed and protected…they're direct information portals. Gambling town…heroin alley…different vices…different quadrants." Tweeker said.

"The shelves for meals are thin and the lines long. It's not worth the wait to get nothing, and it leads to a lot of complaining, waiting in long lines, leaving empty…but there's nothing else to do—and even doing something that amounts to nothing… becomes part of a span routine." said Shin Yen, a hint of mischief pulling her dark scowl upward.

"Whoever drew the map I saw…staked his life on all the rest of the coordinates falling true, based off the first coordinate."

"How come you didn't draw your burlap curtain in the streets?" asked General Kubrib, suddenly suspicious of Clarence, fearing he might have smuggled in an airborne contagion undetected.

"I couldn't breathe." answered Clarence as the children rapidly piped in, one right after the other.

"Draw it." started Shin Yen vehemently.

"Always…" added General Kubrib.

"Get used to it…" offered Tweeker.

"Especially in the streets…" continued General Kubrib.

"Not wearing it…where you come from, under the sun…will guarantee that your last breath will be in here, and not out there." Rognar professed solemnly.

"People die in here from disease, Mr. Camel horse. None of us are here to beat the odds!" shrieked Shin Yen, racing across the hovel and twisting in the air with ease, landing without sound.

"Especially in the streets. Whatever virus they send, breeds in the proximity of others. That's why we've got to get out of the city as soon as possible. Especially if the first wave of whatever they send doesn't strip the uninfected population by half." Rognar warned.

"I have a son…I left a guitar for…" Clarence tried but was unable to continue speaking, bowing his head and the body of Gerba toward the plastic hovel floor.

"Don't count on getting out…until you're out." uttered Shin Yen, shifting her weight across her body like the bending of a bow.

"Once you're in…I don't care what anybody told you, getting out isn't guaranteed." stated Tweeker.

"Do you think any of us would be here if we could get out?" asked General Kubrib.

"Freedom isn't granted…but if you think crossing the hills will get you there…we'll cross the hills." agreed Rognar.

"We'll guide you." added Gerba, speaking to Clarence in his head. Shin Yen, echoing their thoughts out loud.

"Ninety days and a wake up, that's when I'll be back in the sun." said Clarence.

Rognar spoke first, voicing the children's collective thoughts, as they followed, expressing it together.

"We don't' know how things are under the sun, but here…

"Unless we experience it for ourselves or see it, heading straight for us..." General Kubrib interjected passionately.

"It doesn't exist." concluded Tweeker.

"Ours is a stark reality filled with lawlessness and disease. Nothing else matters...surviving is secondary...being true to each other, because for us..." continued Rognar...

"Surviving only means being recycled and used again." concluded Shin Yen.

"We may be sphere breeds...but the humanity we embrace is much larger than your common sun drencher." added Rognar.

"I was born in a house with German roof tiles, above a rolling hill that led to a lake and another house that linked the ocean...all the doors had keys. Whenever we traveled as a family...we never drove...we sailed. That was the only time we were alone as a unit... on the open water...without servants." Tweeker said, wistfully, staring beyond the hovel walls, pulled into the black hole that was his family history along the silver treads of his Radio Flyer.

"I have the escape coordinates in my head as well as in my compass case..."

"Good, you'll need them, but for us..." Rognar said, as Tweeker merged his thoughts.

"We'll never be able to leave, even if your coordinates bring us to a red carpet with a doorman...the closest we'll ever get to an exit is the fruit buffet line! Pineapple toothpick chunks, or bust!" expressed Tweeker.

"They said I could buy my freedom out, with what I earned! What a gyp! They lured me in then took all my savings!" bemoaned General Kubrib. "Fleeced me to my last drachma, or whatever it was I had—they hung me upside down and cut the linings of my pockets! Do you know how many lazy soldiers there are, willing to pay someone to clean their weapons and watch over their socks on the fire? I paid off like a piñata! I'm off the currency bandwagon. It's sweets, dried fruits, or bit coin for me now! I'm not back to trading gold teeth for oranges, but close!" overshared General Kubrib.

"The wretched refuse of your teeming shores…for all of us… no more, no more. The wretched refuse of your teeming shores… for all of us…no more." quoted Tweeker, referenced from the base of the Statue of Liberty.

"Never ever…for all of us…no more." imbued Shin Yen, vibrating with life, the sole surviving member of a laboratory mistake. Living for magic, Marzipan and Finlandia Jellies.

"Never ever…for all of us…no more. Cast off from Ferris wheels and magic lights…" recited Rognar, Inciting Shin Yen to interpret his words into dance, her movements encompassing the pageantry of the big top. "Seek for me when I am gone for all the things I lacked, not in abundance but in necessity, but most of all…"

The entire cadre of hovel children spoke on cue, channeling their inner thespians, reciting the rest of the poem with theatrical gusto.

"Remember the calm of peace I sought that lives in shade on sun lit days…bathing the hours unto myself, and all that joined me then in thought, living and dead, as carousel minds, linked by pipe organs humming in the round!"

"If any one of our bodies finds itself in the light of day…the results for you sun drenchers could be catastrophic." expressed Rognar.

"Is that something you've been told, or something you've learned?" asked Clarence, interrupted by a loud crash upon the door.

"The pedophile tribe...they found us!" yelled General Kubrib, racing for a stash of weapons he'd whittled that morning from plastic fence posts, tossing three of them to Clarence who fashioned them onto his body, marveling at their craftsmanship and balance.

"They followed *you!*" Shin Yen accused Gerba.

"We were too merry! They followed the howling dog!" Gerba screamed through her eyes. Before Clarence could bow to one knee Gerba rappelled down his body, exiting his shoulders, transferring caretakers, swinging onto Tweeker's neck by way of his dreadlocks.

"Keep this door locked...and don't let my dog out!" Then changing his tone to a whisper Clarence added, "Unless you hear the same knock Gerba used—twice—don't answer. Even if you know it's me, if you hear the sequence tapped out wrong, don't open the door!"

Clarence slid the hovel door open, fighting off the press of bodies that tried to get in around him as he struggled with all his strength to force the door closed. The head of one of the children's oppressor's fell inside and was soccer kicked back out immediately by General Kubrib, as Clarence used the door to decapitate a woman, clearing the rest of her body free of the entrance way.

"General Kubrib, hold guard from the inside!" Clarence commanded.

Zorro seized the opportunity, racing over the headless corpse into the fray, ripping at men and women's throats with a crazed determination. Joined in force by a pack of wayward strays that immediately fell under Zorro's command, mirroring his actions.

Once Clarence heard the door bolted shut from the inside, he swung his body toward the center of the crowd, spotting the slit eyed man in the subway, who was orchestrating the attack. Clarence set his course for the man in the scarlet turban, slicing clear through people's skulls with the tools fastened by General Kubrib, their skulls being thin and their bones brittle.

The battle in the hallway corridor, outside the children's hovel was brutal, but brief. Although the tribe of attackers outnumbered Clarence, soldier of one with a dog, they dispersed quickly when met by his opposition, those that could crawl, crawled off, those that couldn't crawl were swept away without fanfare from the germ sphere floor.

Recalling the knock Clarence heard on the door, he repeated Gerba's sequence twice. The door opened and immediately the squad of children and their protector, Clarence, began to speed up their preparations to vacate the main quadrant of the sphere and head for the seven hills before the pedophile tribe returned with greater numbers and heavier artillery.

When Clarence and Zorro emerged through the hovel door to check the corridor, the only thing that remained of their battle with the pedophile tribe was a stream of large cockroach beetles, leading to a gumline of teeth left behind by the retrieval crew. Death clearing was an enterprise the retrieval crew took great pains to keep pace with, since cockroach beetles fed on fallen carcasses and spread disease faster and more efficiently then P Meister & Schoemann could successfully track.

CHAPTER 10

Into the Dark

"Clip the dog to your belt, so he doesn't get lost. We'll run a rope through the second carabineer—that ties *you* to everyone else—so *you* don't get lost." General Kubrib instructed, readying Clarence for the dark, fastening the second carabineer onto Clarence's belt loop.

"I wouldn't recommend he lets his dog go unleashed." cautioned Tweeker, speaking to Clarence through General Kubrib, unable to locate enough courage within himself to converse with Clarence directly, feeling as a boy to a man as an unlaced shoe staring at itself.

"It's not safe." warned General Kubrib.

"This dog's got Sullivan County pedigree. Once he gets his bearings out there...all you'll have to do is keep up." wagered Clarence.

"We'll see..." smiled General Kubrib, exchanging a glance with Tweeker.

"We'll see..." said Tweeker, repeating the General's precise inflection.

"Use this to keep him tied around your waist if you need it. Let him walk free, but keep him close. If he breaks loose in the dark...we'll never find him!" General Kubrib handed Clarence a small piece of rope, then took a longer rope and began to count out the length for the rest of the group.

"How am I going to get lost?" Clarence asked, having gotten so use to Gerba being on his shoulders that he forgot she was there.

"It's darker out there than any American cave-dark." Tweeker said, speaking from the memory of his last trip with his parents before he was isolated into captivity. Tweeker, Joesph Henry Standish under the sun, remembered sitting at a concert in a cave on his mother's lap listening to an orchestra in the pitch blackness, feeling he was floating in outer space, believing that if he slipped off his mother's skirt he would slide into a void of musical darkness.

"The manmade dark is like no other dark." uttered Rognar, as he collected water from his filtration device. Handing a full canteen to Shin Yen, who fastidiously secured it onto her rack, running her hand over a tear shaped, vending machine trinket, strung on a satin ribbon salvaged from a prom dress. Shin Yen believed the trinket contained magical power.

"There's a difference to the dark you're used to. Where we're going—nothing's natural and nothing makes sense." said Tweeker, attempting to put a collar he fashioned from his belt around Zorro's neck. Zorro backed away wedging himself between Shin Yen's rickety legs. "It's like that, humph! I've had dogs, you chose your protector well!" said Tweeker, refastening the belt round his waist.

"We need to muzzle your dog unless you can keep him from barking." instructed General Kubrib.

"He'll only bark to warn us of something…wouldn't that be useful?" replied Clarence, inspecting the children's racks, taking items off theirs and securing them onto his own.

"What if he gets scared?" General Kubrib asked.

"It's darker than any dark you know out there." Tweeker insisted, preparing himself not to slow the others down, reaching after serving spoons drawn through his mind.

"Will he howl or whine if he's frightened? We need to know." insisted Rognar.

"If he howls, every disciple from hell will know which direction we're heading. Before they put the lights on, we could all find ourselves hanging over a meal spit, even you!" cautioned General Kubrib, motioning toward Clarence, closing the gap between them. "The sphere cannibals could keep you alive, on their menu, for the length of the span! Shaving your flesh for brisket and deep frying your hands for finger crisps!"

"This dog's bred better than to howl at scentless shapes in the dark. He's from a long line of crop dogs. His father killed sixty-three rabbits in one day, thirty-seven under the sun, twenty-six more…after the moon fell! The blood moon rose with the sun and they sat in the sky together side by side…spectacle orbs to his kin's slaughter." The children listened with a reverent attentiveness that made Clarence want to seem as mysterious to them as possible. The more the children welcomed Clarence the more he felt his wife Clara thrumming through him.

"You trust him? We trust him…but if he howls, we cut your line and leave you both. You can find us at first light by a trail we'll leave—or one of us will circle back, and *fetch* you." declared General Kubrib, his cavernous, dark eyes, offset by the forged look of mirth he posted onto the "No Trespassing" parchment of his Khyber Pass skin. The horror General Kubrib witnessed was not unlike what other children endure, raised between warring factions in an unsettled corner of the world. A settlement child, born square shouldered and low to the ground, General Kubrib ran ammunition, suckling life amid rations, tent gangs and tamped floors, until he was poached, packed, and purchased by the pound—shipped in a container where asphyxiated bodies, slumped around him.

"Trust your position in the line and follow where you're going—through us. Let your mind wander, it's going to wander… but never stop moving your feet. Keep the pace, but don't believe your mind." Tweeker advised, his eyes darting beneath his dreadlock fronds.

"Keep faith in things unseen because…you won't be able to see anything!" purred Shin Yen, climbing onto Clarence, finding a way to stand on him, speaking nose to nose. Clarence could feel his wife Clara, reaching to embrace Shin Yen. The child's dull brown eyes, sunken into her face like coffin nails, contrary to her effervescent spirit. Clarence, having little experience with a girl Shin Yen's age, melted amid her vulnerability and mighty strength. "You might think we're a bunch of runts compared to you, but first night is ours—*we* own it!" trumpeted the joyful tigress.

"*We* earned our right to walk at night! *We* earned it!" Tweeker growled, clenching his teeth, forcing himself to make direct eye contact and hold Clarence's glance. Staring into Tweeker's turquoise eyes, Clarence likened the boy to a sea urchin, perched in a crow's nest, scanning for land. Clarence couldn't help thinking that it was all capes and costumes for Tweeker; that at any moment the twelve year old hostage would be summoned by a porch bell and strike off on his skateboard home.

"We've adjusted our eyes to the dark…but not to the evil that men do." said Rognar, filtering water for a second canteen and handing it to Gerba, who secured the canteen onto Clarence's rack by tying a reef knot with her toes.

General Kubrib crushed a walnut between his palms, doling out the nutmeat equally as he spoke. "The pedophile tribe, like the mayfly, has a short season. They all get sick and lose the force they feed off—from their own kind, because they travel together…"

"They go down hard in the first virus." Tweeker interjected, sticking out his tongue for nutmeat, biting his portion in half and sharing the other half with Shin Yen, spitting her share across the hovel. Shin Yen caught her chunk as she was want to catch flying insects.

"The remnants of the pedophile tribe scatter, but if recognized alone, they'll be stoned by other recipients. Stones are hard to come by…anything heavy that can be thrown…is more accurate." General Kubrib concluded, dropping a pinch of nut meat into Rognar's hand, who savored the tiny amount, nibbling around the edges, clamping the final bite with his fingernails before the treat dissolved.

"It gives sphere dwellers things to do, organize, create markets, exchange goods, hang and stone pedophiles…" Tweeker caught his canteen, thrown by Rognar, taking a quick gulp before Rognar could stop him then stashing it among his rack.

"It's going to be impossible for you to keep up, we've honed are senses to the dark, but follow along—best you can!" encouraged General Kubrib, gripping Clarence's bicep.

"You keep us safe during the day, we'll keep you safe at night. First night is ours! *We* carved it, *we* own it!" Tweeker shouted defiantly.

"*We* claimed it. In spite of who *we* are! In spite of how *we* were born." spewed Shin Yen, taking in a deep breath and preparing herself for the enveloping darkness while beginning the Peking form of Tai-chi, the rest of the children flowed into the form, joining her at different intervals. Gerba went through the twenty-four postures of the form, balancing atop Clarence's shoulders, shifting her weight around the back of his neck.

"We always move at night." finished Rognar, topping off the final canteen for himself and beginning to break down his filtering apparatus.

"It's harder for anyone to track us—because they haven't spent time…learning to see in the dark." offered General Kubrib, doing his battle speed version of the form, adding military thrusting advances into every posture.

"There's cannibals in these spheres. They don't put that in the brochure, but we all know people that witnessed children eaten alive! Cooked crisp in their skin, crying for help." said Tweeker, swooping crane like.

"I'll kill any cannibal who attempts to dine on my friends!" hissed General Kubrib, drilling bayonet thrusts, attacking at precise angles conducive to his stature.

"Me too…" echoed Tweeker, staying true to the form, floating in stillness.

"Who's the man with the golden sash and the red turban?" asked Clarence, feeling a shudder of horror pass through the hovel.

Rognar began to speak over the protests of the other children urging him not to.

"Hush! Don't say his name and bring him to our door! Don't tempt the fates and say his name! Don't say it!" insisted General Kubrib.

"It's superstition, General Kubrib, not science." Rognar respectfully retorted.

"Don't risk it Rogs! It's not worth it." implored Tweeker.

"Don't say his name! Please don't say it! Please! I'll let you carry my omelet!" begged Shin Yen.

Most of the children finished the form settling into the final pose, Shin Yen, though she had started first was still several postures behind.

"An omelet you rob nests for...your amulet has special powers. Someday we'll clean the capsule and see what kind of devil kryptonite you've squirreled away in there, what magical stone you have, or eye of extinct newt." Rognar addressed Shin Yen, softly, then changing his tone and speaking quickly he blurted out, "The evil one with the blood turban..." General Kubrib and Tweeker both tried to capture Rognar as he evaded them, scampering around the hovel. "His name is Abdul the mad bull! Rumor has it, if you say his name...he seeks you out, and finds you...every child in captivity fears Abdul and his squad of ghouls." finished Rognar defiantly, attempting to scream Abdul's name again, but General Kubrib subdued him lovingly cradling his mouth with his bicep muscle.

"There was a drooling eyed woman, when I was in line, getting shots. "Young lamb"—drool eye said, "I'd like to eat you after a long race!" Run me around...until I sweated my own salt!" uttered

Shin Yen, completing the form, pressing into the earth, deepening her breath.

"They'd eat your dog, too!" said General Kubrib, flipping Rognar over his shoulder and down his back, then seizing Zorro, running his hands the length of the dog's body, wrapping the dog's belly against his throat. "They'd seize him while he's still fat and skin him alive! Dog jerky is a delicacy—but bug eating cat, or lizard chicken on a stick, is common fare! Hizzah!" trumpeted General Kubrib.

Clarence marveled how gentle General Kubrib was with Zorro, washing the dog into his skin. Though General Kubrib was legally not old enough to drive, there was a sad, prestamped maturity upon him, as if he had skipped his childhood completely as one would a tottering stone at the crossing of a creek.

"Based on what you remember about your map, we think it's about three and a half miles from here to the base of the first of the seven hills. That's three and a half miles in pitch darkness!" spoke Rognar, his thoughts pirouetting across his eyes.

"That gives us another bell before the lights go…" calculated Tweeker, counting through his twitching fingers. "We gotta' bust, man…forget the bells, forget the bells! The tribe's gonna' come back strapped with dinner spears! We're all going to end up on spits, man!" Tweeker could not comprehend what the bells tolling from the center tower of the sphere meant. To Tweeker, time didn't break, or reset, it only returned without end, wherein immediate paths to survival and the wellbeing of his sphere clan were his only concerns.

Rognar, fearing Tweeker might spiral out of control so close to the twelfth tolling of the bells; tossed him a gaming Switch, which he immediately grabbed hold of, retrieving his last game while projecting it onto the hovel wall. The children became engrossed watching Tweeker play, echoing every move that rippled through his body.

"The first set of coordinates on your compass will supply us with whatever we need to get over the first hill, my guess…it's an underground post of some sort…" continued Rognar.

"The coordinates represent safe houses for all of us—stuffed with gear…" added General Kubrib, his attention fixed on the clan's communal game image, his body thrumming.

"…and greals." concluded Tweeker, his face flashing gaming winces under his dreadlocks. The other children conjured up images of monsters from the dark, Tweeker saw only saw his parents, surrounded in plush, murky luxury.

"And two kinds of candy…known and surprise!" screeched Shin Yen, silently. Exuding a joyous expression she mastered screeching without sound, nestled in Tweeker's lap, exchanging a glance with Gerba, who raised her eyebrows up and down, expressing her enthusiasm for surprise candy.

"Half face always knows how many trinkets we need to staff the party." Tweeker said, dreaming of bulging his cheeks on wads of Big League Chew, his favorite treat.

Rognar spoke directly to Clarence, readying the giant stranger for the oncoming dark. "The second set of coordinates we think is placed in the valley, over the first of the seven hills. We'll be heading north—Ursa Major won't be accessible, maybe a Chevron sign, but stars aren't visible from the base of a sphere kettle. Once we open that door…we won't strike a match until we reach the first set of coordinates. Trust following us...knowing *we* know where *we're* going."

"All of the lights are out on first night. You can see a single spark for miles." expressed Shin Yen, who let slip a twinge of sadness, preparing to enter the dark hold ahead. The laboratory born Shin Yen was terrified of the night, harbinger of additional horrors when the limited sun broke.

"It might take two or three days to get over the first hill... we can set up camp in the valley at the second coordinate and restock there." General Kubrib rehashed the plan, keeping part of his attention on Tweeker's game while lacing his rope through each of the carabineers on their belts, knowing that the chiming of the twelve bells was nigh.

"By the end of the long night, when they relight the day, we'll be at the base of the first of the seven hills. By day three, we'll have a full hill or more to separate us from whoever might be tracking our movements." said Rognar, attempting to comfort Gerba.

"The pedophile tribe will be back at this door at first light! Tripling their numbers, armed to the hilt...but we won't be home! Nobody goes out on first night...only us." General Kubrib declared valiantly.

"Only us." echoed Shin Yen, sensing Gerba's fear of Abdul the Bull pressing into her thoughts.

"Can't we get out on the trains?" asked Clarence, feeling Gerba's fear of Abdul the Bull, as well.

"Everything closes at first night. Nothing stirs, that's the law. All the lights go out...everyone's locked in tight by the twelfth bell." answered General Kubrib.

"Except us!" whispered Shin Yen.

"The trains run from the middle of one city encampment to the middle of another…" General Kubrib explained.

"They don't stop at either of the furthest ends—only in the middle!" Tweeker added, sensing from the others that the sounding of the bells was coming, squeezing out the last remaining minutes of his playing time.

"Trains are a good way of injecting viruses into cramped quarters. Once a virus is transmitted, it doesn't matter how lethal it is, or who it takes with it when it passes, only how fast it spreads. That's all the data keepers are interested in. Speed of transmission." Rognar concluded. Uncertain what would become of them if Clarence unraveled in the manmade dark.

"They track us wherever we go, remember that! We all got chip jabs! They could pluck us off any of the seven hills or between the five valleys…hunt us down…drop us into any quadrant they want, just like that!" warned General Kubrib, filling the many sheaths that draped his body with his handcrafted shivs.

"Prescribers are immunized for different things—some viruses fell all but a few, some…only a few…but not all." expressed Rognar.

"Ninety days and a wake up, I don't expect to notch any sick days." offered Clarence.

"No one can dodge every virus, not even you." General Kubrib advised Clarence, exchanging a glance with Rognar, concerning the impending bells, knowing they had to shut Tweeker down.

"Everyone is vulnerable to keeling over, we choose to know when and where we fall! And if we get so lucky…who will bury us!" spouted Tweeker, arching his head back, dreading the suffocating, oncoming dark, then plunging himself back into his video game.

"Just because we can get out of the city...that doesn't mean we're safe from whatever the city is suffering from week to week, it just means...we'll suffer from it ourselves, but away from where the majority of people are suffering the most. Tweeker, it's time... finish your game or save it." expressed Rognar.

"You don't want to be near any separated quadrant when they break a virus over it." uttered General Kubrib, shuddering at the thought.

"People defecating in the streets...hanging their inflamed butt cheeks over balcony rails, shitting over whoever passes..."

"Tweeker! Give up the game!" Rogner scolded.

Tweeker refused to turn it off, holding it over his head, playing it as he paced the hovel, finishing his game as he spoke, "The suffering people put on to others, for the sake of their own suffering! This world knows no poetry. Rognar, you spoke the un-named name, I'll speak my mind! They'll be concerts, soon, to drown out people—wailing in sickness! Sporting events to take recipient's minds off killing each other! Banquets held... after starving us on scraps! Tell me that isn't true, Rognar! Tell me they don't sound a gong and everyone stampedes, shouting for crab paste! Nobody stays indoors. Most of the people during the day...they ride the trains, they wander from sector to sector, working at odd jobs doing nothing. They can't help themselves— trading, bartering. Gamblers gamble...others pray. Numbers... don't tally the babbling masses—here, take it!" Tweeker shut down his unfinished game, handing the Switch to Rognar, which he secured onto his rack.

"If this world holds no poetry, Tweeker, then we'll write our own! In our time on the plastic walls of this Petri dish, scrolling graffiti eighty stories high! Even if our words and images are ground to dust, we will paint them to the very brim of the dish— not to be seen, but to quench our spirits with color, through the wake of our span!" said Rognar, taking deep breaths in coordination with General Kubrib, Shin Yen and Tweeker, all of them beginning to breathe in sync.

"In order for an experiment like this to work, they have to have numbers, ten thousand prescribers? That's what they said you came in with, isn't it?" asked Rognar.

"That's the number they told me." Clarence responded.

"There are tens of thousands of people here...each jabbed with different company chips. Paid specimens from many different countries. The spaces in any sphere, occupied by prescribers, are sold at a premium. Retrieval of a single chip would be worth a small fortune. There are people here, filling vector spots, for tracing purposes only. When we get to the ridgeline, on the first of the seven hills—see for yourself. The number of living quadrants will be visible from that vantage point. There's housing for ten times the ten thousand people they told you were harbored here, but if you never go outside what you're inside of...you'll never see it." expressed Rognar.

"That many people—how?" Clarence asked.

Tweeker responded, "Anybody that falls through the cracks, ends up here. The elderly, siphoned of all their hourly worth, they arrive in shipping containers, like General Kubrib did, poached by the pound."

"I got caught on the wrong side of a new regime and was thrown into a shipping container, bound for my first span, as tip weight! Tip weight!" blurted out General Kubrib, "A captain's bonus purse, presuming half his merchandise is near dead leaving port!"

"Anybody that's in here, old enough not to remember who they were when they lived under the sun...they're here because somebody got paid to put them here." said Rognar.

"My father helped bank roll this world. Because of some company flaw, he was forced to sell me off to make amends and save face." finished Tweeker flatly.

Rognar continued, "The number of bodies are crucial to the data. It's all...in the numbers! The path of evil repeats itself... people shake their heads...after the dust settles...as if they were surprised!"

"Older recipients are important, too..." Tweeker added, "They're direct hits, soaking up every virus that's sent out—but I'm here to paint! Not to count fruit collectors!"

"Swoooooooshhhhhh!" burst Shin Yen, without making a sound, "Bring me wings or wish my death!"

"Pretty soon..." General Kubrib began, "Sectors will be divided up. Dementia city. Homeless city. Alcohol, heroin, pedophilia, every vice forms its own quadrant. It doesn't matter that our domicile is where it is, if enough people survive that want to shoot dice night and day, then this area becomes...the dice shooting capital of the sphere..."

"Currency is worthless ..." added Tweeker.

"Not even a three month currency." said Rognar.

"Canned goods, soda pop, alcohol, drugs. Everyone and everything is tradable. Especially your dog!" concluded General Kubrib.

"Your friend that gave you that compass..." Rognar said.

"Half Face…" added General Kubrib.

"My friend, the map holder, that's Half Face?" Clarence asked.

"His code name for us is Half Face. Half Face and whoever helps Half Face—we know Half Face doesn't have a whole face, but his heart…" each of the children, even Gerba and Shin Yen, who had ventured into the deep end of her trance, pounded their fists over their hearts, in a solemn show of respect.

"Half Face…" continued Rognar, "and his friends, they're our last remaining links to the sun."

The lights in the hovel flickered as the tower clock sounded its first of twelve strokes.

"It's time…" somberly tallied Rognar, summoning his own spirit as he looked at his friends around him.

"First night is ours!" expressed General Kubrib.

"Get ready for the dark!" Clarence heard Gerba speak into his mind as General Kubrib released the bolt on the hovel door.

CHAPTER 11

Traded Child

A body pulled on a string, Clarence marched along in solid darkness. Whatever it was the children walked him through, around or avoided, Clarence had zero knowledge of it, his eyes never adjusted. He was solely dependent upon keeping his place, marching his feet forward, deafened by the sound of his parties' footsteps echoing off the plastic tower walls and thermoset pathways—casting an eerie, synthetic broadcast of their shuffling progress.

Clarence served three tours in Afghanistan, but he had nothing to reach out to or balance his weight upon, except for the lives of the five children he was tied on to, holding him in place.

Wood grains from Clarence's great grandfather's hunting lodge seeped into his vision. *The scent of peppered sausage, spicing the air from an oven hosting dozens of stuffed pheasants. Clarence felt his cousins' many hands, crossing over his, plucking bound turkeys, comforting the birds while brining their skin in frigid water. Clarence's clan gathered seasonally, salting venison, pork, and beef in hollowed poplar troughs, parceling off the hunt, canning and distributing yields, whiskey and song. A tradition revisited as Clarence felt his cheeks brushing fleeced flanks, reaching his face out in the dark, stumbling below armloads of applewood, waiting in line for a pear slice from his great grandfather's blade. The grizzled patriarch, scrutinizing his progeny. Shadows of countless deer draping the porch hang, the soft whine of fiddles and folk guitars*

intertwined with women's voices, humming into tune, deer blood
draining into pudding pans, keeping time...the children's scratchy
footsteps shuffling in.

Shin Yen kept pace at the rear, behind Tweeker, progressing by walking backward as well as forward, alternating karate kicks and standing on her hands when the wet strength of her foal legs failed her. Shin Yen trusted her vendor trinket's power to hold the collapsing darkness at bay, repeating, *"Get thee behind me!"* every roundhouse kick of the way.

General Kubrib probed the air with speartip swipes and sword jabs. Zorro kept pace with the teen age avenger, bonding child to beast with each forward press into the swallowing blankness. Zorro snarled into his half-hound mind, smelling the vagrant pack of domestic strays whining mercilessly in the lost dark, following Zorro's scent which lead them away from the Tupperware Cities where an uncrowded spot on a barbecue stick was their destined end.

The moment Gerba met the dark, she pressed her tiny palms into Clarence's temples, burrowing upside down into the nape of his neck, shuddering fitfully. Gerba felt the quietness of her own death in the infinite darkness tithing her every breath, frightening her beyond anything she'd previously experienced. Born into famine, living among contaminated refinery tanks, polyester heaps and industrial bile, Gerba was not the savior of lab children, but the burier, preserving only Shin Yen. With most of her remaining strength Gerba assuaged her fear by knotting Clarence's future Mohawk, fastening the yet grown stripe into its nautical, flag colored weave.

The darkness brought images of Tweeker's parents formal pleasantries into the light. The falseness of their concern, dismissing his existence, and the tidiness in which they managed their lives unearthed resurgent horrors for the transplanted twelve year old, adopted into his first sphere before the age of four. Unable to scuttle the swaddled fineries bred into him, Tweeker chose to baptize himself with a new name, "Call me, Izod!" was his first choice, inspired by Moby Dick, read to him by Rognar passing time between their first and second spans.

Nothing was as frightening to Clarence, his second firefight included, as the moment the children's footsteps went silent and they stopped moving. Without his body pushing through the darkness, the broadness and depth of the surrounding nothingness collapsed upon him—crushing every sensitivity of known humanity from its coil.

Clarence became unhinged listening to Zorro, search-sniffing maniacally, the sound of the dog's dead ending snorts, echoing into the void, traveling onward without return. Clarence and the children stood without making a sound for an endless hitch of time, until the hatch to a concealed hut was discovered by Shin Yen, passing across it, pacing on her elbows after her hands gave way.

The press of Gerba's palms weren't released from Clarence's temples until she was passed into General Kubrib's extended fingers. Once Gerba was safely stowed away, Clarence fumbled through the hatch, sending the children fleeing for safety as he crashed helplessly onto the tamped floor below. Shin Yen standing on Tweeker's shoulders shut the hatch door and sealed its lock with a mighty body twist, fixing her knees into Tweeker's ears for leverage.

"Shield your eyes from the light...open them slowly." Rognar said as he lit a candle, then gave the nod for Tweeker and General Kubrib to light the lanterns overhead.

"Butterfly fluff your eyes open! The light will sting at first. Butterfly fluff them...we're safe here as an empty mine. We're the only diamonds left!" Shin Yen said sweetly, whistling as she spoke.

Color coordinated stacks of brightly wrapped boxes of treats and greals filled an entire corner of the tiny shelter.

The children ran to the boxes casting shadows on the barren walls from the dancing lantern flames strung from above. The walls looked as though they were bored out, revealing striated layers of plastic.

General Kubrib tossed Tweeker a brown papered package. Tweeker spun the package around, juggling it, reveling in his opportunity to present the gift to Clarence. Unable to rein in his joy, Tweeker chest passed the gift, laughing with the other children as the box launched off of their caretaker's forehead. Clarence's eyes were unable to adjust to the incoming package, his mind still pressed within the density of the manmade dark, unable to command himself.

"Open it! That one's for you, it's yours! And if there's anything in there that we haven't had before..." said Tweeker.

"We share it!" shrieked Shin Yen, singing loudly above a whisper, along with Gerba, speaking into Clarence's mind for the first time since crossing the dark, where she edited thoughts of her own death, throwing up the face of Abdul the bull as a firewall.

Clarence was unable to unwrap his gift, his motor skills inaccessible, he sat listening to the children's empty stomachs growling in stereo as they gathered around him, starving, but feeding on Clarence's reaction as they unwrapped his package together.

"How do you pronounce it?" asked Shin Yen, examining the tiny bottle of Jagermeister.

"It's adult syrup, for adults…" Clarence mumbled.

"Medicine?" asked Rognar.

"Not really. But we'll save it…in case anyone gets sick."

The children all let out a loud roar of laughter.

"In case anyone gets sick…good one!" shouted Tweeker.

Clarence never recognized Gerba's presence, nestled against the side of his head, resting on the flap of his ear. Gerba huddled safely, soaking in the joy of her friends unveiling their greals, dispersing her own trinkets among them, reducing her entire banquet to a solitary macaroon, sharing the cookie end to end with Shin Yen, until their smiles met face to face on the last crumb.

CHAPTER 12

Desert Sack

After navigating the many hours through the manmade dark, the children awoke, refreshed from the short sleep they plummeted into—freefalling without the fear of waking up. A delectable occurrence, cherished among them as any Half Face trinket.

"Oh heavenly earth, breakfast!" squealed Shin Yen in a high pitched screech that though silent, was on par with any siren's vocal squall. Shin Yen's infectious mirth was evocative and pure. The music she exuberated living drowned out the sadness of her laboratory birth. Billeted, much like fast food chickens in factory pens, rampant with forecasted disease and commercially instilled neglect.

Clarence was seated crosslegged in the underground shelter, Gerba sprawled hammock-like across his shoulders. The children converted the lotus position of Clarence's body into a picnic cactus; perched, like desert tenants, they devoured their morning greals, a Half Face specialty of the hovel, sausage and lake perch paddies, scrambled in powdered eggs, with peach cobbler.

Clarence waited until the children had finished their greals, which they savored, sharing last licks off their personal cutlery, as Rognar furnished his final conjecture concerning the garbage range they were about to cross, comprised entirely of magazine issues dating back as far as the seventeenth century. Rognar and General Kubrib determined that the mountain range spanned a mile and a quarter end to end. As field examiners they were two miles off their original estimate, neither traveler knew the perils that lay ahead. The magazine mountain, shifted continually— though the crew were supplied with bayonet sharp crampons and saber tipped hiking poles, the magazine hills would prove treacherous, and the elusive ridgeline—nonexistent.

"There's something I need all of you to see, before we embark. I think it's best if you stay here, and I go out and show it to you, through the hatch, so you all know where it is, and we can put it at our backs, when we begin our climb." Clarence said, handing Gerba off to General Kubrib.

Tweeker seized Gerba's pass off as an opportunity, running his finger across a tiny compartment in his rucksack, checking his stash of Big League Chew, surmising that somehow Clarence had discovered his treasure and was in the process of exposing him to his comrades as a treat hoarder. Tweeker only shared the treats he didn't covet, rationing his Big League Chew to a strand a day, joining the new strand to whatever remained from the day before.

Clarence climbed deftly through the hatch followed routinely by Zorro which elicited an exasperated howl from a pack of hairless cats, who scattered, protesting the dog's reappearance. Zorro smelt the air, deciphering the fewer numbers of surviving strays through the lifting of the dark.

"Come to the opening of the hatch and look up!" urged Clarence.

Shielding their eyes the children gathered around the opening at the bottom of the hatch, looking up at Clarence and Zorro, who was circling a burlap sack, fending off the remaining hairless cats, most of which were already kicking up shards, padding back toward the Tupperware quadrants. Because the children had learned to see in the dark, their eyes were sensitive to the early first glare of reflected, manmade light. Behind the sack lay the miles of shredded shards the children crossed during the unlit hours; a barren plain of used tires, destination stamped knick-knacks and bric-a-brac, ground into repurposed rubber sand.

Clarence reached into the sack and pulled out what looked to the children like a rock with a wig on it, wrapped in a scarlet towel, until Clarence turned the object, face side front and adjusted the turban. The children gasped and bowed their bodies to the safe house floor, covering their heads with their hands and the hems of their shirts.

"Behold, this is the head of Abdul, the Mad Bull, his headless body with his golden sash, I piked, for others to come across—to deflect our passage when they find him! Don't fear to speak his name, his head and his body, and all their evil deeds, will never be joined to wreak havoc upon the meek again!"

CHAPTER 13

Magazine Mountain

T he light streaking through the recycled plastic sides of the germ sphere carried an intense heat, off-gassing inky clouds from the magazine mound where millions of individual subscriptions completed their final circulation, forming a curved wall around the lower quadrant of the germ sphere, a quadrant reserved for waste.

The squad scaled the magazine mountain at a slow pace, gaining three treacherous quarters of a mile daily while sliding an eighth of a mile back…while they slept. The crew's footing shifted constantly over the glossy pages of words and images and even with the crampons, and saber tipped hiking poles supplied by Half Face, the travelers were never without the unnerving fear of losing their balance. The bulk of the burden was levied upon Zorro. The crew would never have progressed without Zorro's ability to burrow into the magazine mounds, anchoring enough line for Clarence to follow and pull the rest of the band forward, angling along the mountains ever-shifting slopes, seeking the elusive ridgeline that always seemed to dissolve, restacking in a distant pile at an unreachable end.

The squad grew accustomed to the volatile hills of bound, glued, and stapled issues gathering speed in avalanche proportions, creating self-stacking sink holes. Craters sucking inwardly with centrifugal force, holiday issues, yearly catalogs and such, pulling opioid pamphlets and thinner stocked manuals downward, until the swirling holes they created filled themselves in.

Rognar deduced that a melodic rainstick sound flowing continually through the mountain was caused by a sibilant of staples, cascading in innumerable tin torrents across miles of glanced over pages.

At the end of the sixth day, laboring through the putrid heat, the travelers accomplished only a fraction of their daily trek. The cliffs shifty and slick, caused Clarence and the boys more difficulty stacking and hollowing out their sleeping lair then previous nights.

Gerba, knowing the troop was desperately low on water, tied a bowline knot from a strand of Shin Yen's trinket ribbon to a minature boxkite she constructed out of cellophane and swizzle sticks. She entrusted Shin Yen to hang the kite into the wind from the highest point she could climb, then Gerba went to work blending a pot of tea with herbs gifted to her from Half Face. The tea sent a soothing aroma of roasting chocolate swirling through the hovel.

Another sterile night bore down upon the travelers as they shared a protein loaf of hard tack, passing around cotton for their ears to dampen the screams coming from the tenement towers. The screams carried across the micro-shard desert, which the crew had traversed under the cover of the manmade dark.

"This is just the toehold on the first wave." said Tweeker, sensing what the *recipients* living in the Tupperware cities were going through, while secretly slipping a strand of "Big League Chew" underneath his tongue, clinging to its sweetness as another smothering night draped the span, the feelings of vertigo sinking equally deep within them all. Even Zorro sat up spinning until he collapsed while the crew set up camp.

"The exported body count, quadrupled since yesterday." General Kubrib informed the group.

"You got that off the radio?" Rognar asked.

"I didn't receive it from a carrier pigeon, I don't think one could fly through this slop. The winds were pretty oily today." replied General Kubrib.

"That's a huge jump in dish exports." said Rognar, comparing the number of infected recipients in his head against other spans.

"There's estimates already from sources inside the infirmary that say this first wave may strip the initial prescribers by *more than half!*" added Tweeker.

"If that's the case there could be a huge wave of prescribers headed to the hills to escape the virus." cautioned General Kubrib.

"That's the way it happened in two other spans." said Tweeker, reflecting on the extreme hunger they all endured during their fourth span. The children had survived five pharmaceutical spans together on three different continents.

"If it's that bad…we know what happens—sadly, it's the only history we do know. A history no one will ever study, write about or question. The history of our fourth span. The hunger span." Rognar said, continuing a test on a magazine page that he collected from the mountain, measuring it against samples collected from prior elevations.

"We should have collected a few more shamed crew members—like myself, after that fiasco! Silo raids for gruel! All my old man ever did was rubber stamp a faulty chip!" said Tweeker, praying beyond the polluted sky and through all the pages below, that he stop spinning. Securing his mind to a flickering elevator light trailing forth out of the trout brown darkness.

"Even if it takes us another two days to get to the ridge..." General Kubrib began.

"Maybe it's better we forget about the ridge and proceed forward without looking for it? It's a mountain of magazines, maybe...a manmade mountain of magazines, doesn't have a ridgeline, or never flattens out?" interrupted Tweeker vehemently, venting his frustration, unable to dislodge the feeling of instability from his limbs. "What the hell is it doing here, anyways?"

Clarence noticed that Tweeker was chewing something and Tweeker immediately dodged Clarence's glance, locking his jaw and summoning his preteen, camouflage dreads to canopy his shame; hoarding stashed greals from his giant friend. It was no mystery to the other children that Tweeker was unable to part with his Big League Chew. Tweeker was a sun drencher through and through.

"We can set up camp in the valley at the second coordinates and restock there—worst case scenario, we send a water party ahead, and reconvene midway between both points." General Kubrib floated the plan out to the group, who all nodded in agreement except Rognar.

"Our water supply won't last another two days. Based on the particle readings I took over the past thirty-six hours, I won't be able to safely extricate any moisture from the air at this elevation— it's too contaminated. It seems when they dropped the first pathogen, they stilted the air flow to dampen and keep the virus active." said Rognar, thinking aloud while continuing his test on the paper and sliding a piece of the material he was evaluating under a microscope; that by changing lenses, and unscrewing the tube from the base, doubled as Rognar's monocular.

"They're testing something extreme. They want to see how fast this first contagion spreads—on steroids." raged General Kubrib.

"Drop one big A-bomb virus then send out its derivatives! That's why the lockdown for this span is ninety days and out!" said Tweeker, catching the fire of Rognar's thinking and adding kindling to it.

"Why?" asked Clarence.

"Most spans are less crowded and run six to nine weeks." answered General Kubrib, nodding his head, agreeing to the direction his cohorts were thinking.

"They might only be testing one thing!" said Rognar.

"That would make sense…" added Tweeker, sucking the last strain of taste from his hoarded chaw.

"We need to set out as soon as the brown light lifts and make up some of the ground we lost. There was so little light to travel by and the air was thick as gravy. At the end of the day tomorrow we assess our progress, then we make our plans to split up or not. Put today behind us." encouraged Clarence, giving a wink of absolution to Tweeker who received it, squelching a Catholic twitch to muddle the cross.

"As we get higher up the pile…the paper is collecting a film that turns into a chemical dust, making the elevated areas slicker. It's a dry precipitation, with a high mercury content; an acid filmy dew that either forms or falls through the brown dark, but the higher we climb, looking for a ridgeline, might be a waste of time." Rognar explained, drawing his conclusions and contributing his information from the paper he finished testing.

"Tomorrow…let's see how far we get holding direct north—maybe we have to descend a little lower in order to progress further." Clarence contributed.

"Maybe." General Kubrib agreed, knowing that it would be best, if they had to splinter the group, that he and Tweeker go forward to retrieve water, but General Kubrib wanted to splinter with Clarence to question him about how he had tracked Abdul the Mad Bull through the manmade dark.

"Unlit sky! Why am I always hoping to see stars? Something is flickering out there…twinkle, twinkle, little star are…you a satellite…or a space car?" said Tweeker, outside the entrance of the hovel, lying in the stagnant air.

"The pollution content was thicker today than any day so far. We're looking up through clouds, inside the sphere, with the consistency of sludge. We might see a scaffold light somewhere from the dish wall, eighty stories high or below. Maybe the flare from a work light, but not a star." said Rognar, unaware that the flickering glare Tweeker observed was cast off an elevator panel spinning so fast it appeared fixed.

"Do any prescribers live across these hills where we're going?" asked Clarence.

"Renegades and outcasts…maybe." offered General Kubrib, stringing a bow he forged from tooth and hairbrush handles, his fletching ends strung with horsehair from a push broom.

"Any place outside of the city is usually unoccupied." said Rognar.

"Usually, but not always." offered Shin Yen, feeling drowsy, ferrying Gerba's tea.

"The Tupperware cities they cram everyone into…that's how they obtain information. They want everyone to be contained like leftovers…so they can scribble a date over you, when you're likely to spoil." scoffed Tweeker.

"Nobody ventures out beyond the burp of their own quadrants…that's why we call them Tupperware cities, because everybody stays put, within a burp of space." General Kubrib interjected, as Tweeker continued.

"There's no need to venture out. Where we're going there's no drinkable water. No edible food. The criminals that end up in spheres…dish bodies…extra numbers…they gravitate to unpopulated places. Prisoners hide out…thinking they'll escape… they end up being eaten by roaches or perish in the green gas." said Tweeker, becoming more agitated as the sky closed upon him, spinning, and struggling to dispel the plummeting—climbing feeling of vertigo.

"Isn't that where we're going?" asked Clarence.

"We set out before everyone else, getting the jump through the manmade dark. No one moves until they've gathered enough food and water. Our greals are stashed ahead of us. At your coordinates. Look what was stashed at the last checkpoint, crampons, climbing poles, hundreds of feet of lightweight rope. What does your Bible say about a lily's garment and the needs of man?" asked Rognar.

"If the flowers are painted so…God will tailor the living in similar finery…" Clarence stated, churning through his own staggered recollection of church meetings. His father ceased believing in God after the great flood, when the soil he had been cultivating for years, carried downhill to a handful of less spiritually endowed neighbors. As Elijah Whitney Clay's farm choked dry, he began conversing more with his many stillborn children than his eleven heirs, keeping greater company with the dead.

"It says…" started Rognar, interrupted by General Kubrib.

"If the pedophile tribe catches us on these magazine hills we'll be slaughtered! That's what it says! We've got to get off these hills, Rogs! We can't maneuver! We're sitting ducks—that's the only God I know! Yama the God of Death breathing down my back!"

"There's nothing we can do until morning…and by the composting grace of God…we will be safe until then." said Rognar, attempting to calm the acne pasted General, who posted himself for guard duty at the hovel entrance, facing outward into brown darkness.

"When the day's lit…and we're the only thing visible traveling across these hills—this many days in? Who do you pray to then? I'll pray to my aim, if necessary, thankful for the time I have tonight, whether I sleep or not, to make at least two dozen quills!" said General Kubrib, notching a shaft for a future arrow against his bowline.

"Perhaps going directly north will be easier than seeking the ridgeline, or God for that matter, if one didn't know where to find him, or whether God fancied such a thing as cucumber sandwiches." Rognar said, throwing General Kubrib a piece of peppered jerky from his rations. Calming the muscular savage, who couldn't resist feeling diffused of his anger when teething on the jerky, having long devoured his own rations on the unsettling hillsides.

"Everyone is packed into Tupperware cities. Food bins. Material exchanges. Bartering markets. The germ counters don't want people indoors, they want them out—imitating life so that they can trace how fast a virus spreads." Tweeker said, drinking all of Gerba's tea in a gulp and handing the chalice back to Shin Yen, who cleaned and prepared it for Clarence, who was next in line.

"Once a virus takes root, they extricate infected people as fast as they can, ninety percent of the time before they die— ten percent of the time…they don't. During extraction, which is what's happening, now—those that get out first—they're the lucky ones. If export gets clogged down, then you wait to get admitted, while the initial infected mass is put through…incommensurate levels of care. Different prescribers are administered different vaccines…if the first wave strips more than half the prescribers from the dish…that creates…a bloated amount of data to input. If we stay healthy…that can give us a seven day window…or what we sphere borns like to call…a death spa! Since none of us are here to throw horseshoes!" concluded Rognar.

"Or sip sassafras!" Shin Yen and General Kubrib joined in…

"Or sip sassafras!" Gerba spoke laughingly into Clarence's mind.

"Or sip…" Tweeker heaved a huge sigh and fell asleep.

Clarence carried Tweeker back inside the hovel, noticing in the boy's fist that he clutched a tiny wad of chewed gum, planning to recycle the wad back into play tomorrow.

"He's fast asleep." declared Clarence, unable to remove the gum from the boy's hand, he placed him down onto the crumpled up pages that feathered his bed.

"He will be anxious without sleep…restlessness will attract the wave of sickness that's coming. Tweeker is not sphere born, his immune system is sun strong, like yours, even mine, responds in part to a known foe, once they've been introduced. He's anxious because he doesn't want to get sick and keep us from going forward. He is only anxious in his thoughts…when he's not moving… and now…he doesn't have them." Shin Yen said softly, separating Tweeker's dreadlocks to wipe streaks of colored ink stains from his cheeks with the sleeve of her oversized shirt.

"How did he get here?" asked Clarence, looking down at the twelve year old boy, sleeping soundly amid the paper wasp like walls of the hovel pages, the issues stacked around them, editions fluffed, or with their bindings facing out.

"His father shamed the company that built this kettle… Tweeker's parents…forfeited him here. Rognar said, "He was originally from a place called…""

"Sea Born Heights…" Shin Yen said slowly, dissolving a seaweed spoon into Clarence's tea in order to mellow the harsh taste of the various roots, tree barks and herbs.

"Why do you call him Tweeker? That can't be his name? Who names their kid, Tweeker?" inquired Clarence.

"It's the name the guards called him. For a short time…while he was still very angry…we called him Izod. Tweeker was always climbing electrical fences to get out, writhing in fits, from the shock. The guards found him amusing…making bets and letting him fall from great heights. " Rognar explained gently.

"He kept the name! It helps him remember what he was climbing after…he has to remember…somehow…that he doesn't belong here…so he keeps the name." expressed Shin Yen.

"…in case he forgets altogether!" Gerba spoke into all of their minds.

"My mother didn't have a choice…" squealed General Kubrib, the words dragged out of him through his teeth, as he tried to suppress himself from speaking of his mother's memory, a passing depot stranger lurking in his mind, reeling in upon his brain from a thousand bending lines.

"Casualties of war don't get to make choices, General Kubrib. How many times as a child did you serve on one side in a battle, then in a month's time, the other? Your mother's choice was the same as yours…hosting a pot on the stove to survive…feeding both factions." said Rognar, with a measured understanding, cultivated well beyond his nine innings of life.

"To die from hunger or to live here…what would be your choice, Mr. Camel Horse?" asked Shin Yen of Clarence.

Clarence could not remember responding yet he knew it was the last thing he thought about before falling asleep and the first thing on his mind when he awoke. The second thing he recognized once he stood to his full height was that his shoulders were empty and Gerba was gone!

CHAPTER 14

The Indigenous Scholars

Zorro raced out of the troop's bivouac trailing Gerba's scent. Clarence was close on the masked hound's hocks. General Kubrib followed, carrying every spear and shank he had carved to a point. His brush bow and several arrows he bestowed upon Tweeker, who was entrusted to keep watch over Shin Yen and Rognar. Although the younger children's limbs were frail they scampered up the side of the magazine cliffs at a frenetic pace, fearing abandonment, pulling each other along, sending magazines sliding down the mountain behind them and causing mini-staple flows to gush with each tumbling step.

Clarence caught up to Zorro on a small plateau where the dog was long snapping magazines between his legs, tunneling at the spot where Gerba's scent dissolved.

Clarence's eyes were drawn to a copy of the Farmer's Almanac, sticking binding side out from the mountain wall, while all the other magazines were immaculately groomed page side flush. Clarence had received that issue a few months back, reaching his outstretched fingers towards his own name and address labeled on the binding.

Pulling the issue forward, Clarence let fall a sea of magazines, stacked to dispel fountain like, layer by layer, in a continual spiral swirl, revealing a red and black Encyclopedia Britannica stairway, scripted in gold leaf leading into the mountain.

Before Clarence could issue any warning Zorro recaptured Gerba's trail, scampering down the stairway as magazines and catalogs of all sorts sheared off the walls showering the point dog's hot pursuit with no avail.

The stairway led to a hollowed tunnel with a barrel vaulted ceiling, where all the magazines that formed its circular walls were visibly aligned in an immaculately supportive way. The tube-like corridor was lit by solar lamps, and had the feeling of a Publishers Clearing House catacomb giving off a much finer vibration than any possible trap set by a violent pack of child eating fiends.

As Clarence wound his way through the tunnel he saw that the curved walls surrounding him were constructed of similar magazine issues, molded into supportive cap stoned archways. Traversing the passage Clarence could see that the same types of magazines were used for equal spans of distance, Better Homes and Garden, House Beautiful, Redbook, Country Living, the pristine positioning of their binding spines visible along his route, their titles decoratively arranged in mosaic patterns.

The sound of Tweeker, Rognar, and Shin Yen squealing as they entered the stairway echoed through the vaulted tunnel just as Clarence came upon a cavernous room, much like the center of a library, or the nave of a church. The room sat beneath a dome spanned of hard covered books, the walls, built too of books, scaled hundreds of feet in the air, all miraculously balanced, one upon the other.

The room was bathed in light emitted from an enormous chandelier comprised of the skeletal remains of a Blue Whale, drizzled in colorful ink stained stalactites wired with optic mirrored fibers that brought in sunlight from outside the dish.

The book walls in the room were accessible by scaffolded planks, with stairways connecting levels on each of the opposite ends.

Gerba sat submersed in a reading trance, perched on a pedestal chair constructed of needle craft publications, her eyes never lifting from the page. She was accompanied by nine mop haired, indigenous looking men, each wearing enormously thick reading glasses, who all looked up eventually from whatever books they were engaged in, blinking intermittently at Clarence and the battle ready General Kubrib, who, after measuring the tranquility of the room, immediately stood down.

"As soon as the rest of your party arrives...we'll seal the entrance. Then...*Turcia ad opus disputatio!* That's Latin mountain wanderers for...let's talk turkey!" said the chimp muscled man, with a large steel harmonica bulging from a pocket on his bat tail fringed vest.

When the rest of the party arrived, a tumble of magazines was heard falling noisily into place to secure the encyclopedia stairs behind them, followed by the sound of staples that cascaded over unseen pages, growing stronger and louder until it traveled and died, somewhere inside the mountain.

After the visiting troop were provided for, the leader of the indigenous scholars huddled Clarence, Tweeker and General Kubrib together for a parley, while Rognar, Shin Yen and Gerba feasted on the reading material referred to them by their hosts. The other indigenous men, some seated about the room, some standing, all reading, were not the least bit concerned with Clarence or the troop of children that accompanied him, however, they did select a representative, and he negotiated for separate petting sessions with Zorro, whom they embraced, drying their joyful tears upon his fur.

Fallen Eagle, the fastest reader of the tribe, spoke candidly. "Who told you you could cross the magazine hills? They can't be traversed! Every quarter moon these mounds are re-shifted by huge stabilizers that re-shuffle the mountain, like an enormous deck of cards. This heap has no stability but where we hollow it out, and stabilize it—wherever we see fit to do so, *Per ipsum core! Quia non potest!* Securing our position, among every word and image that shifts around us."

"This span for us, began weeks ago…when did you arrive to do all this?" asked Tweeker, still amazed as all the others were by the living structure of the indigenous scholars, hollowed out within the mountain.

The leader of the dark haired bibliophiles cocked his head oddly toward the trio, first one way and then another, much like a cockatoo, but did not answer Tweeker's question, reaching for his harmonica instead, waving it around as he spoke. "We're always the first to enter, without invitation…and the last to leave…we're what you might call the Jackson Brown quality control team of the pharmaceutical digestive process…we've been in business since the Lindy Hop. Then…it's off to what's next. Nam anequam piano!"

"Old piano!" shouted Rognar, revealing the translation cresting over his book.

"What's next?" asked General Kubrib, awestruck by the stalactite chandelier hanging from the ceiling, its greasy colored shafts, drizzling ink down the whale carcass, dissolving from the editorial soil above.

"What's next, we never know, only what's now—but there has always been a what's next. We're forever assured of that. It's a stark reminder of our last remaining attribute and the dual cause of our own near extinction…our reckless embrace of the diminution of time! That was our crime, transferring our beliefs onto others as if they had been with us since the first rain!" Fallen Eagle's muscles rippled through his jockey sized body as he let out a musical moan from his harmonica. The sound traveled upward, filled with anguish and hope. Fallen Eagle's eyes flickered as he played, his lithium necklace chains, beach glass and soda tab bracelets, jangling in tambourine time. His hair, like his cohorts, cropped in a bowl cut, with a solitary braid running down his spine. Fallen Eagle's braid ran directly through a back tattoo of John F. Kennedy, inked from the 1961, August issue of Life, Martin Luther King, April 1968 filled out his chest. Other tattoos on Fallen Eagle's arms and shoulders were visible though simious matted hair, his vest was covered in amber buttons, concealing living images of extinct species, all fogged over as if clouded with breath.

The last note of Fallen Eagle's harmonica riff swirled about the dome of the nave, as scholars consistently lowered requested books by use of a pulley and bucket system. Finished books were placed in the bucket, pulled up by a scholar, reading on a plank. The scholars reading on the ground sent the books back up, almost as soon as the new ones arrived.

"All these walls of books…" asked Clarence.

"Were buried in the mountain…all pearls. That's what we call them, pearls. Most of our work in this span…is done. We're by no means finished, but for now we can engage our minds, wait, keep watch and read." Fallen Eagle said.

"Can you help us get over this mountain?" Clarence asked directly.

"Over it, by no means, but we can allow you access, *per ipsum core*…through the middle! But…we can only escort you as far as the valley between the next hill and this. The area where you're headed, is not for us…our work is here—and to resist completing it, when we are so close, would run contrary to our nature—finishing the work of the undone. Taking recess when there is so much to sit down with, here…to read…and so little left to do…but wait. "Time for you and time for me and time yet for a hundred decisions and revisions before the taking of a toast and tea. *Tosti et tea!*"

"T.S. Eliot…" offered Rognar, clarifying for his travelers from whence Fallen Eagle's tangent sprung.

"What is it that you're doing here, carving through the mountain?" Tweeker asked, overwhelmed by the largesse of the room, the books traveling up and down in pulley buckets, juxtaposed to the tranquility of the indigenous scholars devouring literature and flipping pages.

"Creating caverns for the bats. We're the guano bakers! When the moon hits your eye like a big pizza pie…we bake yeasty guano!" answered and sung Fallen Eagle.

"Bats? Chiroptera Scrotifera? Flying mammals? Is that what you mean?" asked Rognar, raising his head up from his book, baffled by Fallen Eagle's answer.

"The bats come before the birds. We filter them in…the cockroach beetles follow the bats. Bat guano is the cockroach caviar. Not a single cockroach egg can survive this span—German, Oriental, Ectobius vittiventris…Frankenstein-roach!

When the halls we've hollowed are packed and the exits sealed… then we can assure…that all the tactile spined tenants are properly expired. If a single bat or roach escaped, there wouldn't be "a what's next" for our tribe, or anyone else. That's how delicate this balance spins. Modern man…tinkers in the dust, thinking he's making tracks in the mind of the Great Spirit! The Great Spirit remembers…as it forgets. Man forgets before he has made any effort to remember. Creating a world in a Petri dish has many disadvantages. You and your conquering humans, with your muddy, big-buckled, Mayflower boots…and hypodermic flags! Humans are consistently careless. We were an enduring peaceful tribe, withering now…down to nothing! Summoned here to make sure your species doesn't destroy itself. As done onto us— sharing your religion in our sacred lands, where nature prayed, undisturbed by man, long before your Jesus cured the blind with mud. Now, we are dependent on mankind to survive, fixing your mistakes to absolve our own. When you get back beneath the sun, even a crinkle of it, promise me you'll remember the names of our sacred leaders. Intone their names out loud under the first rainbow that you wish for! This will instill the survival of our nation. But you must remember all of the saviors names, in the proper order or your blessing will fall among deaf stones. Recalling our names in the direction of a rainbow, helps free us of the anger we hold over human kind…destroying our livelihood and relegating the pursuit of our own happiness to the overseeing of your mishaps. Repeat these names after me, and say them in this order…the very order as I set down, memorize and practice the order among yourselves, so that you will never forget them. This is all we ask for safe passage through Magazine Mountain.

Recalling these names, as a prayer, will bring you peace when fevered, and calmness where you cannot find it. These names… are the only compass points you'll ever need. I can only disclose these names aloud a single time. Commit their order to your memory, their names when intoned in full ignite the power found in old prayers still in orbit. Their order rises from within me…not from memory…Meaen Show Hoe, Chai Schwa Chi, Tiow Tay Toe, Leu-tee Tine, Beknow Bo, Finchknee Pleck, Wayme Moe, and my name to be said last after all the others, my name, and pronounce this perfectly, my name is Moo Shu Pork!"

Fallen Eagle's comrades raised their heads from their books, howling with laughter, the children didn't know why, but they joined in, the merriment of the indigenous scholars being so infectious.

"Ours is a serious lot, so a little levity befits us all!" said the leader, laughing into his harmonica, musically enhancing his merriment.

"Moo Shu Pork!" one of the mop haired book workers screamed down from his place on a library plank near the ceiling. "I had no idea what you were talking about…Moo Shu Pork! I almost fell off my plank!"

Comically inspired, a tribe member began shouting memorized text from a Buddy Hackett joke book…another began quoting TV Guide films of comedic category, while another recited a Herb Gardner play, as the others sorted out the parts to be played as the act progressed.

"A posse of our corridor stackers have gone back to your camp and transported your belongings to the end of our tunnel. Your gear will be waiting for you on the other side of the mountain.

Bask in the comfort of our halls, the tide you need to traverse is too high to overtake until the treatment waters subside. Fish heads will be your pavers soon and wings your astral limbs, but mind the purple creek, the stench will twist your stomach sour! Life, Popular Mechanics to start your trek, Time, The Atlantic, Harper's Weekly, The Nation, when you hit the Vogue halls you'll be almost to the end, there's a chapel in the Reader's Digest Hall, divest yourself of any prayers there, and prepare yourself to exit. The Reader's Digest Hall…will lead you into Field and Stream, and that will lead you out. Be at ease…the devil's comforting thorns… cannot rest upon you here…not for the man who severed the head of Abdul the Mad Bull!"

Clarence thanked the leader for the hospitality of the indigenous scholars, then knelt down to allow Gerba to climb on to his shoulders. The spirit of the child scampered aboard, but her body remained engaged in her book, devouring each page like a dot matrix printer.

The children set off, Tweeker and General Kubrib leading the way along with their flute wielding guide, Trusted Fool.

Clarence stood over Gerba waiting for her to break from her absorption with the book. Without looking up or losing her place, Gerba spoke into Clarence's mind.

"Go…rejoice…my death is summoning my birth! The time that I have filled with breath I need for study, to learn about the space between this air, and the corridor of light to come. Thank you, Mister Camel Horse for the scruffy ride! Your beard was rough, but I grew to know it like a mane! I'll miss your human strength! Never once did I fear that you would let me fall…or abandon our way for easier passage!"

Clarence reached over and kissed Gerba on the top of her head. Her protective afro, warded off his lips as the sweet scent of Gerba's flesh burrowed into his memory, the weight of his lips nearly dented Gerba's yoke soft skull.

CHAPTER 15

Fallen Eagle's Visit

After traveling peacefully through the groomed passages of magazine mountain, the crew set up camp for their final night in a corridor where the Field and Stream bindings prominently faced out. They sat around a beam, emanating from a rock crystal the size of a truck tire. The beam from the crystal fanned its light outwards, the opposite of a dancing glow thrown from a candle. After Trusted Fool unfolded the final installment of his Pamphylian tale, he left his flute sheathed and instead took a request to recite The Player King's speech, but before he began, mammoth industrial plates reshuffled the magazine range back into form, causing an avalanche of staple rushes, pouring metal torrents around the cored out archways. The noise rumbled through the mountain leaving the crew in awe amid the fearful magnificence of the "metal rain", a phrase conjured by Clarence. When the staple rains subsided, Trusted Fool began his speech, but it wasn't until he completed the Bard's tale, recalling Priam's last days and the fall of Troy, that the squad became aware of Fallen Eagle's presence among them, though it was Fallen Eagle himself, who had requested the soliloquy— so powerful was the trance of the "metal rains" coinciding with Trusted Fools complete transformation into the Player King.

The leader of the indigenous scholars put his hands to his lips to quiet the crew's questions while scooping into an ice cream tub, passing out waffle cones stacked with various flavors. The tattoos on Fallen Eagle's face and neck made more sense to Clarence as he studied them. Rognar missed their significance, spelunking through the scoops of Rocky Road. Fallen Eagle was inked with marks found on federal currency. When he twisted a certain way, Clarence could see the hint of watermarks, inked on different epidural layers of Fallen Eagle's skin, visible at certain angles in the crystal light.

Fallen Eagle's words wound through the sash that masked off half of his tattooed face, leaving his cheeks and above his eyebrows visibly inked in changing images of disaster photos, famines, fires and John Muir's footsteps in the flooded valley. "When you wake, follow the sun to the end of Winged Foot hall, outside there's a canal, filled with a dark paste that runs through a towering chasm. The paste neutralizes the undigested residue from toxins—purged through the sphere's prescribers. Passage through this paste, acting as an organic kidney, is the only way to reach the Refuse Forest, where all loose debris collects. The entrance steps to the bag lands are built into the side of the chasm walls. Once you cross the tree bag glen, fish heads will be your stepping stones and then…you must all fly! Soldiers too! Though soon, too soon, fond guests, you will curse Great Nature's architect, wishing for gills, instead of nostrils!"

Fallen Eagle was interrupted by the sound of Shin Yen coughing spasmodically, shifting restlessly in her sleep.

"The thin skinned one is early with the virus, her barrier against disease is only a fortress of mist."

"Have you been following us all this while?" Clarence asked, unnerved by Fallen Eagle's presence.

"We could not harbor you and risk inhaling the same death that stalks your friend. Drawing the Eight of Wands, Trusted Fool won the honor to be your guide. Your friend is no longer contagious to anyone but herself—the cycle of this span's virus has two heads, devouring the child, full circle, at both ends. She contracted the virus outside the mountain, before you crossed the shard desert through the manmade dark. This hermetically sealed vial, Agave Trismegistus…is why you're not all writhing in agony. The nutrients we fed into her will ease some of the inflammation to come but not her pain. She's the last survivor from ten thousand specimens. We've packed roots and herbs to coat her throat and keep it open while the virus strangles her. The chasm walls await…the paste you must route through…has been too high to penetrate or cross, but now the tide has ebbed, and the ransomed moon has pulled the waste along. Follow the stagnant flow. Every step will count for you as valiant deeds…when heels and toes collect!"

Fallen Eagle turned his attention to Rognar, while he continued scooping ice cream into cones and distributing them. "*Balaena verins…corde maris!* (Whale headed brain monster!) This flavor I packed exclusively for you, for its melded treasures. When the wind blows unfavorably, lead the charge! The lemon sorbet for our fevered waif, bubble gum for the lost raisin, butterscotch toffee for you general, yours Clarence, I scooped into a large gourd with room for many spoons. Zorro, the scholars froze you cubes in herbs and grease, the tribe wishes you back but spells you on! It's too dangerous to mingle a moment more—until our roads return." A gelatinous breeze passed over the rock light, extinguishing the flame as Fallen Eagle and Trusted Fool vanished before the rock-wick could self-ignite, revealing a swirling wisp of ashy smoke, circling the places where the indigenous scholars had sat. On Trusted Fool and Fallen Eagle's exit, the pages amidst the Field and Stream section of the tunnel shifted, as if the issues in the entire hall were thumb fluffed, all at once, fanned by a mighty hand.

After Rognar savored the end bite of his ice cream cone, with sticky hands and drips lapped by Zorro, running the length of his arms to his elbows, he administered Shin Yen's IV, supplied by Fallen Eagle. Though it was hours until Shin Yen stirred and discovered her lemon sorbet, the dish was still cold, quenching the fire in her throat as Shin Yen and Gerba's spirit, from a single spoon, made a shared meal of the icy delicacy.

CHAPTER 16

Oxy Creek

The band waited at the end of the tunnel until the first slices of light trickled through the many pages of the mountain corridor, signaling their exit from the cloistered refuge of the indigenous scholars. A door dissolved in the squad's presence, resealing the mountain behind them as they stared down the banks of a dark canal.

"Plug your noses!" barked Rognar, leaping into action, following Fallen Eagle's prophecy.

Tweeker, General Kubrib and Clarence donned the green rubber waders over the triple layers of Tyvex jumpsuits each member had wrestled into at the Reader's Digest chapel.

"These zombie algae blooms formed all this...cyanobacteria sludge. Keep your faces covered...make sure nobody opens any canteens to drink from through here...use your water hoses, but keep them capped. Don't let the air from here get into anything." proclaimed Rognar, looking across the murkiness of the canal, which reminded him of a grey, toxic slab of Jell-O.

"Hold me back, man! This is slurpyville! I was just reaching for my bamboo straw to suck up a big gulp of this muck! I always love an Ebola flavored smoothie to start my day." said Tweeker, forcing himself to find humor while pulling his gas mask from his rucksack, holding his breath as he suited up.

"Keep your gloves on, your masks up, and stuff your nostrils wide with the cotton Half Face supplied—bulge it out your nose and ears." instructed Rognar, as the stench from the canal began to climb up to the magazine plateau where the troop was strapping into their protective gear.

"I'm not bulging any cotton out of my ears!" protested General Kubrib. "What if someone flushes toward me from behind, and I can't hear them, slogging through that pudding crud down there? I don't want to be trapped in a swamp, that stinks like a body rotting in the sun!" General Kubrib spoke glibly about the certainty and smell of death, as readily as a young adult his age might compare one right field fence distance to another.

"The cotton is pre-fitted, even for your ears—those nubs you have, designed specifically for battle; those ears of yours, more like the thought of an ear, left incomplete." chortled Rognar, gagging from the smell of the swamp as he crammed his nose with cotton, previously stored in cedar boxes stuffed with pine needles to snuff the scent.

"If they fit and I can hear…I'll wear them. If they don't fit, or I feel I look ridiculous, like some kind of Lynx…no way! I don't want someone to attack me while I'm looking ridiculous! How does that befit me in a troubadour's song? Fighting my last battle clothed like an idiot!" General Kubrib declared, stuffing his nose with the pine cotton to dampen the waft from the canal that made a violent assault on his nostrils.

"What if looking ridiculous gave you the upper hand? Isn't that possible, Clarence? Couldn't looking ridiculous be actually used as a weapon?" queried Tweeker, wavering on tightrope tips awaiting Clarence's direct reply.

"It's a primitive tactic." said Clarence, catching Tweeker as he fell back, adjusting his waders.

"Everything that's living in this swamp is already killing itself! We're just passing through, but I don't know how far we'll have to go to reach the end." Rognar said, drawing his monocular from his rucksack and looking down the canal that ran through the chasm. Rognar explored the massive, plastic-block walls, stacked hundreds of feet in the air, but still far below the rim of the dish, eclipsed from the sides of the plastic gulley which appeared to curve slightly inward, like tusks, parted by the fetid swamp.

"What is this swamp doing here? Or do I not want to know that? Really, is that something I don't want to know? If it's something I don't want to know, don't tell me." said Tweeker, pulling on his waders, his stomach twisting from the intensity of the poison he engulfed from an unguarded waft of the canal.

"From what I could gather from the notes scrawled by Half Face's crew, and my conversation with Trusted Fool...this slop trough is an effluence of treated Tupperware city water."

"Treated?" blurted Tweeker, as Rognar continued.

"First or second use—I can't be sure—maybe third, maybe fourth. The water is trickling through all this sludge. This canal holds the runoff from Tupperware cities, filled with whatever chemical refuse flushes through a spanners' organs. Dilutions from greals, rinsed fertilizers from greal preparations, everything served in a span is crammed full of genetically modified soy beans, rice and potatoes. Whatever the body can't absorb...junk food pheromones from greals...it all ends up here...opioids, fentanyl, Vilibryd, Celexa, Zoloft, Porza, Desyrel, Lexapo, Paxil...we have to walk through all this pharmaceutical—bile, before it branches off into a purification tank of some kind...somewhere—I just don't know where. The exit we're looking for is a stairway built directly into the side of this gorge. It exists along the downhill flow. According to Fallen Eagle, this chasm, Oxy Creek, just got flushed, so it's safe to travel through. The gorge is built over a Mayan filtration system. We're atually walking on multi layers of various filtering substances, gravel, quarts, zeolite minerals and lava rocks. Cave mollusks too, aggressive microscopic clams that filter out the impurities in the water, eating microbes, heavy metals and nitrogen compounds before this goop runs through the filtration tank at the end of the canal. The water is thick like this because it stagnates while it separates…until it's flushed along…because of all the chemicals."

"This is all some kind of runoff—and we're gonna' walk through it—waiting for a flush? That doesn't sound good, Rog. That doesn't sound good at all!" General Kubrib spat out, pulling his waders over his jumpsuits, testing their constraint on his body by replicating a number of assault lunges.

"Water waste not solid. The blue colored cotton goes in your ears, it's fitted, the green cotton goes in your nose, under your mask." Rognar explained.

"You're kidding me! I can barely breathe already." scoffed General Kubrib, checking to make sure he stuffed the precise colored cotton into its proper orifice.

"This is the time we might all wish for gills, like Fallen Eagle said!" Rognar reminded himself, feeling the oppressive weight of the stench as he tested the depth of the muck with a hiking pole, revealing to himself and the other travelers that the sludge would gather just below his chin, which was too high for Rognar to travel through. "I got fit for waders, too. I can walk through this…we're probably at the deepest point." Rognar said, sheepishly knowing he would have to be carried.

"If this is the direction we need to go…then let's mount up and step it off!" issued Clarence guided by a sense of urgency.

Gerba's spirit melded into the body of Shin Yen as she climbed into the harness strapped to Clarence's shoulders. Shin Yen hid her ailing symptoms from the others, wrapping her shawl around her head, though they knew the tiny warrior had been infected. A laboratory survivor conceived in conditions…*prepared for future times.*

Clarence carried Shin Yen, General Kubrib shouldered Rognar. Tweeker, carried Zorro who nestled and buried his nose securely into his harness, his muzzle swaddled in a breathable fabric, fitted around his canine gas mask.

The squad traveled through the algae infested, foul smelling canal for three straight days without rest. Their military gas masks, pre-soaked with jasmine and lavender canisters, helped clot the awful stench that wafted up from the slimy gruel. Traveling without sleep the pod pressed forward, the claustrophobic span of their journey being a hundred times more bearable in motion. The crew had no idea that the run of the canal would take three days to traverse. Scaling or going around the towering plastic gorge was impossible. The chasm walls were built to withstand a waste flush at the highest and final cleansing point of the span.

There was nary an oasis for the crew to take refuge, only clots of colorful bacteria clumps, dispersed with a bayonet swipe from a hiking pole.

The crew shared anything that came to mind swearing off even the slightest hint of complaining—lest they be plummeted into a deeper depth of dispair, doubling their troubles by adding additional weight to their burden.

The odor trapped in the chasm was so strong it caused their ears to ring while squelching any thought of attaining sustenance—their stomachs wrenching in agony. Zorro buried his own high pitched whine, muffling the intensity of his suffering from the others.

Slogging the paste, Tweeker spoke of the large gatherings he attended and the palatial estates he roamed. He spoke of racing grassy slopes, sledding the same hills in winter, sliding onto an adjoining lake. The sound of his Radio Flyer cutting the ice, echoing the shoreline, but whenever his mind stumbled upon his siblings he succumbed to a numbing paralysis, rendering himself speechless—euthanized emotionally. "Everything…was beyond abundance…and we never bothered to take the time to be thankful, only pointing to a favorite dish…motioning for a twist of pepper. Carving trays on wheels—gravy boats in fleets sailing linen tables…so many sets of hands knotted my shoes…they never stayed tied. I knew attendants by hair combs, bald spots and bad weaves!"

General Kubrib remembered the candy scented smell of his birth mother's hair and burping up phlegm because his mother's breast milk, he protested, was thick as cream, and syrupy sweet! He retold the many jokes he'd heard in war, and how he counted his fingers as a prayer each night, as they were precious to be kept safe in a set of ten.

Rognar never mentioned his life under the sun because he had none to recall, but he entertained the crew, reading books selected by Fallen Eagle, a collection of Thurber stories, Robinson

Caruso and Anne of Green Gables, reading by way of a headlamp, switching power chips whenever the energy waned.

Clarence spoke of the guitar he left for his son and of the acres of lemon balm, spearmint, heliotropes and yellow olive he planted after his wife died. How he wept smelling their fragrance blowing over his porch, bringing an intoxicating plume of relief that helped wring his heart dry of an unfathomable sorrow. He spoke of his struggle to climb out of a medicated haze, of pill piles, the slowing down of battle and the unbalancing of human nature through manufactured fears.

Shin Yen clutched her eyes within her gas mask panels, listening to every syllable her friends swapped. The sound of her pod's voices kept her mind floating out of reach from the circling virus, set to pounce, like an orca, waiting to drag the tiny child from the surface of life into its drowning depths.

After the third full day of swamp marching, the sun squinted through the plastic resin of the dish, finding the squad in mid-debate concerning whether or not they'd gotten used to the horrid stench of the canal or if the filtration system was having a positive effect, converting the density of the sludge they initially set forth upon into a viscous gruel.

Shin Yen aided by Gerba was the first to see the steps, molded into the side of the chasm, shouting, "Up we go! Stairs ho, stairs ho!"

Once the squad could see the steps for themselves, they seemed forever in the distance until the team were making their spiral ascent, each tread a premolded foothold, welded into the tusk curled chasm. Upward the crew climbed, sucking madly on their water hoses to keep their bodies hydrated as egg rotting vapors, trapped against the chasm walls, overpowered their respiratory devices.

When they had nearly forty final footholds to ascend before reaching the exit, they smelled the chlorine scented gust coming off the dark water, rushing along the path they had trudged.

The squad looked back, knowing every step meant not being washed away by the brackish water swirling in the footholds that they had just climbed above.

"If they Chutes and Ladders us all the way back to the beginning of Oxy creek…let's wait for the flush and request that Half Face send us a raft! Huck Finn the gorge on the release!" offered Tweeker looking down upon the sluice of brackish water that filled the chasm, his body drenched in sweat.

CHAPTER 17

The Plastic Bag Forest

T
he clan entered the flatlands of the plastic bag forest with
only a portion of light left before the dish day collapsed,
sputtering like a diesel van as it did on most truncated
evenings, through the carted to the curb like sky. Emissions from
methane, coal, and oil refineries, producing fuel for the Tupperware
tenements, muddied the air and filled this higher elevation the
crew had reached with a pungent, chemical scent. Renegade
tracers and prisoners were often the only sphere residents to reach
such heights, the heavier contaminants eventually trickling into
the psilocybin reservoirs and open bathing areas below.

As the crew shuffled and high stepped their way through the
littered ground, pulling single use carriers from their bodies or
off their faces, they debated whether they received direct light
from the sun or from a series of Vitamin D bearing bulbs of some
fantastical sort. The entire traveling clan were in agreement that
the dish light never felt warm or inviting, but strained its way
through the dense walls of the quadrant tank, bereft of nutrients,
trickling down to the spanners like some sort of government
stimulus. Rognar's conclusion was that the walls of the dish
possessed some mirrored component that reflected the sun's rays,
magnifying their intensity, but defiling their connection to the
source.

"It can be defined in the simplest terms...for me...this has
been my wish...but not my way... " prefaced Rogner, as they

dodged the tumbling bags that rolled and flew between them. "A father looks at his child and his expression is read off the man's face, but if the father were wearing, say, mirrored sunglasses and a virus shield, then the child would read back its own reflection and have no interchange with the parent directly, expression to expression, skin to skin. The purity of the sun has been adulterated in the same manner. We feel its presence, but through the grip of a manufactured scrim—similar to the white gloved hand of a mother, chucking her child under his chin…"

"Fearing…leaving ice scream smudges on her evening hands!" Tweeker interrupted, "I stroked her beaded purses! Custom spun for gala gowns!"

"I had a mother and she had gala gowns and beaded purses, too!" squealed General Kubrib, pinched in anguish, wishing for an ice pond to plunge into. "I had a mother, too!" he said, gutting himself. "And she had beaded purses…and I stroked and stroked them!"

Brown night came quicker in the plastic bag forest; the ration of evening light diffusing from the dish; as unsettling as a murder of trademark bearing crows, blotting whatever strangled sun that had slithered through the discarded flock.

The plastic bag trees formed around poles scattered in the flow of a forest where vagrant bags clustered and multiplied. There were bag trees sixty feet high and forty feet in diameter, collecting and growing as more bags found themselves pinned upon the ever expanding structures. Smaller poles spawned rows of bush bags and higher poles, pergolas, hedges and trash mazes. Scuttling bags dragged, twisted, or wrestled against others, colliding in crowded flight paths. The fluttering sound of rustling plastic severed the squad's wits, their senses being stamped out in the chasm, re-enlivened the further distance they gained from Oxy Creek.

"She's burning up! We're far enough away from the smell of the canal to reach us here. Let's break, and look to make camp." suggested Clarence, feeling Shin Yen's feverish body ironing the skin between his shoulders.

"Can't we keep going, just a little further? We've been through the worst of it. Maybe there's an IV at the next checkpoint? It's worth trudging forward just in case." pleaded Tweeker, hoping that Half Face's people had prior knowledge of the opening virus and had medicine and possibly an antidote for Shin Yen stored ahead.

"I've saved one field bag for her. It's best we get this IV into her as soon as possible and connect to our next checkpoint tomorrow. Maybe not spend the entire day there, but resupply and move on straight away." suggested Rognar, allowing his mind to begin to consider the idea of his body lying flat. He felt good, voraciously kicking through the tumbling floor bags after spending so many hours reading aloud, shouldered between Tweeker and General Kubrib, unable to wade the swamp himself. Rognar was mindful that his fellow comrades had not slept in seventy-two hours; awakened many times by their laughter as he dozed off in midsentence, quoting utter gibberish as Morpheus pulled him from the page he was reading, his mammoth head tied off to the book, bobbing upwards, lest the story become lost in the Oxy crud.

"Straight away to what? Does the next place we're going to have a pool? If it's safe at the next checkpoint, I vote we bunk down for a few days and regroup. My nostrils are caked in skunk death! I want to fillet my entire nasal cavity, power wash it, then…sand blast my guts!" General Kubrib said, as he and Tweeker tarped a roof between two high tree bag hedges, fitted against the back of an immense bag tree that expanded outward and upward at such an odd angle that it was beginning to bend itself back downwards from its culminating height, resembling a carnival ride.

The squad barricaded themselves out of the prevailing direction of the wind, but the bag lands were set between two wind turbine strips, shifting bags in many directions. The crew wove a barrier made of six pack rings to keep the bags from their lair, taking turns poking the gate free to circulate air.

Rognar hung the military IV into place and fed it through Shin Yen while Clarence cut out a bed for her in the trunk of the giant tree, leaving layers of molded bags in place to fold over Shin Yen's body, like massive, neoprene banana leaves. The children lovingly coaxed Shin Yen to swallow extra sips of liquid, helping her conquer several canteen caps of hot tea and lemon water laced with ground roots and herbs. After the children swaddled Shin Yen into every blanket they could muster, forfeiting everything they had, they nestled her into the trunk of the plastic bag tree to sweat her fever out.

Rognar, Tweeker, and General Kubrib danced under their make shift lean-to, praying with their hearts for Shin Yen's recovery, while shaking their bodies with interpretive wish movements. Shin Yen could be heard laughing in the trunk of the bag tree as the boys made up silly get well songs for their comrade, soothing her plummet into misery, which came full force when she shut her eyes.

Shin Yen knew that the images of her early childhood would accompany her fever, causing her to swoon, blocking the intensity of certain memories. Swaddled in the bag tree, shuddering with fever, Shin Yen saw herself penned in among other children, body to body, crowded in circling clouds, wailing. Shin Yen passed among the hordes of fellow children hand in hand with Gerba, only one of them had lived in Shin Yen's past, but through her paralyzing fever they both bore witness to the same memory, passing a barrier held in place by the senses. Gerba used Shin Yen's fever as a plank to join their minds. Comforting Shin Yen through a time when she was otherwise alone.

"We can only wait now…she's burning up! *The waiting is the hardest part. Every day you see one more card. You take it on faith, you take it to the heart…the waiting…is the hardest part!*" Clarence serenaded the children with the last part of the refrain.

"That's a rock song?" asked Tweeker, knowing he had heard it before, the words stirring his brain.

"Banjo Dave could play anything—killing time…put his guitar down…fall asleep snoring lyrics." Clarence said wistfully, his prone body molding itself into the many layers of bags beneath him.

"Sing a song…" Shin Yen requested from within the trunk of the bag tree.

"Like the one you were singing through the muck…that's the same song? I don't get how the waiting fits into the purple rain?" asked Tweeker, feeling his own body beginning to float upwards as he too stretched himself out, lying on his back, happily sharing the warmth of his own blanket, which was swaddled around Shin Yen.

"The metal rain song…yeah…how did that go? Sing that!" seconded General Kubrib.

"Sing it…the metal rain!" shouted Shin Yen, peering out of her blankets into the plastic dark, potted as a boiling lobster.

"It's a song I was making up as we went along…singing Metal Rain instead of Purple Rain…" answered Clarence.

"What's the Purple Rain…sadness or light? Hatred or resurgence? Purple is a majestic color symbolizing wealth, majesty…sometimes magic?" rapidly fired off Rognar, his mind bubbling on the edge of sleep.

"Light!" said Clarence, reflecting on the many hours he logged listening to Trusted Fool weave Rognar's mind to slumber. "The Purple Rain is sung through this Minnesota guy's fingers. Bending the notes all the way from Minneapolis through the Milky Way. That's why I left my son the guitar…I didn't have anything else that could speak what I heard Prince play—the prayers *he* spoke from."

"Prince made the Purple Rain?" asked and answered Tweeker.

"Prince did?" questioned Rognar.

"He might have gotten the idea from the Vikings…" Clarence said, half way between being awake and asleep.

"The Purple People Eaters…not the iron curtain…" General Kubrib continued.

"Steel curtain…" corrected Rognar, his mind settling softly.

"Black and Yellow, not purple?" inquired Tweeker, invested with his traveling comrades in the simple pageantry of truth.

"Right." confirmed Clarence.

"Prince made the Purple Rain, then he became a symbol, like a comma. He was The Prince who made the Purple Rain and then… the artist formerly known as Prince…the symbol." summed up Rognar.

"That's what I was dancing too…when I made my future wish moves!" said General Kubrib.

"Me too…" affirmed Tweeker.

"I never meant to cause you any sorrow…" Rognar began singing quietly to himself.

"I never meant to cause you any pain…" joined in Tweeker.

"I only want to see you laughing in the Metal Rain!" they all sang, including Clarence.

"Staples falling, Staples crawling…

"In the Metal Rain…"

"Metal Rain, Metal Rain…"

"I only want to see you laughing…"

"In the Metal Rain…

Before they sang the second verse the crew was sound asleep. General Kubrib snored louder than a charging elephant, but punctually forced himself awake, every hour upon the hour. Placing his tiny cauliflowered ear to the wall of the bag tree, straining to hear Shin Yen's rattling struggle for breath before rejoining his watchful slumber.

At one point the entire crew was awoken by Shin Yen deliriously belting her own made up version of Purple Rain, then chanting Fallen Eagle's prayer, feeling her body lifting above her fever as she intoned the names. "Meen Shoe Hoe, Chai Schwa, Tiow Tay, Leu-tee Tine, Beknow Bo, Finchknee Pleck, Wayme Moe…Moooooo-shooooo Pooooork!"

The crew laughed in their sleep with Gerba and Shin Yen, while their astro warrior spun head over heels, wrestling the contagion, body and soul as if she were tumbling in a dryer heated from the deepest coils of hell.

CHAPTER 18

Shin Yen's Respite

The pod were all seated in a semi-circle beneath the lean-to when Shin Yen awoke, pulling a shawl around her scalp, hiding the beginning spikes of a tight afro that had begun to grow in during her passing fever. Shin Yen staggered nobly, catching herself against her rucksack; screeching, "Mount up, you scurvy dogs, especially you, Zorro!" Bereft of fever, Shin Yen feasted upon this expansive morsel of time, polar bear riding that acheless, dwindling ice, until she felt the virus rising against her, tempering her breath as the crew broke camp around her.

The squad barely reached the next checkpoint as a squall blew up, sending clouds of vagrant bags fluttering through the forest, cluttering their passage. Clarence could barely forge their way and several times the team had to stop and rescue Rognar, who had completely disappeared in a swarm of rapidly collecting bags, forcing the youngster to forge himself a tube to breathe from, while his crewmates peeled him free. Zorro found safer passage crawling on his belly.

The winds raged so ferociously they were forced to remain pinned down in their quadrant headquarters for four straight days. Waking upon a dreary cellophane wrapped morning, the crew found that the winds had ceased and they passed on through the remainder of the forest, amazed at how much trash had collected, waiting out the vagrant bag storm.

CHAPTER 19

Somersaulting the Tickling Carp Pond

The crew squished their way up to a marshy liquid leading to an undulating pond.

"Keep your boots up!" ordered General Kubrib.

"They're…jellyfish …parts?" posited Rognar, as he sifted through the mush cautiously, avoiding the veiny tentacles streaming the clotted waters.

"Is that what they are?" asked Tweeker, "I've seen them as a kid, washed ashore…they were more eye-bally than this stuff."

"Hydrated jellyfish put through a thrasher, maybe!" commented Clarence, relating the fish mush in front of him to the additional enzymes he stirred into his septic tank before he left the farm.

"Jellyfish bits? Jellyfish sting…right? They don't have teeth?" pondered General Kubrib, rolling the idea of a jellyfish through his brain, conjuring up an image of an individual schmear packet with dorsal fins and a tail.

The crew sloshed through the whitish-blue muck, high stepping around a thin swamp of shredded dead or possibly still living jellyfish.

"Up, up, up!" Clarence commanded as Zorro scaled his back to the place where he was less of a burden for his human to carry, straddling Clarence's shoulders. Shen Yen swung around to his chest.

Using a hiking pole General Kubrib speared a clump of whatever they were walking through, holding it up into the dim sphere light for inspection. "They're not jellyfish…they're…" General Kubrib wondered aloud, interrupted by Rognar, standing beside him, doing the same.

"Surgical masks!"

"They're face masks!" continued General Kubrib.

"It's a swamp of mushed up medical masks!" Rognar blurted, happy not to be wading through a garbage bred version of a man o' war.

Without the fear of being stung by jellyfish, the crew picked up their pace, advancing on the pond ahead that exuded a dank, fish stench, so severe it temporarily wreaked havoc on the crew's balance.

"Here we go, again!" General Kubrib erupted.

"Mask up! Mask up!" Clarence ordered, reaching for his gas mask, stumbling from the pain of the smell.

Zorro let out a frightening whine, his paws dancing unsteadily on Clarence's shoulders, pacing off the agony until the pain forced the animal to break his human's command, bounding forward, attempting to outrun his suffering. Zorro raced along a short levee wall that stretched above the massive conveyor belts which labored under the strain of the fish that breached the walls, churning them into the canning plant below.

"What in the name of Ozymandias' great refuse is that?" questioned Rognar, baffled by the large mass of undulating water and belching spouts of oily dust.

"It's all moving." uttered Tweeker.

"It's live bubble tea!" screeched Shin Yen, joyously, believing what she saw before her was the very thing she dreamed it to be—bubble tea! Shin Yen never tasted bubble tea, straddling that wondrous place that suspends a thing from what it is, converting it to an undiscovered article of mystery. With Gerba clinging to her mind, the infant warrior embraced her struggles now in tandem, buoyed by the embracing spirit of her friend—a converted believer to the magic of bubble tea.

"It's exactly what Fallen Eagle said it would be. It's fish!" trumpeted Rognar.

"It's the carp farm!" muttered Clarence, scanning the vibrating water, reminded of headless Abdul the mad bull, holding Gerba's life ransom for a can of carp, water pressed or oil!

"It's moving. All of it! It's all moving!" Shin Yen declared, squealing with equal portions of wonder and fear, spider crawling up and down Clarence's body, using her hands, knees, elbows and feet, dancing gleefully, her uncontainable excitement, overflowing through her limbs.

"Remember what Fallen Eagle said" Rognar stated, quoting the fastest reader of the tribe, "*One end reaches into the other, sometimes you fly, other times...*"

"*Take off your shoes and step upon the heads of breathing fish!*" General Kubrib joined in with Rognar.

"Today...we walk the fish! Let's walk the fish! Tomorrow the plank, who knows?" declared Tweeker, kicking off one boot and throwing the other behind him, pacing along the edge of the carp pond, repeating basic Capoeira forms of dance fighting, his golden dreads flowing around him.

The pond was crowded with mud brown and white catfish, tri colored carp and dappled koi, their billowing gills scattering a blood lit flame across the surface, their gaping mouths churning behind every ripple. Scale scraping cartilage scratched against fins, flapping as wistful wings. The carp pond was four full soccer fields wide and more than a mile and a quarter long, filled with murky fecal fish water, high enough to cover only three fourths of the biggest, slithering fish's back and tail. There lurked also a scum feeding species of scavenger fish that coated the bottom of the thermoplastic pond in reflective, slithering sheets.

"Are fish, bite sharks?" asked Shin Yen hanging over the side of her carrier, her eyes bulging out of her ashen face, enamored by the multitude of fish mouths, their gills clicking and clattering, filling the air with the sound of cricket leg castanets.

"Travel on the heads of the biggest fish swimming away from you, so we don't gash our feet on scales. None of us can risk an open wound." Rognar said, staring at his own murky reflection, pierced by the mouths of gasping fish penetrating through it.

"How come Half Face, didn't leave us aqua socks? We had aqua socks once. I loved those aqua socks. I wore them until they became sandals!" General Kubrib crooned, nestled on his haunches, peeling off his socks.

"Don't worry to step on their bodies, but keep straight through the middle of the pond! Don't stray anywhere near the end…at either side. That's where excess fish flop off and get canned." ordered young Rognar, fumbling through his commands in the hope it would help him overcome his own fear of crossing the crowded carp pond.

"As long as there's a spoonful of earth under my feet, even if the soil is fish crap, I'm happy to make the cross!" crowed General Kubrib, the first to barefoot test the fish crossing. "Ahoy, these fish steps have the same consistency as stomach bowels! I've stepped on those before, slipped and almost broke my neck! But all this, fish roe caviar, stepping on carp bellies, is sturgeon shag! Step on and slime a ride!" roared General Kubrib.

"It tickles! It tickles!! It tickles!!!" squealed Tweeker, laughing hysterically as he danced forward from fish head to fish head, doing cartwheels, running full blast and laying out, head over heels! The tickling sensation vibrating through Tweeker's feet, released his hatred for all the things he could not name. The sensation of laughing, tickled by fish backs, catfish whiskers and Koi tails, sent Tweeker hurtling joyously, expressing himself in an unbridled acrobatic manner, dragging his fluttering ribs through the stars. Reversing the polarity of his anger, Tweeker unhitched himself from that tiny sled driver in his being that wished to unmush his mirth, hushing and shushing him from flipping and skipping on the tickling fish heads at toe.

"Are they supposed to be swallowing my feet?" Rognar sheepishly telegraphed the direction he was leading, prompting the fish to snap up his toes as bait, pulling his big toe from one fish's mouth and yanking two toes from another.

"Don't leave your steps hanging in front of their mouths, be martial, Rogs! March across their heads so they don't bait your toes!" advised General Kubrib, having found a way to skate from catfish to catfish, carp to carp, circling Rognar, skate fishing with his hands behind his back as he tutored his friend on the nature of fish travel. "The Koi are less aggressive than the carp! Stick to the Koi, Rogs! Aim for the fans of their tails and you'll catch the next one by the belly roe to make your cross!"

"They keep attacking my toes!" whimpered Rognar, lifting up his tiny feet, circling himself, attempting to walk forward on his heels, struggling to balance himself on a slimy fish back. "It's all alive! We're stepping on everything living in layers!" For the entire spanning mist of an eternal instant, Rognar experienced the overwhelming feeling that he was stepping upon living matter. Unlike Rognar's beloved quarantine grass, the six sod piece strips Rognar cared for, this entity had eyes and clicking gills. Rognar's sod pieces watched over him and they cradled his head when he slept, but they never disturbed his balance or expressed discomfort pillowing his head.

"We're always stepping on one thing to get to another! Forward ho! Forward ho!" shouted General Kubrib, encouraging Rognar, running full speed and leaping onto a large catfish that he surfed, skateboard paddling the fish with his feet, while looking for his next fish to ride. "Keep going, Rognar! If we hear a fish choking on your toes, we'll apprehend the creature and make sure it coughs up every crube! Even your smallest foot pegs! Not to worry, your shoes won't slide off your feet without them! I cleaned plates for a bomb maker. He shared four toes, between both feet! Three fingers on one hand, two on the other! The finest fiddler, playing his heart out on the stumps of his hands! Unfortunately, bomb making was his first trade!" General Kubrib crooned, his hands outstretched, fish surfing.

Tweeker was the first to travel the length of the pond and dove onto a small embankment, welcomed by thistles and blooms. Bathed in hysterical forgiveness, Tweeker severed himself from the human race, horse traded by his parents for an undisrupted lifestyle.

Tweeker cartwheeled his way back to help Rognar as his span mate struggled to extricate his entire foot from the mouth of a large catfish that seemed to be in league with other bigger fish, creating a whirlpool, circling for a taste of Rognar's toes.

Shadowing Rognar, Clarence often found himself standing on one fish, waiting for a big enough fish to wade by in order to take his next step. Clarence didn't fish skate, he crossed the pond in methodical, crane-like fashion. Shin Yen hung from Clarence's finger tips, giggling, as she dangled her callused feet over the gulping fish mouths.

Before the crew finished their crossing, chumming up several trails of dead fish in their paths, Rognar, losing both his feet in two different fish at once, was forced to do the splits, toppling into the wading waters head first, setting off a feeding frenzy! The pond erupted as every fish flapped to get close to where the food had been served! Thousands upon thousands of fish swarmed Rognar, overwhelming his mask, sucking on every pore of his face and hair, his feet pinned down by a giant koi and a white catfish, both tugging equaling for their reward as other fish fought to suck out Rognar's cantilevered eyes, hordes of scavenger fish plugging his nostrils. Rognar flopped onto his back and managed to get a short breath of air as the fish assailed his body, suckling every piece of his flesh, forcing their way into his mouth, seizing his tongue, clamping around his lips and his teeth. Every pore on Rognar's body was vacuum gripped in a suckling fish lock. Rognar could feel the head of an entire fish pressing against his upper gum ridge, and beneath it, inside his mouth, another fish, stretching his jaw open, attempting to swim down his throat! Unable to scream, Rognar could feel he was moments from passing out as Clarence swept him up, twisting him like a pinwheel, brushing him free of fish, Shin Yen, yanking handfuls of fish tails from his nostrils.

The pond undulated in a frenetic feeding frenzy. Tweeker and General Kubrib ploughed a path for Clarence carrying both Rognar and Shin Yen, pushing against the fish drifts with the strength of their thighs.

Tweeker shielded his private parts by strapping them into his gas mask, his clothes flung aside during his first pond crossing, his golden dreadlocks shimmering amid a grimy crust of sunlight.

Zorro followed the levee wall where the unseen conveyor creaked below. Zorro had nearly reached the end of the pond when the feeding frenzy forced the dog to seek safer passage, trampling over the snapping heads of wilding fish to reach his human pack.

CHAPTER 20

Kitty Hawk

The echo of General Kubrib's battlefield smoked laugh, returned from out of the canyon of medical refuse that stretched beneath the guardrail, marking the edge of the GMO infested clump the crew stood on, no bigger than an infield pulled in for a bunt. Below the guardrail mealworm eels slithered among primary colored valleys of needle tip caps and cotton swabs. From the crew's vantage point the canyon of medical refuse looked like flesh colored mountains with stretches of snowcapped hills from stacked band aids, flipped, hydrogel pad side up at their apex, surrounded by latex glove pools of blue.

Rognar was drawn to the sound of ratcheting fish bones and rustling scales. "It's a fish wave! Get the wings!" shouted Rognar, looking across the pond, recalling what was foretold by Fallen Eagle.

"They're up on the rail!" Clarence responded.

The surging wave of carp, koi and catfish, traveling upwards, grew as the fish climbed against each other for height, sacrificing their bodies as ladder rungs towering forward in the collapsing distance.

"What wings? What are you talking about?" General Kubrib responded as he ran from the rail to the place beside Rognar at the shore, tilting Rognar's giant head back and flushing his mouth out. General Kubrib leaned his body into a defensive posture, cradling Rognar as he watched the wave of fish climbing upwards and moving towards them.

Clarence found his flying suit left by Half Face and pulled it over Shin Yen, who was nestled into a joey-pouch on his chest, then helped Zorro into his suit which came complete with four legs and a rudder hole for the dog's tail. Zorro's suit was connected to Clarence much like an umbilical cord.

The multitude of fish climbing upon each other in the giant wave kicked up clouds of scales and excrement, pulled upward amid the swarm, seemingly climbing for the sphere rim, coughing bunged up gills.

Rognar and Tweeker quickly donned their suits, stuffing miniature protein bars into their mouths, chewing them savagely, not fully realizing that their flying suits would be needed to cross the canyon below.

"I'm not going anywhere near the edge in that flying suit. I don't fly...I rappel!" General Kubrib howled.

Clarence approached the young soldier in militaristic fashion, then softened his gate, parting through General Kubrib's Ghillie suit, startled at how young the General was. An untended garden of a boy, trampled by war as a collateral boot print. "That fish wave will send you over the edge—you won't survive that kind of fall without this suit. My family crop dusted off the back of a flatbed to avoid leaving the earth! Half Face's flying suits are the only option." Clarence pulled a second umbilical cord from his suit and connected it onto General Kubrib's suit. "When Half Face was full face, I could have left him, too. Don't let fear mark your gravestone anywhere but where you choose, kid. Choke on a grape, but fall to grace on your own time." Clarence spoke to General Kubrib as if he were talking with his son, knowing, too, in an ancient way, that no child can resist the spell of a moderately crazy scheme, as anyone who has ever ridden a shopping cart down a steep hill can attest. "Stay and die alone with all these carp...end up in a can yourself...or jump with us and live...maybe just until the bottom, who knows?"

"Thanks for the vote of confidence! How sharp is the learning curve in one of these things?" General Kubrib said, pulling up his suit and letting out a loud tearful roar, his body trembling from Clarence's mere proximity. "What the hell is a grape?" General Kubrib howled mournfully.

Errant fish bloodied to a pulp, their exposed spines swimming tailless, catapulted onto the weeded tuft.

Clarence double checked his connecting cords, huddling the crew together by reeling them in as the battered fish continued to drop violently around them. "We have to get up enough speed to clear the edge, in case some part of the cliff that we can't see, juts out below. Once we get into the canyon we'll find a stream and guide ourselves out...stay with me! Don't let go!"

The shadow of the oncoming fish wave darkened the tuft as the crew huddled together, blocking flying fish while working their way to the furthest end of the weed patch.

"I can't do this! I can't do this! I can't do this..." General Kubrib repeated, preparing himself for the inevitable by voicing his disdain. General Kubrib wasn't afraid of heights, he was afraid of being hung upside down and lowered into a human container as tip weight. Kubrib was nearly skinned alive for his platoon earnings, lowered into his first span, upside down, every upturned pocked sliced and drained.

Shin Yen buried her head into the divot in Clarence's sternum, aligning her body into his in order to reduce any drag and sucking wildly on her water line cooling her burning thirst.

Tweeker couldn't wait to hit the open air and left his cord to Clarence's suit unattached, confident that he would be more useful to the crew outside the scrum.

"One…two…go, go, go!!!" They all yelled, heading for the guardrail, arms locked, as the wave dropped battered fish, stacking several feet high behind them.

Clarence neared the edge pulling the others along until he lost his footing, Fosbury flopping over the guardrail into the chasm; all of the crew, except Tweeker, summersaulting in mid-air around him.

Tweeker was swatted off the ledge by a torrent of fish that forced him into the chasm, trapped amid the thickening swarm, pressing him downward, showered in blood and guts as fish splattered inches from his face. Tweeker fought to right himself, willing every ounce of his weight downward, plummeting deeper into the chasm before catching a current and soaring upward, watching the fish as they continued to separate from the edge and fall.

The cords connected to Clarence's suit were wrapped around his body, sending him spinning as his crewmates panicked to right themselves. Zorro, sensing danger, bit through his cords but the line was pulled-in by General Kubrib, who seemed to forget he was falling, reaching out and snagging Zorro's cord before the dog spun loose on its own.

Tweeker reached his tangled crewmates and began sorting out Rognar's cord first as Kubrib strengthened his grip on Zorro, tying Zorro's cord around his own body. With Tweeker's help, Clarence managed to twist himself free, flying with Rognar. The General holding Zorro.

Catching a tailwind, Clarence shot up from the dead fall into the canyon, looking to exchange a hand signal with Tweeker when a large catfish crashed against his temple, knocking him senseless.

General Kubrib released Zorro who met the air as infant skaters sometimes do, taking to ice for the first time with reckless abandon.

General Kubrib and Rognar fought valiantly against the drag caused by Clarence's body, plummeting them downward. Tweeker collided with Clarence in midair, in an attempt to slow him down and found himself part of the dead weight as Clarence reeled him in, holding on to Tweeker, instinctively, as his body, sent out the alarm that he was falling. Clarence held strong to Tweeker and though Rognar and Kubrib tried they could not unpry his grip, falling fast together in a clump as the blueness of the glove pond came glaringly into view.

After making several passes, Zorro got close enough for General Kubrib to grab the errant cord severed from Clarence's suit, wrapping the strands around his fist several times as the champion hound with Sullivan County pedigree pulled his own parachute, rocketing his cohorts upwards, lessening their impact into the pile of surgical gloves. General Kubrib released Zorro's cord just as he bounced and rolled atop the rubbery glove pond, setting Zorro free.

Zorro soared the length of the glove pond, reached the valley of the colored hypodermic vial caps, buttonhooked and returned, circling the crew from above, dodging fish and playing in the winds with ease.

Clarence sunk into the sponge pile of latex gloves, swallowed by the unsupported mass unaware that he had plummeted into a heap of medical refuse, clinging to Tweeker who struggled to press himself out from beneath the weight of Clarence's body, desperately pushing Clarence upward with the strength of his legs.

General Kubrib felt the pile moving below him, dug into it, hooking Clarence under both armpits, wrenching backwards with all his might, prying both Clarence and Tweeker free from the suffocating glove mass that absorbed them.

Gasping for breath, gagging on micro flecks of latex, silicone eels and their gelatin larvai slithering around them, Tweeker and General Kubrib frantically struggled to turn Clarence over, fumbling for footing on the slimy, spongy mass.

Rognar managed to crawl to Clarence and open his suit as Shin Yen, her red veined skin, bruised in color from lack of oxygen, let loose a musical gasp for air. Her head, usually wrapped to insulate her body, was visible against the tarmac of medical refuse, her dark locks woven into cornrows, a mossy green glow seeping into her brown eyes.

CHAPTER 21

Yuma U-Turn

The animals that made up Barrister Holmes' *entour-herd* wasted no time filing out of the train doors, flung wide by the exiting goats. Liondra posted herself dead center of the door header, making sure she was positioned to unleash one final throat cluck upon her sparring mate, master of seeds, De Gama.

"What's next for you deadbeats, back to burying nuts for animals too lazy to dig their own? How about you save me some pheasants you're not fond of for *my reward*? That would be a tasty bonus for this mission. We could set up...*an arrangement.* You have your trial...you give me the sign, I swoop in and eat the convicted felons! Some animal unearthed another's nuts? I eat 'em. Too many crows pushing onto a sparrow's turf, I swoop in...we do lunch. One puff of feathers or fur and all the *prawns* align. It's important to control the balance of power from those who relinquish it freely, fearing the might of it! Throwing a little bloodletting into the mix keeps the animals fearing the above. I'd relish the role! Put it in your crumpled bonnet, Shar-Pei rabbit! Maybe I can get one of those falcon masks and glitz it up like a Luchadore! Death Hawk, mistress of vengeance! Catchy name, ha?"

"We were thinking we might stay on, ride to Yuma, hit the black tip lettuce there, then hitch the train back." De Gama responded a tad coldly, not having shoulders per se, the rodent still arctic-ly shrugged the hawk off.

"Wow…all that way for lettuce. That's the kind of a thing a chipmunk and a rabbit would bump whiskers over! And you… tattered rug of fur, you're going, too?" Liondra addressed Striker.

"Yes, I'm going, too. For the companionship, not the kale."

"Lettuce." De Gama and Barrister Holmes both corrected.

"Lettuce." Striker barked, corrected.

"Wow! Cluck, cluck, cluck! All that way for a vegetable you're not even sure of?" Liondra quipped.

"Not just lettuce, black tip, black tip! There's a lot of us, we meet in Yuma for black tip season. Black tip, black tip!" Barrister Holmes answered, thumping his tail, unable to control his agitation, exhausted by Liondra's relentless sniping, unearthing worms within every pause—poisoning passing time with her incessant hawkness.

Liondra primped herself, leisurely grooming her feathers, "To think of all the things I'd dive for, I wouldn't fly across a pond for lettuce! Black tip or romaine…and I love skimming ponds! Well… chipmunk, maybe I can drop you over a dam sometime, for a white water swim!" clucked Liondra, stretching her wings across the railcar header, showing off their speckled span.

De Gama, preparing for the long black tip trip, fastened a shop rag over the hole in the center of the cable spool, putting the finishing touches on her makeshift hammock, "Lording over the sky because you were gifted with wings is a funny way of showing your appreciation for being a bird! We won't need any flying services for a while, thank you, we're taking this train and I'm sure the trip will continue pleasantly, once we are bereft of your annoying company! Have a nice journey back to New York

City, (cluck, cluck, cluck) please be so kind to forget yourself, fly low and go splat on a bus!"

Liondra took her final lap inside the railroad car, gliding in a prey seeking circle. The remaining rodents in the car were aware of the pattern, causing Striker to growl, in a menacing way, protesting the hawk's display.

"A rodent convention over lettuce, cluck, cluck, cluck! I'm sorry I'm going to miss it. But this is the year the animal kingdom allows me dining access up the Hudson! Snakes and locusts cycling into season together...aye-Chihuahua, pass the worm sauce! Locusts! Juicy little poppers! I can barely make sense, I'm full of spit! Snakes and locusts cycling in abundance! I would never grow tired of eating snake, but they're so hard to expose. Following locust they emerge tasty fresh from crowded nests! A blue plate special, wriggling in the grass! Bones-are for Pete!" Liondra soared out of the boxcar, snapping her wings towards a low patch of rain clouds, hoping for a shower as the conductor blew the train whistle to clear the tracks.

Striker, from the boxcar door, barked wildly into the sky toward Leondra. "What are you cawing on about a snake cycle?" Turning his attention to Barrister Holmes, "There's a snake cycle? What's a snake cycle?"

Unalarmed, Barrister Holmes circled a blue flame around the bowl of his pipe, "How is it I didn't know both species were cycling into the same season this year? Good heavens, the fragrance grower's Almanac!"

"We couldn't get our paws on it this year...and it's always out for recycle...barely thumbed!" concluded De Gama, remarking at the phenomenon.

"We've always relied on it! That was our downfall! We've been flying blind all season because of it! Snakes and locusts, parlaying in abundance!" Barrister Holmes raged on, his ears flopping about wildly.

"Our go-to edition disappeared from the trash before it arrived!"

Liondra swooped down, circling the outside doorway of the railroad car, keeping pace as the train began to grind its way forward.

"Have you ever been through a snake season, chipmunk? I thought when I flew with you in the sky you smelled of old food!"

"The snakes cycling into season in abundance...I'm sorry, I've never had the pleasure of living through such an awful experience...I stumbled upon a multitude of sunfish once, all sprung to life in a rain pond...I've fallen out of several trees remembering that nightmare! Having a swim through the cranberry bogs after they've mashed the bushes loose and set the berries overnight to spin! That's the closest I've experienced to a nest full of snakes!" De Gama responded, burrowing herself deeper into the comfort of her center spool hammock. The idea of sleeping without the hawk in her presence filled her with relief.

"The Second and Ninth plagues combined...snakes and locusts...it has to mean something?" Striker pondered aloud.

"Phenotypic plasticity...that's what you're cawing on about? That's snake season?" Barrister Holmes, ruffled in thought, his entire pelt undulating.

"The snakes aren't as abundant as locusts, if that's what you mean, but swarming in sufficient numbers...every stringy yank... dark and ay-Chihuahua tasty!"

"When is snake season?" Barrister Holmes asked, drawing a huge intake of his many blends of seed grass.

"Season? What have you been feeding on? A stash of fermented pumpkins? The snakes are already on the menu and the bugs are coming soon!" Liondra cried, piercing the air with the shrill of her voice.

Striker leapt out of the moving railroad car, his senses pointing his legs toward Sullivan County. "The first summer cliff dives in the quarry...if snakes and locust are bursting, maybe the cliff dives will be moved up, too?" Striker barked.

"What does that mean for you?" Barrister Holmes and Houdini both quipped, tumbling out of the railroad car, hopping triple fast to keep pace with their friend, his beagle emergency switch flipped full on. Barrister Holmes' pipe smoldering somewhere in the wrinkles of his fur.

The trailing foxes, Ghostress and Slickbend fell into place at Striker's head and tail. The three identical guard hares, eager to run their legs, fanned out into traveling position, surrounding Barrister Holmes, De Gama, and Houdini, the Golden Rabbit, who never appeared to tire at any stretch of an arduous journey.

"The quarry is usually filled with snakes, a dozen or two a year at most, easy kills, but if the snakes are cycling high...like locusts...there's an old beaver's hut in the quarry that's always been empty...but if that nest was ever full!" Striker's ears were pinned back against the wind as he churned his legs, pullling himself continually right of center.

CHAPTER 22

Porch Chops

The first notes from Terrance Clay's guitar solo pealed across the farmlands prompting Benny Gates to wave off his imaginary warm up tosses, exciting the swarming cicadas with tymbal chants of what Benny interpreted as *Ghost Ball! Ghost Ball! Ghost Ball!* "He's starting again! I say we pay him a visit...ourselves..." expressed Benny, gripping his famous Ghost Ball, tumbling his fingers from a two to a three seamer, then firing a splitter, completing his rotation without letting go of the ball. "Shazamm! Ghost Ball Express!" Benny was cloning himself in the Roger Clemens pitching mold, presently residing at Clemens' exact weight and height at Roger's high school age, with all the pitches known to The Rocket in his professional arsenal, with the exception of Benny's Ghost Ball.

"What if he's alien fret calling?" Dennis Ezekiel Hines tossed his conversational ante into the forum, stroking his chin with long swipes of his boney fingers, sifting every encounter he ever shared with Terrance Clay, then adding, "There ain't nothing Terrence Clay can't figure t' fix, with the aid of his own spit and a piece a' wire. That's got alien DNA written all over it."

"What about it?" Tommy asked of his brother Dennis, who often made statements nobody responded too, which in a town filled with lonely people, spoke volumes about Tommy's concern for his younger brother.

"I've heard stories 'bout odd timers, lived in this town hundreds of years, nobody sees 'em, until they roust up at the pig roast! Odd time pork eating aliens! Aliens prefer pork to beef, that's a known fact." posited Dennis.

Terrance Clay had warmed up his fingers with a few scales and was now playing a barn rattling version of "House of the Rising Sun."

"He just started all of a sudden playing, so why don't we all of a sudden go ask him *why?* Or we could swim? I could add a swim to Picnic Rock and back to the reps I did today. How 'bout you, Herbie? You gonna' sit on your laurels, three time state champ, or match me for a night crawl to Picnic Rock?" Tommy said, encouraging his training partner, Herbie Bones, flexing his muscles, praying for the chance to witness Rachel Hobbs, swimming in the moonlight.

"Yep, yep, yep. I could go for that." offered Herbie, staring across the fields at the only four way stop in Sullivan County, his mind fixed on Rachel's brother, Charlie, absent during the canoe haul along the creek bed and now a no show at the last Saturday night before summer planning session.

"I don't think I've ever been to the Clay farm, not even when his mom died. Not when his dad…lit their fields with perfume…" said Rachel Hobbs, enshrined in the last pool of sunlight; the evening bowing gallantly around her, drawn to a halt by the simple reflection consuming Rachel Hobbs pillared between thoughts.

Rachel listened to Terrance Clay playing the guitar his father left in his path, unaware, as the breeze parted her hair, that she was being released as her *brother's keeper*. Pulled from sibling duty by the gentlest force known to human kind. Love. More specifically, encroaching love that waits in the wings, playing Cyrano to twisted tongues.

"Who picks up a guitar and starts throwing down Clapton licks? Fret speak. Sending alien Morse code! End of the summer pig roast, I'll point out all the *odd timers*...aliens just can't get enough pork! Deuteronomy, Leviticus! Why would God be irritated by pork eaters? Because aliens come to this planet to suck all our pork clean to the last bone!"

Tommy didn't reply and no one else appeared to be listening either, but Dennis worried him.

"Charlie pedaled off with a torch under his butt after supper. You all go on, ahead. Me and Charlie, we'll double up on his bike, when he rides in." Rachel said, fighting against a pressing feeling to sit down in the very place where she stood.

Thomas held Rachel by her elbow as she looked into his eyes as if from afar, having no idea who Tommy was, or which way her internal compass pointed. Rachel listened cocooned in a pocket, overhearing everything between divides that was previously said somehow or somewhere before. Listening but drowning out Dennis' voice babbling against the wind.

"Charlie's sporting colors, Rachel! Looking street! Silly as a scarecrow, set for supper—then asked to say grace!"

"I'll wait for Charlie, you all go ahead." said Herbie Bones, "I need some air in my back wheel—he's got the pump. We can get to the lake cutting through the Clay farm. I got a whole case of night flies, I'm wanting to try." Herbie had been suspicious of Charlie's behavior ever since Charlie rolled up at the farm loft with new sneakers, brandishing a pro hockey uniform, talking about hanging a flat screen on the wall and pulling electricity from the barn in order to smash a cooler.

Rachel Hobbs, Ghost Ball Benny Gates, and brothers, Dennis Ezekiel and Tommy Elijah Hines, set off following the sound of Terrance Clay's guitar. Tommy and Rachel walked close enough for the hairs on their arms to almost touch, her scent embedded in his senses causing Tommy's tongue to curl, but not speak. Dennis and Benny seized openings in each other's diatribe to exchange baseball statistics and posit whether the owner of Barney's Tackle and Gas Farm Stand was an alien. Their words ran together beneath a mix of scale riffs. Benny walked the soft grass part of the way on his hands, which was his custom, Dennis obliged the aspiring major leaguer with a rare, poised silence, allowing Benny to carry the conversation until they were both vertical.

Terrance played through an amplifier he built by attaching several sets of automobile speakers to his barn wall. All the loose nails, cedar shakes, and wasp holes added to Terrance's farmyard rattle, playing from sunset until the moon split the weathervane over the barn. After church he played gospel hymns then devoted the rest of the Lord's Day to finger picking, from several guitar books with accompanying CDs, gifted to Terrance by the town barber, the North Star in his father's absence.

CHAPTER 23

Romeo Falls

A cusp baby, Tommy Hines repeated kindergarten in order to collect all the red crayons from other tables upon Rachel Hobbs' request. Tommy felt as if he were walking through quicksand, each step toward the Clay farm bringing him nearer to learning that Rachel Hobbs had a heart of her own, and though her heart strands spiraled out for companionship like all others, they aligned in their reach for a union nowhere near his own.

As if the axis of the planet grinded to a momentary pause, Tommy Hines watched the words coming out of Terrece's mouth as if they were flown on a beach banner. Amid this short collection of syllables, Tommy discovered that the love of his life had left the station, that she had in fact, never arrived, that there was no station, and that the relationship he forged with Rachel was embellished by his own imagination, this became tragically apparent to Tommy, standing on the bottom step of Terrance Clay's porch.

"We could start a band. Wean on what exists to grow roots. I didn't learn to play guitar, I just ran out of things to say and people to talk to. I've seen what a hundred pound bag of seed brings...I don't know the same for words. There's a lot of things I'd rather find a chord for...then explain. At least...until my dad comes home."

Love travels at a speed so fast that it often goes undetected, but those gifted with romantic sensors can clock a glance that not even the encrypter knows they've cast. So swift is love and random that it is often left for others like Tommy Hines to admire...the exchange between Terrence and Rachel spanning a canyon's gulp, all the roots of their hairs braided through time.

The next words Tommy spoke, ejected out of his mouth to keep an opportune moment from evaporating...knowing only... *to be involved in something...for all the right reasons was a path he didn't want to miss taking.* "I could learn bass!" Tommy blurted, his heart clutched in pain as a confident, *I know the distance to the right field porch*—grin, split his face, turning the back of his head to Rachel's eyes. "I've been listening to my brother Denny bang on things since he could grip a stick! Bass and drums have to be a tight fit, so...Den...your skins, I'm bass! I can vouch for Herbie Bones' singing voice...he's got serious church pipes...we can harmonize and work security! I can get us all the instruments we need loaned out for summer from Coach Fishback, he's band teacher, too! Not that the amp you built, isn't boss...boss...it's boss, alright, but if we all have to plug into it, we won't sound any better than a lumber house, milling wood...all playing out a' the same wall!"

Tommy said goodbye to his imaginary bride that summer evening in the town of Waving Plains, outside Hayseed, combined population: 863. He also played to a packed gym the end of his senior year, making a friend for life in Terrance Clay, and as painful as he never let it appear to be, stepping aside, letting the natural flight of things to come—find air.

From the moment Terrence spoke, Tommy felt engulfed by the same overriding feeling he experienced after a called second strike on a three and one count. All senses open, Tommy Elijah Hines lived his life going forward embracing that feeling, knowing that he would see another pitch! Tommy would sit on that three and two count amid all things to pass, a forty-three year marriage, six children and thirteen grandchildren. Yet on this night, as the evening waded into forever before pulling its studded curtain, Tommy Hines experienced utter heartbreak, letting go and finding root in a three balls and two strike perspective. Pitching underhand to his grandchildren, Tommy's forearms would often twitch, recalling Rachel Hobb's beauty, remembering too, his crazy brother Dennis, banging madly on the drums in what would end up being the happiest moments of his tragic existence, falling so fast in the wake of years to come, unable to get out of the way. For a short time the Sullivan County Crew played music together, exploring their youth, rocking out, creating bonds never forged in the path of un-plagued life again.

CHAPTER 24

Kush Thief

Herbie headed off in the direction he felt certain to find Charlie, urgently out pedaling his back wheel leak making the trek to Farmer Keys' property.

Saturday was the day the Sullivan County crew picked to drag the canoe along the creek until it deepened enough for them to paddle and ride. The creek funneled into a stocked fishing pond, outboard motors prohibited. They docked the canoe on the pond bank for summer use, saving themselves the return trip through the leech infested creek until fall, or maybe never. Charlie was absent the entire launch day. When he caught up with the rest of the group he first emptied his pockets of all the bottle tops, candy bar and ice cream wrappers he amassed hustling dime bags out of Barney's Farmstand, Tackle and Gas.

Herbie caught sight of Charlie Hobbs' signature sneaker flying over Farmer Keys' stone fence, Charlie followed, falling after scaling only a few stones from the top; pressed on, Herbie reckoned, by the demonic scratching and hissing sounds he could hear coming from the other side of the wall. When Herbie reached him, Charlie was as pale as bone shard sugar, patting Herbie's chest, mouthing the words *"Lizards!"*

"I've been saved! Delivered by a stag!" clarinet squeaked sounds pinched out words from Charlie's body, the wind knocked out of him from falling flat on his back. Charlie continued patting Herbie, celebrating his presence as if he needed reassurance that

Herbie was standing in front of him. "I followed the stag…its rack shook buds from the top stalks!"

"You're high!" Herbie bellowed ferociously.

"The fields on the other side of that wall are full of razor thorns! Dead rabbits everywhere! Dead cats…raccoons… skunks…possums. I was chased by big lizards! Coming at me… low to the ground…from different trails! I was running and something said stop! Stop! And I stopped and there was a twisted run of razor wire—a pea's width from my face! Steel thorns—right there!" Charlie held his trembling hand in front of his face, "The giant stag ran over the first lizard to come clear from a trail…I followed that stag out! That's how I got out, Herbie. You know…I don't stretch doubles…but I ran with superpower, stride for stride with a giant stag!"

"You got your flashlight or did you cop it for a smoke fix?" Herbie questioned, laying on the sarcastic guilt trip as deep as he could shovel.

Charlie forfeited his small flashlight which Herbie quickly took possession of; projecting the light into Charlie's eyes, following protocol, but not really knowing what he was looking for. "You ain't high, just scared. Did you eat or smoke any dope back there? Eat any mushrooms or drink anything smelled like horse crap?" Herbie inquired, pushing his big brother protocol to the hilt.

"I never got to the ripe spot. I got lost—took the wrong path. I almost lost my whole face back there! Herbie…I almost lost my face!"

Herbie draped his arm around Charlie and began to walk with him toward the sound of Terrance's guitar. Herbie had gone undefeated for three years as a high school wrestler, but he'd offered solace and advice many times to fellow teammates during league matches when they had to wrestle opponents who went up or down in weight to avoid facing Herbie.

"I escaped lizard patrol hell…saved by a giant, lizard stomping stag…I'll never go over that part of the fence again, ever!"

"What did you say?" Herbie roared, pressing himself against Charlie, chest to chest.

"I'll never go over that fence again, I swear."

"You missed the canoe haul to jump a dope fence?"

"I wanted to make sure that if I got caught, you all had an alibi somewhere else. I didn't know there were lizards on patrol back there!" Charlie forked his mind to the matter at hand, focusing on separating Herbie from the Sullivan County Crew, knowing Herbie's Achilles' heel was snacks. "Did the canoe sail?" Charlie asked, flashing his perfect teethed grin. Herbie was a full set of chops older than Charlie…as kids Herbie would ask to feel the smoothness of Charlie's teeth as they were growing in. Herbie's teeth were similar to a monopoly board tipped over in a huff.

"No leaks. Bondo was left rough where you left off sanding. Man, that was crazy hard, pulling that canoe one man short, but the laughs were mad wild! A laugh's better than a pull of weed! Maybe dope's the higher yield per acre soil and soul, but dope puts you under mañana voodoo. Pins your dreams around words, without action. If your dad knew you went over that dope fence, he'd fleece your hide!"

"I swear, I'll never go back over that wall, ever. I'll swear on a bible, or my video game collection, or all my baby teeth. I'll swear on all the teeth I've saved, forgoing any tooth fairy money, 'cause

I've never been a material guy! But man oh man, Herbie…the money to be made with two handfuls of skunky weed…"

"You almost lost your face! That was only a few seconds ago…" Herbie screamed, covering every pore of Charlie's skin with his protective rage.

"Yeah…I know…I know…I almost lost my face."

The two walked arm in arm. Charlie shook nervously, shedding the adrenaline coursing through his body, inquiring about the canoe haul in order to find out Herbie's stance on turning him in to his sister, which meant turning him in to his parents.

"Herbie…can we take our bikes to the pond, now that the canoe's there? We could go out even tonight while the moon's full candle! Might be my last…uncondemned night. I gotta' bunch of new flies I tied…night fishing's gotta' be the best, right?"

"I've night fished, yep, yep, yep, it's all that, yep, yep, yep. I tied a lot of new flies too, but I think everybody's too tired from the canoe haul for a swim, especially since we dragged your end." Herbie dropped his final judgmental anchor to make sure Charlie dragged his heels in the errors of his ways and didn't launch off without examining his actions. "I put my foot in a puddle, one step back…I had thirty leeches, sucking on my waders! Even if the moon's full, or hung in a broken slipper…a night canoe ride out to Picnic Island…pitch a tent, that's the summer plan! Still too cold to swim this early. Man…this has been the longest year of my life!" Herbie declared, expressing his love for the end of the school year. Herbie was content stacking long days evenly side by side, never a part of anything that happened after midnight but up eager before the last hush of stillness cued the dawn.

"I've never night fished, or ever been out to Picnic Island… never been…doubt I ever will…"

"You never made the swim to Picnic Island?"

"Half way. Might as well drown, trying! Never get the chance, now. When my parents find out I went over the dope wall, I'll be grounded for life. I'll never make the lake swim! Not now! No way, no how!"

"You've never made the swim to Picnic Rock and here you are, breaking bank on signature sneakers and thieving weed!"

"I got a tab I opened at the Mad Hatter's, for summer. I'll put your name on it, we can share, you can help yourself…just don't tell my sister I was in the dope fields? Please, don't tell my sister I was in the dope fields, Herbie? Please…"

"You can't bribe me with ice cream tabs from dope money, Charlie."

"It ain't all dope money, it's mixed, but if you tell my sister, she'll have to tell my folks! She'll just have to…and she will!" Charlie began to sob uncontrollably, half running, half speed walking, refusing to stop and cry, he sobbed miserably but kept pace with Herbie, who even standing still covered more ground than most. "I didn't think about getting caught. I'll never be able to look my mother in the face, she'll shame me with religion until I'm dead! I'll be wallpapered straight to hell in a bad print!"

"You almost lost your face out there. Don't you see how close you came?"

"I do…I know, I know, I do. But if my sister tells my dad, I'll be kicked out to the fields with Striker's patrol dogs! *Usefulness is next to Godliness,* explain to my dad what's useful in a weed den, and connect that to the hem of Jesus! No way that's happening, I'm a dead goner, dead and gone. My life is over, it's over!"

"Okay, stop, stop! I won't tell your sister you were in the dope fields, not this time, but you betray my trust…you go back over that wall…then all you'll have to pay for it is pain! I'll squeeze you so hard your head will pop off! If it wasn't nightfall, you could see hundreds of black cats dancing in your path telling you the same thing I am. You *got* lucky, Charlie! You *get* lucky *once*! You betray me, you betray yourself, you're lost. Once you're lost to yourself, your useless. Is that what you wish for yourself, Charlie Hobbs? To be useless?"

"I swear on my baby teeth, I'll never jump over or trespass into the dope fields again! I'm still shaking! I can't stop shaking."

"Why don't you want to swear on a Bible? What's swearing on your baby teeth, got to do for anything? You share allegiance to your smile?"

"We ain't got a Bible, here, is all?

"We ain't got your baby teeth, either?"

"We ain't got the baby teeth, but I know where to find 'em! We got a whole house full a' bibles, none of them are mine but one, and I don't know where my mom stores it, Monday to Saturday. But my teeth are all still in my head, grow'd in after the old ones." Charlie flashed his pearly whites, "I never exchanged any of my teeth with the tooth fairy. Tinker Bell always gave me the heebie-jeebies!" Charlie's mind spun onto his next move circling Herbie Bone's Achilles' heel. "When you picked me off the ground…I thought I was gone from life, seeing myself dead."

"We gotta' meet up with the rest of the gang at the Clay farm. My back tire's a little low...I can ride y' on my handlebars, but we won't get far with you on the seat."

"I got my bike stashed here too, with my bike pump. You ain't patched that leak?"

The boys never made it to Terrance's porch jam, stopping first to fix Herbie's flat at Barney's Tackle and Gas, Farm Stand, long closed. Splurging on ice cream and soda from Charlie's tab. Herbie lived coinciding with all things in moderation, but he could lose his Christian manners over a chip bowl spread. With a collection of ice cream sticks stacked between them, clinging to a private stocked Mr. Pibbs, Herbie crushed a bag of potato chips while putting Charlie on notice.

"Ice cream, chips and soda can't buy me off, Charlie. You break our bond and you'll see..." Herbie tore open the bag of chips, pouring the crushed crumbs down his throat and chasing the whole bag, draining his soda. "No mercy between friends Charlie Hobbs, ya' hear? No mercy."

CHAPTER 25

Snakes in a Quarry

C ottonmouth scout Captain Morgan, survivor of countless Striker attacks over consecutive summers, slithered over the surface of the quarry in an "S" path, stirred from his stake out spot on the shore by the trembling vibrations caused by Farmer Hobbs' approaching patrol hounds, escorting the Sullivan Country crew along their traditional first cliff dive of the summer.

Striker let it be known to his brood that he would return before the first swim, but the children were on the march bearing towels, chatting in high registers, calling to arms the mix of mutts from Striker and She's only litter, their progeny kept in check by the state champion trap shooter, Daisy-Jean, who held a rock salt virgil over the purebreds.

The patrol hounds barked back and forth in an excited manner led by Hypatia, the all brown, canine saint of lost and mischief seeking children; Daedalus the surveyor; first nose in, stump tailed Atilla, Ajax the giant, looking nothing like any of his siblings in the extra twenty pounds he carried and Eight the VIII. Eight was the eighth, eight ball spotted hound who morphed into the billiard ball's rolling colors, racing over Hobbs' felt green sod plains. The patrol dogs did not have any snake killing experience but felt secure in the bond they had forged taking over Striker's duties, patrolling Farmer Hobb's corn fields without bloodshed.

Daedalus went over Striker's instructions communicating in short barks, head gestures, whines and growls. "Two dogs…jump first…before any humans…"

"We need to jump before that crazy kid that beef farts jumps!" Atilla added, inflamed by the scent of water.

"Dogs in the water first!" barked Eight, echoed by the other patrol hounds, repeating the eight ball hound's bark to battle.

"Two dogs…dive off the cliff…three dogs…wait on shore…" continued Daedalus.

"To attack the snakes that come up!" barked Atilla.

"Ajax, you and I take first dive!" barked Daedalus.

"I'll beat you in!" barked the giant.

"The first two dogs in the water, retreat to the bank! No matter what happens…follow the plan!" cautioned Hypatia.

"Spot the snakes, kill them coming up!" whined Ajax, his mouth slobbering over the anticipation of snake blood.

"Take kills off the bank…shake dead away from the shore! Away! Away!" barked Daedalus, feeding off the pack's excitement.

"Bite at the back of the neck…" snarled Eight, his rolling colors molding together as he took lead of the pack.

"Sever…shake-kill…swim away…sever…shake-kill…swim away." whined stump-tailed Atilla, prancing for battle her senses expanded beyond their peripheral edges.

"Lay still the head!" encouraged Ajax, forcing the strength of his neck against Atilla's body, pushing her back with ease. Atilla countered her bigger opponent, traveling underneath her brother and climbing over his back to reach his neck, but was met by the full set of her brother's teeth, coating her muzzle with slobber.

"The head is still lethal without the body attached!" howled Eight.

"Shake kills dead…away from the shore…away!" growled Ajax.

"Away…away!" answered the hounds all growling beneath their breath.

"So none of us goes for a sled ride into Hades, facing Cerberus singled headedly…stepping on a dying snake head!" Hypatia finished barking out her last warning as Daedalus and Ajax, running at full speed dove off the cliff; Eight, Hypatia and Atilla, shepherded Benny Gates away from the edge long enough for the first two dogs to hit the water.

"Wow!" exclaimed Herbie Bones, witnessing Liondra swooping down from the sky and snatching Captain Morgan by the end of his tail. Herbie watched the red-tailed hawk release Captain Morgan, letting the snake fall. "Big snake…" said Herbie, his own anaconda framed muscles rippling from his unshouldered, wrestling singlet.

Captain Morgan sidewinded his way in the sky, swimming in the air to alert the nest, submerged in an abandoned beaver's hut below until Liondra reattached her talons behind the snake's head, sending Captain Morgan twisting upon himself as he was flown off.

"Cannonball ghost jump!" Benny yelled, exhausting his lungs, breaking the quarry silence, sending birds fluttering, flashing his ghost ball grip with both hands before clutching his knees.

The dogs hitting the water sent a gentle shockwave to the nest, but Benny's cannonball set off their attack.

"Hold off!" Herbie warned, leaping to the front of the pack with Tommy, locking their arms together barricading the edge of the cliff. "That monster hawk snagged a cottonmouth, big as I've ever seen! A monster snake…and a monster hawk—converging!!! Let the dogs…roust for trouble…that's what they came for. Then we can go full on!"

Benny was brimming with joy as he shot up for air until he received the first bite at the arch of his foot, the second bite was on his glove hand as he reached to inspect the first.

Daedalus and Ajax, sensing the water moving around them, escorted a screaming Benny Gates, to the quarry's edge. Eight, Hypatia and tail-less Atilla, seeing many snakes rising from the nest through the water below, began to pick out their prey from the shore, leaping into the water, adhering to the plan, meeting Striker's splash coming off the cliff from above!

Striker swam directly toward the nest killing three emerging snakes, then followed the trail of others upward, calculating his killing order, shaking many snakes to shreds before returning to the surface for his first breath. Striker spun left and right, separating snakes with every twist of his body, paddling steadily, staving off snakes from below with his extended, razor sharp claws. Striker's death circle made him less vulnerable to the snakes coming at him from sidewinding angles, generating his death shake from a violent twist of his body, rising out of the water like a shark, then diving under to create a path for the next line of victims, flinging bifurcated snakes in the air and swimming away, littering the quarry with wriggling pieces.

Daedalus and Ajax took turns diving under, picking off snakes coming at Striker from the nest below. The three other patrol dogs held fast to Striker's plan, shaking their victims on land until they took their lead from their father's example, creating killing circles of their own, swimming away and separating the snakes that followed.

"Get out of the water! Get out! Get out!"

That was the last bark the patrol hounds heard as Striker was engulfed by a cloud of snakes, dragging his body down by the weight of their slithering mass, instructed to sink their fangs into the furless, pink tufts of the canine assassin's hide. Striker grabbed a last breath before he went under, remembering from his snout the scent of his beloved "She" and the memories he lodged while standing on the bottom of her dairy owner's pond, fully whiskered, nursing his wounds over the cold spring feed.

Striker never stopped biting snakes, one after another, spinning downward, furiously, holding on to She's scent, biting snake after snake until the force that slithered him toward their nest as their prize, was lessened; reduced in bits, giving Striker the ability to snap his way back to the surface, leaving his attackers in scraps, dangling in the water like storm scattered kelp.

The children stood on the cliff looking down as Rachel and Tommy ran to Benny's aid, the quarry was littered with snake pieces as Striker's bloated body bobbed to the surface, accompanied by the patrol dogs howling piteously from the shore.

CHAPTER 26

Bootprints

Liondra swept in, hauling Striker's carcass to the place where Barrister Holmes was waiting along the creek bed. An area rampant with foul smelling waterholes congested with black leeches. Liondra delivered the swollen package and Barrister Holmes, De Gama, Houdini, the three identical guard rabbits and two trailing foxes, dragged Striker's body into a large puddle where the leeches made a feast of his convulsing body.

"Let's all count to a thousand…and then pull him out. Pluck off all the leeches, then send him in again for another count of one thousand! Five counts of a thousand, then…five counts of five hundred, or so. Make sure that the leeches we pluck off of him don't find their way back into this hole! We need clean leeches, so…we may have to clear out a few more leech pools, before we're done!"

The animals repeated the process while the patrol dogs howled incessantly, swimming the quarry until the last escaping snake was set upon and expired into five random lengths.

Benny Gates was taken to Doc Murray's house, driven by late arriving first time cliff diver, Terrance Clay, on the back of his Roadster. Dennis composed a song about how Benny got his picture in The Sullivan County Gazette, secretly concealing his ghost grip in the photo. Rachel's younger brother Charlie, who'd swore an oath to Herbie Bones, went missing in action at the quarry swim and for the rest of the events that summer.

The last leech hole the animals drained before Striker groaned free from his snake coma, held Herbie Bone's bootprint. Similar to the regulation bootprint Herbie would leave taking a fatal step onto a land mine, sweeping a road where female students walked to school.

Herbie left his final print pressing forward. The print he left in the leech hole he made traversing the woods, following the pursuit of happiness with his friends. Herbie put his faith that summer baiting night crawlers to a bobber, spear fishing from the canoe bow while Tommy Hines, (born minutes apart, drawing crowds wrestling in the church basement before they could walk) held a beacon on the kill spot. Tommy would hold a hole in his heart for as long as he lived, mourning the loss of his friend who gave his life for his country. Tommy wanted in so many ways to leave Sullivan County, like Charlie Hobbs did, evaporating first to Seattle, then Ann Arbor, then Humboldt. Tommy seldom left, not even for cheaper gas, knowing he could find Herbie's friendship and comfort anywhere he remembered and everywhere he looked.

CHAPTER 27

Kismet Sit Down

Half Face and Farmer Keys arranged for a meeting to exchange the Chippewa "C", which Clarence had entrusted to his platoon mate before heading north. They met in an office, located at the very end of Barney's Tackle and Gas Farm Stand. Barney's ranch style establishment, extended down the length of his lot in railroad fashion. The gas pumps were a trip around the bases from his office.

Half Face entered the fresh eggs, grab and go area first, curious to inspect Barney's layout; a larger nail in the same hole, no frills establishment, which reeked of cheese. Hats hung three deep upon hats in every conceivable space. The owner, Barney Stetsone, who Tommy's brother, Dennis, suspected was an alien, harbored the personality of a mushroom, craving damp shade with a penchant for sombreros. Barney had only two expressions in his repertoire, a sour sampling suspicion of others, and a pouting cast that fell over him in avoidance of any mounting thing that pulled his attention away from EBay in search of the holy grail of doffing tarps. Barney, wearing a leather kasa, didn't like opening bags. His customers carried their own baskets or bought into Barney's Blockbuster basket fee. Barney was overstocked to his fedoras with corn baskets, squirming to avoid Buck Shelldrake's gaze. Buck, who the sphere children relied upon as Half Face, did have one eye socket jarringly out of balance with his facial alignment.

Having so many military members in his family it was impossible for Charlie Hobbs not to recognize the guardian strain, leaping to his feet from *his* spot on a milk urn, standing at attention, stifling a salute to the massive stranger.

"Pick a basket, fill it, bring it back when you return. You don't return, put some flowers in it, we don't carry plastic or paper bags. Baskets are a dollar thirty-five cents, either way." Barney said the same spiel to every first time customer, using the words in this exchange to pull his entire existence through the back of his skull, unable to bare Buck Sheldrake's visage, demanding full recognition of all senseless human affliction.

"But for you…that dollar thirty-five's on Uncle Sam. I'll send him the bill."

A muddied silence hung in the air.

"I got some local jerky? Unlesssssssss…you want gassss? The boy'll pump it for you, if you do. Anything you don't see here or outside…ask the boy."

"I don't need a basket, but if you had anything in bulk that was on the edge…goin' over…I could get rid of it. I'd pay you for it…bulks more my concern, not baskets."

Barney stuck to his script, swiping his hands around the orbit of his hat, thinking he could touch the crippled giant for a load of grapes. "Wiiiiiiiine? You makin' wiiiiiiiiiine? I got a good price on soft skins?"

"Whatever you got in bulk that you might want to dump and not carry…if I could cut it down…I'd consider but I'm here for an eight-thirty meeting. I could have done six, or six-thirty, but the fish were hitting me like Jesus, today." Buck directed his entire focus on the shopkeeper, forcing Barney to turtle up, then as a bear, smelling over a victim playing dead, Buck shifted his attention onto Charlie Hobbs. "Shouldn't you be in school?"

Charlie stared directly into Buck's face, refusing to turn away from the savage pattern etched across the stranger's skin.

"Class doesn't start until nine, a few days from now...it won't start until next year."

Buck tested the boy's mettle, standing over Charlie so only he could hear him, Barney had returned to EBay. "Were you going to say thank you for your service, son? Letting your tongue...be pulled out of your head, like a jackass...licking for salt? How do you know I didn't go through a windshield sucking on a bong! You reek of weed and it's not even eight-thirty in the morning!"

"I'm sorry for staring, sir. I can't help it. I've always been the lead kid running toward a wreck."

"Stare all you like...this is what three tours and a moment of bad luck can win for ya', kid. It ain't worth agricultural tuition."

"Charlie, run the man to the office...there's a guy...deck shoes, no socks, blue Austin Martin...Connecticut plates...boat slip pass for Newport parking on the dash. Been in there fifteen minutes. It's a two hour minimum, room's paid in full. Beverages are free, sandwiches are extra. No hot food service today." Barney exclaimed, compulsively scrolling derbies.

"What's the weather going to be like next Thursday?" Buck Shelldrake quipped.

Charlie laughed out loud, catching Half Face's dry sense of humor head on.

"Go on, take the man down the office, chuckle head."

"Take him down yourself, you lazy slug. No hot food, today! You haven't had hot food since one of your tam o' shanters fell into the soup!"

"I have to watch the register."

"I'll watch the register, watch itself, you go and get yourself some blood circulation, like you said you wanted. Go on, waddle some of that rump roast off, chop-chop! You don't need any more hats!"

"I can walk myself." offered Buck, taken aback listening to the two quibble.

"You don't know this man, sir, he's so lazy he'd rather get dentures, then bother to take his hat off to brush! Come on, I'll take you."

Charlie Hobbs leapt onto the milk urn, kicked it over and rolled himself on top of the urn to the door, then leapt off the barrel, standing it straight up as he held the door open for Half Face. "I'm usurping all the exercise you're going to get today, Barney. If you have a blood circulation stroke, make sure you put my weekly wages paid until Friday in a tin can. Just like you to go to your grave with snakes in your pockets one last time before you croak!"

Half Face exited the office escorted by the young man dressed as a Halloween gangster, walking down the extended porch line, taking in the aroma of early summer vegetables from the display tables burgeoning with fresh spinach, lumber sized rhubarb stalks, and mounds of thin skinned Pinot Noir grapes, attracting a variety of bees while emitting an earthy fragrance. Charlie escorted Buck walking backwards.

"Maybe you should smoke yourself a mellower grade of weed, kid."

"Ehhhh-ahhhhh..." the young man sighed, "Barney's my circumstantial cousin, of sorts. You don't get out of this town, eventually, you become related to everyone else that stays. Man spends his whole life in the shade! You saw that hat rack he works out of? He's got an outhouse out back for customers, but he installed a bidet in that bonnet shack of his, for himself. Keeps his private bidet locked 24/7! Can I bum a smoke?"

"You got your own?"

"How'd you know that?

"Don't hustle me, kid. You got a good line...it's a long walk... and I move slow."

"Bummed smokes taste better."

"To a bum. I don't smoke, I do though sometimes, if I see fit, stick my foot up a young joker's ass! My foot, this one here, I could be half a mile away, and my foot...would still be climbin' up to get a titanium toe grab on your tonsils!"

Charlie paused to laugh, disappearing into his jersey as he bent over.

"Titanium toe grab on my tonsils...that's filthy rich, mister! I was gonna' say it, I was, I was gonna' say, thank you for you service, but sounding it out...in my head...was like this still born foal I saw spill out flat into the stall...no life in its legs at all. I'm sorry you had to stand in front of so much force and carry your face around to account for it. Talk about your graphic novels, your anime...man, you're the real, O.G. manga in real time... El Greco, Guernica...Goya, La Toya, wrap you in tin foil with a titanium toe grab…so I wouldn't want to spoil ya'! You got that living panorama war horror down. Apocalypse now, right now."

"You got any interests other than smoking weed and annoying people with your…truncated life observations?" Half Face stopped to look over the load of soft skins, hating the fact that Barney had subliminally infiltrated his thinking about making wiiiiiiiine.

"I've been taking college science courses since I was twelve. To tell you the truth, public school is in my way!"

"Like these soft skins you walked into mine?"

"I know grapes…" Charlie Hobbs spit his pitch quickly, guaranteed ten percent of his cut from the soft skins however they moved off the lot, "in my short time…this is the best year I've seen for soft skins. If you're interested…don't bid into Barney by the pound, he'll slaughter ya'. Bid by the yard…he won't make as much, but these grapes are wine worthy. You can get your tonsil hold off on a yard of these bad boys—stomp yourself out a…one legged Sullivan county Beaujolais!"

Inside Barny's rental office, Farmer Keys finished rolling a marijuana cigarette while watching a security camera in the corner. Keys followed a distorted image of a gigantic man, so massive that he blocked Charlie Hobbs' body completely…until the mammoth human stepped out of the frame.

Farmer Keys' Kush crop was overseen by a mist of horticultural ninjas. Keys was in charge of burning dead rodents that overdosed in the fields. The only harvest Keys took part in came after freezing his rink sized pond, gathering pucks that he'd shot into plowed drifts. Storing the shots in his puck shed for the following season.

"Barney had me change the location of these grapes so you and Mr. Austin Martin were smelling them, coming and going.

The bees don't sting…bad as flies on soft skins. Here we are, sir. There's a stocked half fridge with beverages in the corner. If you want something you don't see, give a holler! Barney likes to think he's running an office B and B! Make him run his lazy bones down here, three or four times, that'd be the best thing for him! There's an intercom on the wall, press it as many times as you like! Wish me luck, I've got my last math exam of the year in a half hour!"

Charlie reached the door and opened it inwards, stepping away to allow Half Face to follow, when a voice reached his ears from the inside.

"Sir, would you mind waiting outside for one second? I need to speak to the young man for a moment. It will only take a minute."

Half Face and Charlie exchanged a glance. Buck watched the boy's adolescent swagger—wash pale as he walked ahead of Half Face, shutting the door behind him. Half Face leaned against the door to listen…just in case.

"Young man, can you provide me with a sound definition for the term, *common sense?*"

"Excuse me, sir?" Charlie questioned, fending off the cool blast from the a.c. wall unit, flash freezing his face, thrown off guard by the apparent yachtsman sitting behind the desk.

"Common sense might lead you to question…whether or not I might employ movement sensors and drone cameras flying surveillance over my Kush farm."

Charlie's heart dropped into his shoes, filling into the ample space around his toes, having bought his custom kicks two sizes up online.

"Do I need to tell you how silly you looked playing dope thief, falling over my fence like an amateur? You could have got yourself decapitated. I see you recovered both your shoes."

Charlie began to speak but snuffed the impulse.

"That boy that picked you up on the other side of my fence, the stocky kid? He's your muscle?"

"No sir, he was just looking out for me, I can't explain how he showed up when I fell, but that's the way he is. He had nothing to do with it, just me." Charlie felt he did not do enough to convince Farmer Keys of Herbie's innocence, adding, "He's as good a' man as God grows. There's people and animals he cares for…ain't even been born yet!"

"You want to take a tour of my property, come an hour before sunset, day after tomorrow…ring my outside gate. There's a walkway entrance to the left for guests. I need to secure your word, from this moment forward, Charles Nathanial Hobbs…that you will not venture onto my property, without a proper invitation, ever again."

"You have my word. I'll come…an hour before sunset." Charlie addressed the faux yachtsmen courageously, chilled to the bone hearing his name spoken so clearly.

"You've given me your word, you're dressed like you're begging for candy, I'm sorry I don't have any trick or treats…but your word is *"your"* bond. Come twenty years' on…a man's reputation will be more valuable than all of his imaginary kingdoms, stacked on high…posting selfies in front of other people's property. Please show the gentlemen in."

"Sir…"

"Young man, I have business with that gentleman on the other side of that door."

"The stag, sir? The stag?"

Farmer Keys shifted back in his seat, studying Charlie Hobbs. "That stag reduced my monitor lizards by one, thanks to you. Stag...was my dad's nickname among friends."

"Tyson had tigers."

"How long have you been sneaking into my farm?"

"Little less than a year. I scouted the place out...last winter."

"I think it's best we have a talk before you get yourself into trouble. Understood? I pulled your college transcripts...not bad for a kid, thirteen years old...do you always buy your sneakers a few sizes too big? Those shoes arrived...about a minute and a half before you did!"

Charlie stood in front of his inquisitor, stretching his toes out through the distance, reaching for the end of his sneakers.

"Last question. Last time. Your friend, who stashed his bike in my bushes, he doesn't work with you?"

"No, sir."

"Last time?"

"No, sir."

"You're dismissed."

"Thank you, sir."

"Thank the stag. Cats have nine lives. Farmer's sons have at most three...fertilizing the land and the military claim two..."

"Life number three?"

"What's your college bound middle school guess?"

"Some combination of grain alcohol and bad music?"

"Loose clothing. Winter coats; a man's shirtsleeves hook a fan belt, pull him into an engine, or something he's working under slips off the blocks. You get what I'm driving at?"

"I've got a deeper appreciation for stags, that's for sure."

"The wrong mistakes are fatal, son. Bad company...is worse. Boy's get warnings...men don't always get so lucky. Did you ever play hockey?"

"No, sir."

"Then...I'll spare you the analogy...something my dad used to say...please, let the gentleman in."

"I'd like to hear it."

"You've never played hockey...it wouldn't make any sense, but...you're wearing a Blackhawks throw back uni?"

"Is that what this is? I learned how to skate looking out for stones, frozen up through the crick. My dad relates time to scripture. He's fixed on it. If he gave his mind a second to grow unreligious hair...he'd shave it just as fast! I'm not knocking scripture...just all the riddles don't line up end to end for me is all. Work eleven hours in a field for half a penny?"

"And yet...you...a trespassing thief were saved by a giant stag..."

"I've been scheming to get over your wall ever since I was a kid." expressed Charlie.

"My dad...never played hockey...the last thing he said to me. His last words...*you never laughed as a child...until you chased after a puck...chase after it as long as you can.* Stone...makes for bad soil, kid. I've got some lab work that might interest you. It pays a hundred and thirty five dollars an hour. Do you know what that means...spinning a sample?"

"Yes, sir."

"Have you ever spun a sample?"

"I've half watched…that's like assisting."

"Good luck, begging candy on the way to school. You attend your final college course this evening…make use of it. Please show the gentlemen in."

Charlie opened the door to Half Face's body filling out the frame. Half Face appeared to have swollen in size, towering over Charlie who sidestepped him, disappearing as he closed the door.

"This might be a short meeting?" Buck began, though his body was ravaged, his presence was still a foreboding one.

"I have the room for two hours?" Keys questioned, fully prepared for the visual onslaught that was Buck Sheldrake's face.

"Is that boy working for you? I know who you are, I've done my research…"

"So have I…"

"You're the tomato Kush King?"

"Yes, I am. And you're Buck Sheldrake. That explains a lot… if you know where to look."

"Does that boy work pedaling weed for you?" Buck insisted.

Keys took a moment before answering, staring at Buck who seemed to engulf the room with violent intentions. "I didn't know who that kid was until I saw his face on the surveillance screen there in the corner, see for yourself. There's the kid now, squeezing a lemon over his hands so he doesn't go to school, smelling like the weed he stole from me last night! I saw that kid on my own surveillance video, coming over my wall. It's a small town. I looked on the monitor…same kid…same face…knock, knock, knock… that brings us to here."

"Does that child work for you?" Buck asked directly, unsnapping the button on his blade holster.

"That child does not work for me. Do I suspect that last night was his first foray over my fence? Judging by the cost of his custom sneakers…I don't think so, but it's the first time my drones and cameras picked him up. Do you have my C?"

"I do."

"Any more questions?"

"A few."

"Can I get you a drink?

"Three years sober." out of habit Buck rolled his shoulders, pawing at the ground with his prosthetic leg while fondling his newly strung necklace, containing dozens of AA tokens.

"Soda? Water? Hey…do you want to smoke a joint—sample my yield?"

Buck gave it some thought, then cautiously measured out his response. "I don't usually smoke weed, but I'd like to taste what all the hubbub is about." Buck settled into a metal chair across the desk from Farmer Keys, the chair legs squealed balancing his mass. "Do you mind if I ask…who shot your ear off?"

Farmer Keys pulled a joint from a crimping case, running the joint under his nose as he spoke. "I can't hold liquor—never could. My parents were both alcoholics."

Keys lit the joint, taking a huge drag and waving the smoke back into his nose. "Some kids, don't experience "dad time", but my dad…he gave it out in spades—that father thing. He always drove the same missing parent kids to games. He never said, boo…just rolled up when he needed to…to take out the slack. My dad Stag, the human shim. My dad played his jazz, listened…but didn't speak…after a while…the whole carload of kids would open up about whatever was going on. It would all come out, over the jazz, on its own, without force, driving over the river and through the woods to some…familiar smelling rink."

Half Face studied Keys from across the desk, Keys looked the role of an east coast movie producer, tied off fresh from the dock. The pull the jersey over an opponent's head sort of con man.

"One night I had three beers and a few shots…I'm driving… I'll skip the turtle. I see this gold rabbit on a rock on the side of the road…pulled out a handgun from the glove box, started shooting. I got back in the car, drove off, woke up without my C stud and the bottom part of my ear…M.I.A. My mother was Chippewa. Alcohol and me…no can tango. That rabbit survived my fire pit. You're not from around here…Sullivan County is fertile full of rabbits, ten packed lairs for every seed!"

Keys passed the spliff across the table. Buck handled it like a short spear, twisting it around until he brought it to his lips and immediately began coughing from the explosion that hit his lungs.

"Wow!" Buck declared, seeing spots circling around him.

"Don't be all…King Kong on that stick!" Keys instructed, "This is from the garden of weeden…"

"Do you mind my asking…" Buck inquired, taking a smaller toke with his pinky up as if he were drinking tea.

Keys replied, receiving the joint, "Ask away…you're the finder of the C stud, how could I deny you? Did you play high school ball?"

"Yeah…track and wrestling…"

"Figures…you got no neck stretch marks! College hockey… four years…Percocet's, puck welts and bruises—never missed a line call. Took me an extra two years to finish my degree. Right wing...botany and business. My dad...he'd shag all my pucks... you know...he could have bought me...pucks. He had his own business...but then I would have just been outside...for hours... shooting alone. I bought that C with all the money I had coming out of college, because I wanted to make sure that I never forgot... what my dad willed to me. His time...engraved in person. That C stamped the hours. I signed my scholarship papers and my father's funeral bill...same pen—something the doctors prescribed. I don't know what it was about that golden rabbit, but there has never been a rodent that ever climbed out of my vermin pit and this rabbit that escaped, I swear that rabbit had a Fort Knox sheen!"

Buck reached into his pocket and handed a tiny ring box to Farmer Keys, while refusing the offer of his toking rotation, skipped previously by his bogarting host. "I cleaned it off, the cartilage was dried brittle by the time it came to me."

Keys opened the ring box peering over the red ruby, Chippewa C clustered in diamonds. "I'm sorry...what was it you started to ask? I'm warning you, this is mad tangent weed, we could end up playing golf in Bermuda before this thing burns down!"

"In that case...I'll take one more hit. Bermuda or bust!"

Keys passed the joint back over the table.

"How do you keep lizards in this environment?" Buck asked, his good eye narrowing in on Keys, reading him like an old board game.

"I'm paid to foster lizards and within their environment I produce Tomato Kush...cultivated from an heirloom concert strain."

"I have balance issues. I don't really smoke weed but this…" Buck smacked his lips and clicked his tongue, "this has a sweet taste. I'm glad to taste it…I did three tours with a brother…rolled everything in Swisher Sweet blunt wraps."

"Oh please, Swisher Sweet…Huggies! Pamper wraps! My weed goes with wine, fish, red kegger pong cups and craft beer. There's an extra five thousand dollars in this envelope, Mr. Sheldrake. I appreciate the return of this C. I'm not fond of jewelry…but this C like your necklace, reminds me of things my dad passed on… in winter breaths."

"This necklace reminds me…of where I fell short." Buck took a large toke of the roach and held it in, his war-torn face scrambled happily like a jigsaw puzzle at the first flip of the box.

"My research tells me that you're not as big a redneck as you make yourself out to be."

"Oh…I'm a redneck, alright…red, white and blue, through and through." Buck said, exhaling.

"But you run an enterprise geared toward…pharmaceutical intelligence? How pharmaceutical companies…obtain research? Isn't that your covert line of work, Mr. Sheldrake?"

Buck put his finger to his lips to quiet Keys from questioning him any further, menacingly leaning across the table as far as he could go to accent his point.

"That's a conversation we might want to have back in *my* redneck part of the woods, where all the ears in the walls have been scanned and accounted for."

"Mr. Shelldrake…Half Face…I asked for the keys forty-eight hours ago. I arrived, scanned the room, drove out and returned after the owner pulled in. The Austin Martin was the only rental

I could find with Connecticut plates. You don't strike me as a fanatic, Mr. Shelldrake? Are you a fanatic, or are all your red, white, and blue worms genetically modified by PMeister and Schoemann?"

"I'm a concerned patriot. A little more involved than most."

"That rabbit climbed through flames, glowing…center pedestalled in trophy gold. My old man always told me he was invincible. Until he got prescribed poison. He spent forty years on his knees, soldering couplings and running pipe. We must schedule a meeting in your *redneck* part of the woods, to talk when you see fit! My ire over my dad's death has not been assuaged. I have a lot of money…I'd like to throw my anger behind it!"

"I've got some livestock I need to pick up. Might take me a few days back and forth, once I'm hitched. This livestock set lose, is gonna' 'cause holy hell for the pharmaceutical industry right down to their Keyser Söze ghost balls. You said you had the room rented for two hours? Can you wait until I send a car to take you to a place where we can talk? This livestock, the same livestock that stumbled onto your Chippewa C…he's coming home!"

CHAPTER 28

The Sphere Painters

Clarence came to his senses standing next to Half Face, inside the Sphere walls on the sixty-third floor, his head spinning as he struggled to keep himself upright.

"Stand! Don't move your feet, stay still!" Half Face warned, "We could have taken you out on a stretcher...but I knew...if we stood you up straight...inside the wall...you'd peel your eyes!"

Clarence looked out through the thickness of the sphere wall watching a gathering of children soaring about in flying suits, igniting flames from acetylene tanked backpacks, torch bearing fireflies. Children without suits repelled from the sphere rim down the sides to a place where mosaic floral patterns were being created.

Clarence viewed the children from a compartment similar to the holes inside cement block. The sphere blocks were composed of an industrial, contact lens tissue, infused with a gas that held sunlight like a black hole. The first flock of birds seeking rest neared the rim while thousands followed behind them.

Rognar and Shin Yen flew together, Shin Yen shot ink from a converted toy, changing single shot cartridges from an ammunition belt of tints, mixing colors on the fly. Rognar torched her shades hot enough to infuse the plastic, freeing the gas inside to mingle with the colors and travel. General Kubrib and Tweeker worked behind them with tiny rubber mallets and razor sharp plastering trowels, blending hues and pounding the colors into form. Sphere children flew and repelled along the wall pounding and troweling geometrical graffiti images spanning sixty stories high…*sweet peas and heliotropes.*

The children repeated the process taught to them by the Indigenous Scholars. Their magazine halls filling to the blue whale's ribs with bats, as the children's acetylene flames erupted.

Zorro flew along the rim of the sphere catching any fly painter that fell backwards, helping to speed the process along without the use of a net, flying tandem accompanied in his duties by the last remaining stray.

"When did they start this work?" Clarence asked.

"The equivalence of…eighty-seven days ago, they just about finished this portion, what would have been almost three days ago in the morning. Your fever was so high we had to pull you out."

"Put me back, Buck! I want those last three days, the money accumulates…"

"Your bonus already cleared your account! Darn nickel scratcher…at least your head's okay! Old man Clay, he put that money hex on you, chasing thin air with empty pockets!"

"What do you mean…eighty-seven days…gone where?"

"You'll see…wait until we ride in the elevator. We have to ride it in order to go out. It spins in a circle around the entire sphere, three hundred and sixty degrees at approximately seven hundred and fifty miles per hour. We're going to see it all before you exit, that's why I'm glad your eyes opened. You're pumped full of more antibiotics then a block of Rite Aids!"

"That couldn't be…eighty-seven days? Coming out of the train…we were a day…before we left the hovel into the darkness… several days over the magazine hills before we cut through…

Treasured Fool's story took seven nights to unfold! The tree forest, the carp pond…Oxy Creek! That flush has to be high now…that final release…you gotta' find them kids a raft Buck, let 'em ride that purple chop!" Clarence felt himself drowning, searching for the surface of himself as a grain in a silo surrounded by smothering similarity, devoid of identity and purpose.

"The children worked double shifts, journeying you and keeping up with their side of the mural."

"Eighty-seven days…"

"They come here and create…from a side of themselves…we can't trace or follow."

Clarence tried to speak but his mouth only parted.

"Sphere days are longer, we don't know exactly how long on an hourly ratio, because time varies without the sun. The generators that pump sunlight…kick on and off randomly. We keep time on this side of the glass. Time slips away without record on the other. You've been through ninety days of compressed time. We have to sift through…where you've been…but that red, white and blue Mohawk is classic ridiculous."

Clarence brushed his hand over his Mohawk standing high off his head, anthem shaded with a nautical pattern woven into the weave.

"Your fever ran too high. The children were afraid they couldn't bring it down. They let you soar for three days of compressed time before we pulled you out."

Clarence struggled to keep himself from dissolving, feeling Prometheus' burden inside him, his flayed skin crawling outside of himself as a loud amusement ride sound caused the pit of his stomach to churn, his feet tingling as the ground vibrated violently beneath him.

"Dr. Schworlitzburg wanted to say goodbye. It would mean a lot to him to see you awake, leaving for home on your own power. Schworlitzburg…our I.T. Atlas, he's been holding a place for you to slip in and out of this system ever since he built himself into it!"

Doctor Swarlitzburg appeared as if thrust from the sound of an airplane engine, squatting low before getting to an area where he could stand to his full height as the whirling sound idled to a hum around him. Schworlitzburg waved a long arm of goodbye to Clarence before placing his hand over his heart, saluting him as the children had, stepping backwards, disappearing as the whirling sound re-upped, peaking to a frantic pitch.

"Wait until you see the other side of the sphere, how it's painted in graffiti panels like stained glass. Places in the forest like the panels of a church. Stations in nature. Panoramic views… gathering places. Hunting spots…hundreds of individual trees— swaying with the flow of the gas!"

"What do we do now?"

"You go back home to your son. You were never here. But everything we need to know is on your chip. We took it already. That chip will give us a dim chance to plan ahead and create our own defense, sifting truth from lies, and creating, in time… our own political candidate. Someone who's seen the inside of Pandora 's Box and was cared for by the hands of the children inside it. Children who live without sun…breeding epidemics as impending fashion. The crew is being transferred to a sphere that's twelve years behind schedule—pressing to open. They'll be redeployed after the ceremonial watering of their new sod pieces.

Your dog chose to stay. We needed your chip! *If...you come back with me...you won't have any time to change your mind...or any way to get back to where we are if you decide not to. We secured one exit portal. Once you leave this world you can't come back to where we are...where we are...won't be here."*

Clarence stumbled, catching himself against the sphere wall, looking through it at Rognar blasting flames directly in front of him, as Tweeker and General Kubrib wildly shaped and pounded words from the colors...inscribing:

Thanks for the dog!

Can you guess what we call our fly painting?

Clara's garden!

Clarence pressed his face and hands to the glass as Zorro zipped by taking a moment to acknowledge his human before returning to his post, minding the sphere rim with the last remaining stray.

Shin Yen flew against the wall exposing her trinket, holding it open so Clarence could see miniature versions of the Torah, New Testament and the Koran inside her vendor's capsule, fastened by the prom ribbon she salvaged from the fabric dumps. Shin Yen's afro gleamed thick and dark...her Gerba plated bottle green eyes glowing with emerald fire.

"How do I get home to my son from here?" Clarence asked, marveling at the geometric patterned flowers the children created, flowing all the way to the top of the sphere, scraping away the words they knifed and pounded, returning to the mosaic mural where they left off.

"We follow the moonlight through the pines..." Buck crooned.

"That's what Banjo Dave...used to say..."

"He stole it from Ray Charles."

"He did…but he made it his own."

"Sweet peas and heliotropes…" Buck whispered admiring the children's work.

Clarence focused on Shin Yen shooting tints, watching Rognar sparking flames beside her as Tweeker and General Kubrib pounded colors into shapes.

"This trip on the elevator…" Buck began, "there's a mechanic we work with that slowed the trip down for you…so you can see all twelve murals. You're going out on a maintenance test…twice round. When that door opens behind us…there will be no way to turn back…you're going to see everything twice before you go regardless, so…prepare for two goodbyes!"

The first flock of birds circled the outside of the sphere as the children continued triggering blue flames, shaping color, pounding the glass, hustling to finish their portion of the mural as more birds arrived, resting in flocks at the top of the dome and around the grooved out landing ledges that spiraled the sphere walls.

The children continued shaping and pounding color into the sphere, their floral images shifting magically from one form to another as if turbine blades fanned wind across a stained glass field revealing the inscription…

"Outsource not your soul! Of all things manmade…

let there be art!"

Printed in the United States
by Baker & Taylor Publisher Services